Blood of a Boss 3

Lock Down Publications and Ca$h
Presents
Blood of a Boss 3
A Novel by *Askari: The King of Philly Street-Lit*

Lock Down Publications
P.O. Box 944
Stockbridge, Ga 30281
www.lockdownpublications.com

Copyright 2016 Askari
Blood of a Boss 3

First Edition January 2016
Printed in the United States of America

This is a work of fiction. Names, characters, places, and incidents either are products of the author's imagination or are used fictitiously. Any similarity to actual events or locales or persons, living or dead, is entirely coincidental.

Lock Down Publications
Like our page on Facebook: Lock Down Publications @
www.facebook.com/lockdownpublications.ldp
Book interior design by: **Shawn Walker**

Stay Connected with Us!

Text **LOCKDOWN** to 22828 to stay up-to-date with new releases, sneak peaks, contests and more...

Thank you!

Submission Guideline.

Submit the first three chapters of your completed manuscript to ldpsubmissions@gmail.com, subject line: Your book's title. The manuscript must be in a .doc file and sent as an attachment. Document should be in Times New Roman, double spaced and in size 12 font. Also, provide your synopsis and full contact information. If sending multiple submissions, they must each be in a separate email.

Have a story but no way to send it electronically? You can still submit to LDP/Ca$h Presents. Send in the first three chapters, written or typed, of your completed manuscript to:

LDP: Submissions Dept
P.O. Box 944
Stockbridge, Ga 30281

DO NOT send original manuscript. Must be a duplicate.

Provide your synopsis and a cover letter containing your full contact information.

Thanks for considering LDP and Ca$h Presents.

Dedication

This book is dedicated to all of my fans and supporters, the book clubs and all of the reading groups that show a brotha love. When I first came in the game, I was an unknown author, but y'all gave me a chance and allowed me to create a lane for myself. I truly FOX wit' y'all and words could never express my appreciation and gratitude.

Acknowledgments

First and foremost, I would like to give a special shout out to the #1 crew in street lit - **Lock Down Publications**. The roster may have changed but the objective remains the same - **The Game Is Ours!**

Shout out to my babies - Dayshon, Keyonti, Diamond, and Quamar. I love y'all and I'm extremely proud to have such wonderful children. Keep striving for greatness and never give up on your dreams. The best has yet to come.

Shout outs to my Road Dawgs - Micheal Grant aka Miz Money aka Abdur Rahman (I love you to death, big bro. Without your assistance and wittiness, I would have never been able to pul this off.), Jarue "Masomakali" Lawson (I love you, big bro. Thanks for always having my back.), Cousin Cheese (I love you, my nigga. When nobody believed in my dreams, you did. I know that things are hard for you right now. But be patient and keep your faith in Allah.), Cousin Flaco (I love you, bul. Stay focused.), My little brother, Reginald "Breeze" Cabache (It's your time to shine, beloved. Don't blow it. Stay focused and keep family first.)

Shout outs to all of the brothas on lock that held me down when the kid was suffering from writer's block - Mir from Master Street, Jay-0, T.Y. from Uptown, Live from Cypress Hill Projects, H. Money Bags from Marcy Projects, Mally Bucks from Germantown (Dee Dee, what's up? MAO), Slack from Chester, Nell from 20th and Susque, da homie Dillz, Woo from Chew Ave, B-rad from Southwest, T. Bolda, and the homie, Gotti.

Last but not least, shout outs to the big homie, CASH. You'sa MONSTER with the pen, bro! Thanks for feeling a young nigga's pain, and for giving me the opportunity to tear up this book game. I salute!

Askari

Preface
December 12th, 2014

When Grip and Sonny left the emergency room and stepped into the chilly December weather, they were immediately bombarded by flashing lights and news cameras. News reporters from every local station were crowding the walkway, and they all wanted a piece of The Moreno Crime Family.

"Mr. Moreno? Mr. Moreno?" Roland Rushin, the news reporter from Channel 10, called out as he positioned himself in front of the crowd. He held his microphone up to Grip's face. "Do you have anything to say about the recent attacks on your family?"

The Black Mafia don scowled at him and continued walking towards the parking lot where his driver, Muhammad, was standing beside his Mercedes-Maybach with the back door wide open. Directly behind the large sedan, a black Escalade was parked with the engine running.

"Mr. Moreno," Jessica Summers, the young white woman from the Channel 9 News, called out. "Is this your other grandson, Sontino Moreno? Is he the new boss of The Moreno Crime Family?"

Sonny stopped walking and looked at her with a sinister glare. "Yo, where the fuck is y'all gettin' this shit?"

The young woman stood firm. She held her microphone in front of his face and asked him, "Aren't you Sontino Moreno?"

"Yeah, I'm Sonny Moreno," he quickly confirmed. "But I've never even heard of this so-called Moreno Crime Family. Y'all mutha'fuckas is trippin'."

He pushed the microphone away from his face and climbed inside of the Maybach. The multitude of flashing lights illuminated the car's plush interior, causing him to close the satin curtain on his window. Looking out the corner of his left eye, he saw Grip reclined back in the white lamb-skin seat. He was fiddling with the diamond ring on his right pinky and flexing his jaw muscles.

As Muhammad pulled out of the parking lot with the Escalade close behind, he looked into the rearview mirror and noticed that Sonny was cutting his eye at Grip. Muhammad didn't say a word.

Instead, he reached inside of his suit jacket and casually removed the .45 semi-automatic that was nestled in his shoulder holster. Sonny could feel Muhammad's energy. He looked into the front seat and locked eyes with the old man through the rearview mirror. Disgusted, he shamefully shook his head, and then reclined back in his seat. *Damn, yo, if only Mook could see me now.*

Prologue

"Somebody, help me," United States Attorney Andrew Clavenski shouted as he kicked away one of the rats that were nibbling on his ankle. He was locked in the basement of The Aramingo Diner. The pitch-black room was chilly and damp, and the distinct aroma of moss and mildew filled his nostrils. He pressed his right hand against the gunshot wound to his abdomen and cringed from the pain. The swelling was so intense that it appeared as though a tennis ball was trapped beneath his skin. A dime-sized bullet hole rested at the top of the swollen mound, and like hot lava spewing from the mouth of a volcano, his crimson-red blood was sticky and thick.

"Please," he continued shouting. "If anyone can hear me, call the police." He knew that the chances of someone hearing his cries were slim to none, but just like a drowning man grasping at straws, he was assed out and desperate.

Suddenly, the lights flicked on and Clavenski screamed like a bitch. Under the cloak of darkness, he was completely unaware that he was trapped in the midst of such horror. A couple of feet to his right, the owner of the diner was stretched out in a pool of his own blood. His naked corpse was covered with rats, and the large rodents were feasting on his dead flesh. A gaping bullet hole was embedded between his bushy, caterpillar-like eyebrows, and his mouth was frozen open as if The Angel of Death snatched away his soul in the middle of a scream.

Irritated, the rats stopped eating. They looked at Clavenski and stared. Their beady little black eyes shined like Arabian oil, and their blood-covered whiskers twitched in the air. One by one, they hopped off of the owner's dead body and scampered towards the wounded prosecutor.

"Oh, my God," Clavenski screamed at the top of his lungs. "Not like this. *Please!*"

Askari

Chapter One

It was 6:43 p.m. when Muhammad pulled into the parking lot of The Aramingo Diner. He parked the black, 2015 Cadillac Escalade beside Gangsta's Excursion, and then looked into the back seat where Sonny and Grip were seated in silence. He glanced at Sonny, who had been texting on his iPhone for the past half an hour, then settled his eyes on Grip.

"Mr. Moreno," he addressed his boss. "Shall I wait for you here, or would you rather that I come inside?"

"I think it would be best if you waited out here," Grip replied as he buttoned up his trench coat and ran his fingertips along the brim of his Bossalini. "This shouldn't take too long." He looked to his right where Sonny was stuffing his cell phone back in his Ferragamo slacks. "Sontino, you ready?"

"Yeah, I'm ready," the younger Moreno stated with an icy undertone. He opened the back door and hopped out of the Escalade. His heart was full of rage and his mind was set on revenge. His younger brother was laid out in a coma, their beloved father was dead, and their entire family was nearly eradicated. Certainly, those responsible had to be called into account.

Grip could feel his grandson's aura, and a devious smile spread across his light complexioned face. This was the exact way he needed Sonny to be, heartless and cold. He cracked the back door and returned his attention to Muhammad. "Call Gangsta and tell him we're here."

As Muhammad grabbed his cell phone from the leather console that separated the two front seats, Grip climbed out of the SUV and inhaled the crispy, cold air. He looked across the street where a replica of his Cadillac Escalade was parked at the corner with the lights off and the engine running.

The large vehicle was jet-black with dark tinted windows and black 26-inch rims. His bodyguards, Ahmed and Mustafa, were sitting behind the tinted windows strapped with AR-15s and watching his every move. Grip nodded his head, giving them the green light to murder anything out of the ordinary, and then stood beside Sonny at the diner's entrance.

A couple of seconds later, Gangsta appeared on the other side of the glass door, and Sonny took a step backwards. He was completely caught off guard. How in the hell was his Pittsburgh connect tied into Grip? He screwed up his face and ice-grilled his grandfather. "Yo, what the fuck is Kev doin' here?"

The door swung open and Gangsta emerged from the diner with a brown folder tucked under his arm. "First of all," he spoke to Sonny in a calm voice, "my name's not Kev. It's Gangsta, and I'm your cousin."

Sonny was fuming mad. His breathing was heavy and his nostrils flared. "You's a slimy mutha'fucka," he hissed at Grip. "Every time I turn around, ya crafty ass got a trick up ya sleeve."

Ignoring Sonny's outburst, Grip remained calm. "Everything that I do is for the sake of this family," he viscerally stated. "And the moment I realized who you were, I knew it would only be a matter of time before my enemies turned their aggressions towards you. So naturally, I took the necessary measures to ward off any possible advances."

This pussy must think I'm stupid, Sonny thought to himself, referring to what he perceived to be Grip's condescending way of justifying his reasons for killing Mook. He desperately wanted to address the elephant in the room, but he realized that now was not the time. Not only was he out-manned, two to one, he was also out-gunned.

"But I'm sayin', though," Sonny shrugged his shoulders, "What does any of that have to wit' Kev, or Gangsta, or whatever the fuck this nigga's name is? What the fuck that gotta do wit' him?"

Grip nodded at Gangsta, and Gangsta handed Sonny the brown folder. He opened the folder and the first thing he noticed was a 10x12-inch picture of himself. He was draped in diamonds, wrapped in a waist-length mink, and leaned against the chrome grill of his Rolls-Royce.

"What the fuck is this?" Sonny asked while staring at the picture.

"It's the wrath of my enemies," Grip explained. "Essentially, it's the totality of the evidence that the federal government was building against you. And as you can see, it entails everything from drug distribution to murder. It was scheduled to go before the grand jury on Monday, but as a result of my due diligence, we caught it just in time."

While thumbing through the documents, Sonny came across the Title III wiretap transcripts. "Damn," he said with a raised eyebrow, "this conversation took place at my sports bar. This is Suelyn's work. That stankin' ass bitch was try'na line a nigga up the whole time."

"Oh, it wasn't just her," Gangsta smiled at him knowingly. "Kev," he used his index fingers to indicate quotation marks, "was on that ass, too." He removed his platinum necklace with the lion head pendant and handed it to Sonny. "The red rubies on the lion's face are actually hidden cameras," he revealed. "There's a microchip built inside and it downloads video footage, similar to a USB."

Feeling betrayed, Sonny looked back and forth between Grip and Gangsta. "Aye, yo, hold the fuck up. Nigga, you's a fed?"

Gangsta chuckled and shrugged his shoulders. "Yeah, I'm an agent with the Drug Enforcement Agency. My government name is Terrance Long, but my birth name was Terrance Moreno."

Sonny didn't speak, he just looked at Gangsta skeptically.

"Yeah, I know, right," Gangsta said as he nodded his head, "that's some wild shit. But dig, though, the Italians killed my parents when I was a baby. So, to protect me from his enemies, Uncle G had my name legally changed to Terrance Long. He shipped me off to boarding school and then to military school. After that, I spent four years in the Marines and another five years working as a police officer with the Pittsburgh Police Department. A few years ago, with the help of our political allies, Uncle G got me a gig with the agency. My sole mission is to undermine or ward off any federal probes directed at the family. Ironically, the same day that Uncle G found out about you, your file came across my desk."

"My file?" Sonny inquired. "What file?"

Gangsta sparked up a Newport and took a couple of drags. "Remember Diamondz and Shiz?" he asked while exhaling a cloud of smoke. "Them niggas from Frankford?"

"Yeah," Sonny quickly replied. "Diamondz, that's my mutha'fuckin' man. Why? What's up?"

"Your so-called man, that's what's up. That bitch ass nigga was settin' you up."

"Settin' me up," Sonny shot back, looking at him with a confused expression. "I was showin' him and his homies crazy love, so why would he try to line me up?"

"Because Shiz lined him up first," Gangsta said, wondering how Sonny could be so naive. He tossed his cigarette to the ground, and then gently caressed his goatee. "Lemme give you a quick rundown on how the federal government operates. They make a list of all the short-term offenders who they believe have the propensity to continue selling drugs when they're released from prison. Each potential target is assigned an undercover agent. The agent, playing the role of a major drug distributor, is housed in a cell with their target for a specified amount of time."

"Yo, ain't that entrapment?" Sonny interrupted him.

"Not at all," Gangsta replied, shaking his head. "The undercover agent walks a very thin line, carefully avoiding anything that would invite his target to engage in criminal activity. At the most, he'll spark up a conversation that glamorizes his drug operation, hoping that his target will express his desire to do business with him. Now, the second that actually happens, it's hook, line, and sinker. A deal is established where the target, upon his release, will link up with someone from the drug organization, who by all intents and purposes is another undercover agent. And the second he attempts to make a buy or receive a package on consignment, he's arrested and charged with conspiracy."

"This," Gangsta continued while sparking up another Newport, "was the method that was used against Shiz. His stupid ass led us to Diamondz, and ultimately, Diamondz led us to you."

Sonny held up his hands and signaled for Gangsta to slow down. "Yo, lemme get this straight. You're tellin' me that Shiz lined up Diamondz, and then Diamondz tried to throw me under the bus?"

"Correct."

"A'ight," Sonny continued to make his point. "The last time we kicked it, you told me that Diamondz and Shiz was locked up in Cleveland for a body. So, which one is it," he folded his arms across his chest, "are they locked up in Cleveland, or are they locked up in the feds?"

"Neither," Gangsta confirmed in a stern voice. "Both of those Chucky Cheese, provolone-eating rat mutha'fuckas are dead. It's just like I told you, my only mission is to protect this family. And whether you like it or not, you are a part of this family."

"That's enough for now," Grip interjected. "It's time to get down to business." He stepped inside of the diner and looked around. "Gangsta, where is he?"

"I've got his punk ass downstairs in the basement," Gangsta revealed. He put a little pep in his step, shot pass Grip, and led them towards the kitchen.

"Yo, who are y'all talkin' about?" Sonny asked his grandfather.

"A pain in my goddamned ass."

As they followed Gangsta to the kitchen, they heard a man screaming for help, and when Gangsta opened the basement door and flicked on the light switch, the man screamed even louder.

"*Aaaagggggghhhhhh*. Get me the fuck out of here."

As they stepped through the door and descended the stairs, the pungent odor of feces and fresh blood invaded their nostrils. Halfway down, Sonny noticed that a fat white man was stretched out in a pool of blood. A congregation of rats was feasting on his bloody corpse, and off to the side, his eyes settled on the screaming white man. His shrieking cries were nothing short of soul piercing, and his physical appearance gut-wrenching. He was seated on the basement floor with his back propped against a rusted septic tank. His head was swollen to obscene proportions and the whites of his eyes were filled with tomato-red blood. The buttons on his dress shirt were unfastened and his right hand was pressed against the gunshot wound to his abdomen.

The rats hopped off the corpse and scampered towards Clavenski. The largest in the pack climbed on his right leg and crawled towards his stomach. Hungrily, it sniffed his blood-covered fingers. "Oh, my God," Clavenski shouted at the top of his lungs. "Not like this. Please."

As the large rodent nibbled on his fingers, Gangsta whipped out his P89 handgun and aimed the barrel at Clavenski. He finger-fucked the trigger and squeezed off a round.

Boc.

Instantly, the rat exploded. He was suddenly no more. His friends scattered and quickly disappeared through the cracks in the walls. The wounded prosecutor cried like a baby as the rat's warm blood dripped down his swollen face. Itty bitty pieces of fur-covered flesh clung to his chest and shoulders, and he was beginning to feel nauseous.

Grip reached inside of his trench coat and pulled out a black .22 semi-automatic that was equipped with a silencer. He towered over his prey, and then looked at his grandson.

"Sontino, I want you to meet United States Attorney, Andy Clavenski. This no good, dick-sucking, son of a bitch has been sniffing up my ass since the late eighties, and I never understood why. But now," he aimed the barrel at Clavenski's right knee, "I overstand."

Pfft. Pfft.

"Ummm," Clavenski grunted as he desperately tried to fight through the blazing hot pain. "Fuck me so bad, you bastard of a bitch."

Grip handled the pistol with ease, making it appear as if the .22 was an extension of himself. Swiftly, he aimed the barrel at Clavenski's left knee and let off a few more rounds.

Pfft. Pfft. Pfft.

Hopelessly, Clavenski rolled over on his side and squirmed around like a fish out of water. "Please," he begged in a soft, dry voice. "Just fuckin' kill me and get it over with."

Pfft.

Grip shot him in the ass, and then returned his gaze to Sonny. His blue eyes were cold and deadly, and his light complexion had a burgundy hue.

"This pussy mutha'fucka..."

Pfft!

"Had been working for The Gervino Family."

Pfft. Pfft. Pfft.

"You're talking 'bout your brother, Angolo, and his grandson, Carmine?" Sonny asked.

"Precisely. And when those cowards realized that they couldn't handle me in the streets, they tried to use his punk ass take me down." He pressed the bottom of his wing-tipped Stacy Adams to the back of Clavenski's neck and applied pressure. "Obviously, I'm far too advanced to succumb to such nonsense. So, in the alternative, them mutha'fuckas came after you."

"But why?" Sonny asked him. "Me and the Italians ain't never bump heads. We've never even crossed paths, so why the fuck is they comin' at me?"

"Honestly, it's not even about you," Grip explained. "It's about the blood that's running through your veins, my blood. And this is something that you'll never be able to escape. My enemies," he applied more pressure to the back of Clavenski's neck, "will always be your enemies. But on the flip side, as the boss of my family, you'll reap the benefits that come along with it."

Sonny looked down at the wounded prosecutor, and then returned his gaze to Grip. "What kind of benefits are you talking 'bout?"

"Political connections," Grip stated like a true boss. "You'll receive a percentage of the local unions, and a profitable stake in national and international commerce, including, but not limited to, the mining of natural gas in the Poconos and the mining of diamonds along the coast of West Africa. But most importantly," he placed his hand on Sonny's shoulder, "as the boss of this family, you'll join me as a co-chairman of The Conglomerate."

"The Conglomerate?" Sonny asked, gently pushing Grip's hand away from his shoulder. "What the fuck is that?"

"It's a secret society consisting of the major crime families and drug cartels from the Americas to Asia. It is," he theatrically paused, "the motivating force that indirectly runs the world."

Grip returned the .22 to his holster, and removed the diamond ring that adorned his right pinky. "Now," he held the ring in front of Sonny's face, "will you accept this and take your rightful place as the boss of this family?"

Damn, Sonny thought to himself as he silently weighed his options. *This nigga's grimy as shit. He left my grandmom for dead when she was pregnant wit' my pops. He killed Mook and Nasty, and if it wasn't for him and his bullshit, I'd still have Riri and the baby. They're dead, and it's all because of him. And on top of that, for all I know, he had my pops killed and sicked the feds on me just to put my back against the wall. But at the same time, if it wasn't for him and his peoples, my entire family would be dead right now. Damn!*

"Sontino," Grip continued in his deep voice. "It's time for this family to turn the page and begin a new chapter. I've been running these streets for over fifty years now. I'm burnt out. It's time for some new blood."

Sonny took a deep breath and anxiously bit down on his bottom lip. He'd hate to admit it, but his grandfather was right. The Moreno bloodline was something that he couldn't escape. *My enemies*, he heard Grip's voice in the back of his mind, *will always be your enemies.*

Slowly, he nodded his head in the affirmative and held up his right hand, embracing what he perceived to be his destiny. *My enemies will always be your enemies.*

Grip looked at Gangsta and smiled. The first phase of his master plan was finally complete. He grasped Sonny's hand and carefully slid the diamond ring on his pinky. The younger Moreno stared at it. The diamonds were so clear and precisely cut that he was momentarily blinded.

"A'ight," Sonny sighed. "Now, what's poppin' wit' the Italians? They bodied my pops and tried to kill my whole family. Them bitch ass niggas gotta go."

"Most certainly," Grip agreed. "What's understood doesn't need to be explained. This is something that I take very seriously, and just so you know, I already placed a hit on Little Angolo. He'll be dead by the morning."

"What about Carmine?"

"We're going to let him breathe for now. As you can see from the attention that we received back at the hospital, we're hotter than fish grease. We'll get him eventually. But after we take care of Little Angolo, we'll have to fall back for a couple of months."

"And after that?" Sonny asked.

"We crush him," Grip confirmed.

"More or less." Sonny nodded his head, and then pointed at Clavenski. "And what about him?"

"Whatchu think?" Gangsta replied. "I'ma send his ass to the place mutha'fuckas go whenever they cross this family, the depths of hell." He aimed his P89 at the back of Clavenski's head, but Sonny waved him off.

"Nizzaw," he looked at his cousin. "I'ma park his stupid ass myself." He crouched down and motioned for Grip to move his shoe from the back of Clavenski's neck. He then snatched him by the back of his hair and pulled his head back

"Agh," Clavenski groaned.

"Pussy, shut up," Sonny snarled at him through clenched teeth. He held his left hand in front of his mouth and spat out the straight razor that was concealed beneath his tongue. As he dug the tip of the razor in Clavenski's neck, he leaned forward and whispered in his ear. His words were so low that only Clavenski could hear them. "When you get to the next life, tell my niggas that I send my unconditional. And don't worry about Grip, I'll be sendin' him to you real soon."

Slit.

***

"Oh, shit, baby, yes," Simone, a beautiful brown skinned woman, cried out as Carmine dipped his thick meat in and out of her pussy. "Hit that shit. Fuck."

"You like this Sicilian sausage, don't you?" Carmine asked while busting her ass from the back.

"Hell yeah," Simone panted with her head buried in the pillow. "Ummm." The young crime boss couldn't get enough of black women. Their beautiful skin and shapely figures killed him every time. And just like any other Friday evening, he was staying at the Presidential Suite in the Marriot Hotel with one of his chocolate bunnies.

"Oh my fuckin' stars," he shouted, mesmerized by the sight of her fat pussy swallowing his dick. He snatched her pony tail and pulled her head back while violently thrusting his hips. "You like gettin' fucked by a gangster?"

"Yeah," Simone whined. "I love this fucking gangster shit."

"Oh, yeah," Carmine challenged her. He grabbed his .10mm from the nightstand and pressed the barrel against her right cheek. "How 'bout now?"

"Ummmm. Fuck yeah," Simone shouted. She was instantly turned on by the sight of the large pistol. "Whatchu think a bitch can't handle two cocks at the same time?"

"I don't know," Carmine said, and then smacked her on the ass. "Show me."

Simone didn't hesitate. She turned her head sideways and deep-throated the barrel while making her ass twerk. Carmine was no more good. His toes began to curl and he grinded his teeth together. "Ummmm," he groaned as cum shot from his balls and filled up the tip of his condom. "Damn it."

The feeling of his fat dick throbbing inside of her pussy made Simone go crazy. She moved her head away from the pistol, and then reached back with both hands and gripped his ass cheeks. "Uhhhnnnnn," she cried out as thick, creamy cum erupted from her pussy and slid down her inner thighs.

Exhausted, they both collapsed on the bed and wiped the sweat from their faces.

Vrrrrrm. Vrrrrrm. Vrrrrrm.

Carmine's cell phone vibrated on the nightstand. He'd been receiving incoming calls off and on for the past thirty minutes, but he was balls deep in Simone, and refused to answer.

"What the fuck?" he complained while reaching for the phone. "It's like every motherfucker who knows my number is callin' at the same goddamned time."

Sitting up and resting his back against the headboard, he looked at the screen. "Yeah fuckin' right," he mumbled to himself, referring to the text message that he'd just received from his underboss, Alphonso Picatti.

Carmy, somebody broke into the fuckin' club! Drop whatever you're doin' and get here ASAP!

"It's gotta be that fuckin' Grip," Carmine surmised. Although he had no involvement whatsoever with the ambush at Easy's funeral, the six o'clock news indicated that his family was responsible for the gangland hit. His soldier, Paulie Rizzo, was pronounced dead at the scene. His bullet riddled body was stretched out in the middle of Broad Street and a black Uzi sub-machine gun was clutched in his right hand.

"This is some fuckin' bullshit," Carmine said aloud.

"Baby, what's the matter?" Simone asked him.

"Nothin'."

After sending a text message to his war capo, Peter 'Fat Petey' Cappazola, telling him to meet him at Club Spontaneous, he hopped off of the bed and quickly threw on his clothes.

Askari

Chapter Two
Sonny's Montgomery County Estate

Zaire was standing outside the west wing of Sonny's mansion, just a couple of feet away from his six-car garage. The December weather was windy and brisk, but the gray Dennis Basso wolf-fur coat that Daphney let him borrow from Sonny's closet was cozy and warm. A burning Backwood was nestled in between his right thumb and index finger, and thoughts of resentment and confusion clouded his mind.

"This nigga's bugged the fuck out," he said to himself with Kush smoke rolling off of his lips as he said it. For the past hour, he'd been receiving text messages from niggas all over the city. Evidently, everybody and their momma were watching the six o'clock news when Sonny and Grip emerged from the Temple University Hospital and climbed inside of Grip's Maybach.

Yo, what the fuck is up wit' Sonny?
Y'all niggas fuckin' wit' Grip? Smh!
Yo, how Sonny gon' do Mook like that?

Those were the main questions that flooded his inbox. Zaire was baffled, to say the least. After everything that happened between them and Grip, how could Sonny even consider fucking with the enemy? Disappointed, he shook his head from side to side. "Damn, Big Homie. What the fuck is you thinking 'bout, bro?"

"That's the problem," his twin brother, Egypt, stated while walking up beside him, "he wasn't thinking. Not about us, anyway."

"Yo, Eyg, this shit is bananas, bro," Zaire said while turning his head to face him. "After all of the shit that happened between us and them, how Sonny gon' call his'self fuckin' wit' the ol' head? Mad niggas is blowin' up my jack talkin' shit, and everybody's feelin' the need to express their mutha'fuckin' opinion. This shit is embarrassin', bro."

"Shit, how the fuck you think I feel?" Egypt replied as he zipped up his Polo coat. He grabbed the Backwood from his twin and placed it between his lips, carefully keeping the cherry away from the wolf-fur that lined the rim of his hood. "I still got bullet fragments in my body from when them niggas clapped me up." He took a nice long pull on the spliff and inhaled deeply. "And fa'real, fa'real," he exhaled the smoke, "fuck what happened to me, I'm still alive. But what about the big homie, Mook? What about my nigga, Nasty? What about Riri?"

"I'm sayin', though," Zaire replied, "it's gotta be a logical explanation behind this shit. I'm not gonna front like I know what it is, but it's gotta be somethin'. Sonny wouldn't be fuckin' wit' this nigga if he didn't have a reason."

"Oh, this nigga's got a reason a'ight," Egypt accused, nodding his head up and down. "It's money."

"Money?" Zaire questioned.

"Yeah, nigga, that almighty mutha'fuckin' dollar," Egypt shot back, raising his voice a couple of octaves.

Zaire looked at him skeptically, "Yo, Eyg, you trippin', bro. Straight up."

Egypt chuckled but deep inside he was steaming mad. "Oh, so now I'm the one that's trippin'?"

"Yeah, bro, just a little bit."

"Just a little bit?" Egypt retorted. "Nigga, look around," he snapped at his brother, then held up his left hand and waved it from side to side. "This nigga's livin' in this big ass mansion wit' all these mutha'fuckin' cars and shit. I'm tellin' you, Zai, that's the only thing he cares about, money. He don't give a fuck about me. He don't give a fuck about you. And he damn sure don't give a fuck about Mook."

Zaire looked at the six-car garage. The doors were retracted, revealing the luxury automobiles that occupied the spaces. Aside from Daphney's Benz truck and the red Rolls-Royce that Sonny had been driving for the past couple of months, he spotted a Porsche 918 Spyder, a Bentley Continental G.T., a Maserati Ghibli, and a Ferrari 458 Italia. Each vehicle was the color of burnt charcoal and had shiny chrome rims.

After taking an assessment of the luxury vehicles, Zaire shrugged his shoulders. "Come on, bro. Sonny was caked up from the jump, and just because he has a couple of whips that niggas ain't never seen before, that doesn't really mean shit."

"What?" Egypt screwed up his face. "That doesn't mean shit? A'ight, well what about this big ass house? How come he was hiding it from us?"

"I don't know," Zaire answered. "Maybe he wanted to keep Daph and the kids away from everybody. You know he still blames himself for what happened to Riri. He was probably just try'na keep his family safe."

"That's bullshit," Egypt countered. "The only reason he was keepin' niggas at bay is because he didn't want us to know how large he was livin'."

"Aye, yo, Eyg, cut it the fuck out," Zaire chuckled. "You're seriously buggin' right now."

"Naw, nigga, you're the one whose buggin'. You see this big ass house?" He pointed towards the mansion behind him. "This nigga has an elevator up in this mutha'fucka. A real life mutha-fuckin' elevator. And what we got? Two punk ass Panameras and a duplex in Chester County? Nizzaw, I'm not feelin' this shit, Zai. We're the ones movin' all the fuckin' work, and what we got? A couple of crumbs? A couple of crumbs for some crumb ass niggas."

He took another pull on the Backwood and quickly realized the cherry had burned out in the middle of his rant. Frustrated, he tossed the spliff on the ground and kicked it away from him. "Man, fuck that Backwood."

Zaire was flabbergasted. Where was all of this coming from? He and Egypt came a long way from scraping on the streets of North Philly, but Egypt was talking as if they were broke. Obviously, they didn't have everything that Sonny had, but they were far from broke. Moreover, Sonny went out of his way to put them in a position to win. So, why was Egypt so mad?

"You're my twin and I love you," Zaire stated with sincerity, "But I've gotta keep it a hunnid witchu. You're seriously outta pocket, bro. Sonny brought us up from puppy dog status. And if it wasn't for him, we'd still be stuck in the hood, posted up on Marshal Street, bumping heads wit' the roaches and rats. He took us under his wing when he didn't have to, and on some G shit, where the fuck is all of this comin' from?"

"From the heart," Egypt shouted while pounding the left side of his chest. "Right mutha'fuckin' here, I deserve more. We," he pointed back and forth between him and his brother, "deserve more! And until I get what my hand calls for, I'm done!"

He stormed off in the direction of his Porsche Panamera and Zaire reached out to grab his arm. "Get the fuck off me," he snapped while yanking his arm away. "If you wanna continue being his little errand boy, then that's what the fuck you do. I'm doin' my own thing. Fuck Sonny."

Zaire sighed. He searched for the right words to calm Egypt down, but he couldn't find any.

Unbeknownst to Egypt and Zaire, Daphney was standing outside on the balcony. She was sipping on a glass of wine and listening to their every word.

***

Club Spontaneous

Carmine pulled up to the club in his cranberry, 2015 Infinity Q50. Fat Petey was behind in a forest-green, 2015 Chevy Silverado, and simultaneously they pulled up on both sides of Alphonso's white BMW. It was precisely ten minutes after 7 p.m., so the fact that Alphonso's 745 was the only car in the parking lot didn't raise any red flags. There was, however, another factor that instantly caught their attention. The club was dark, a little too dark.

"Why the fuck are the lights turned off?" Carmine asked while stepping out of his vehicle.

"I don't know," Fat Petey answered, shrugging his beefy shoulders. He closed the driver's side door and walked up to Carmine.

"When Phons sent me the text message, he was already here," Carmine said. "But, now the place is friggin' empty. All of the lights are turned off."

Again, Fat Petey shrugged his shoulders. The brisk December wind was gliding off of the Delaware River and sending chills down his spine. "I say we go inside and check things out," he suggested as he shuffled from side to side, doing his best to keep warm.

Carmine looked at him like he was stupid. "Dah... I thay we go inthide and check things out," he mimicked the fat man in a goofy, retarded-like voice. He blew into the palms of his hands, and then reached into the front right pocket of his Gucci parka and pulled out his .10mm handgun. With his right hand wrapped around the rubber-grip handle, he looked Fat Petey square in the eyes. "You're goddamned right we're gonna check it." He gestured towards the front door with the barrel of his gun. "You go first and I'll follow."

Feeling mistreated and slightly disrespected, Fat Petey shook his head in contempt, but followed Carmine's orders nonetheless. After removing the nickel-plated .45 that was tucked under his rolls of fat, he cautiously glanced around the parking lot. A dark colored Lincoln Navigator cruised down the block at a calm 15 miles per hour. It slowed down at the behest of the yellow traffic light at the corner, then slowly made a right turn and cruised up Spring Garden Avenue. Fat Petey and Carmine looked at one another for a brief moment, and then returned their attention to the strip club. As they approached the door and peeked inside of the front glass window, the only thing they saw was an abysmal darkness.

Why the fuck are the lights turned off? Fat Petey wondered. *Who in the hell does Alphonso think he is, Batman?*

Gently, he tugged on the door handle. "Carmy," he whispered over his right shoulder. "The door, it's friggin' open."

"No shit," Carmine snapped at him. "What am I, a friggin' idiot? Obviously, I can see that the friggin' thing's not locked. And stop whisperin', wouldja? You're makin' me feel like a goddamned cat-burglar."

Again, Fat Petey shook his head in contempt. *Fuckin' jerk.* He slowly pulled the door open and looked around the club's interior. Initially, it was so dark that he couldn't see anything. But after squinting his eyes for a couple of seconds, he was able to make out the silhouettes of the bar, the stage, and the V.I.P. area.

"What are you waitin' for?" Carmine asked, and then nudged him in the back with the lips of his pistol. "We'll be able to see better from the inside. Now, stop actin' like a little bitch."

Fat Petey sighed. As a result of him and Carmine growing up together, he was accustomed to his sarcasm and wise ass remarks, but now was not the time. "Where's the light switch?" he asked, still hesitating to walk inside of the club.

"It's on the wall, off to the left," Carmine informed him. "But in order to reach it, you'll have to step inside."

Nervously, Fat Petey took a deep breath and sighed. *All right, Petey, here goes nothin',* he pumped himself up before slowly stepping inside of the strip club. His head was on a swivel, and his .45 was ready to wreak havoc. His first step was firmly placed on the polished hardwood floor, but his second step was greeted by a slick oily substance. His chunky right leg shot up in the air and his flabby arms flailed wildly. He desperately tried to regain his balance, but when the bottom of his left shoe came in contact with the oily substance, he landed on his fat ass and accidentally fired a shot into the ceiling.

Boom.

The bright muzzle flash illuminated the club, allowing Carmine to get a quick glimpse of the carnage that lay ahead. Quickly, he stepped over Fat Petey and hit the light switch.

"Goddamnit," Fat Petey complained, realizing he was lying in a pool of congealed blood. His black slacks and gray Ralph Lauren overcoat was covered in the slimy goop. He tried to stand up, but he slipped once again and crashed on his side.

Carmine struggled to help him back to his feet, but not once did he take his eyes off of his surroundings. The pool of blood was connected to a bloody trail that led down the hallway towards his office. At first glance, he instantly reached the conclusion that a violent confrontation had taken place where him and Fat Petey were standing, and that the person on the losing end of the confrontation was drug into his office. In the middle of the blood pool, he spotted a fist-sized piece of human anatomy that was attached to a long, gray rope. The fleshy rope was thick and lumpy, and it trailed the length of the hallway.

"What the fuck is that?" Fat Petey asked while leaning forward to grab his gun from the floor.

Carmine kicked the fleshy pouch with the tip of his Nike boot and flipped it over. "I'm not sure, Petey. It looks like a friggin' organ." As he stood there wondering what the bloody pouch could be, it suddenly hit him. "Get the fuck outta here," he said, shaking his head in disbelief.

"What?" Fat Petey asked, looking to Carmine for an answer. As a war capo, he was accustomed to violence, but this was a little too much. "Carmy, what is it?"

With squinted eyes, Carmine evaluated the lumpy rope that was attached to the pouch. "It's a friggin' stomach," he replied, and then gestured towards the lumpy rope with the tip of his boot. "And that's a large fuckin' intestine."

Fat Petey, a seasoned killer in his own right, was horrified. Sweat covered his brow and the confused look on his face reminded Carmine of a constipated toddler. Fat Petey's hands began to tremble and his bowls released a long sloppy-sounding fart.

Plrrrrrnnnnn.

"Goddamnit, Petey," Carmine complained as he covered his nose.

Plrrrnnn.

"Come on, Petey. Really?"

Fat Petey just stood there looking stupid. "I'm sorry, Carmy. But this," he pointed at the organs laying on the floor, "this shit is fuckin' up my stomach."

Plrrrrrnnnnn.

Disgusted, Carmine shook his head from side to side. He raised his .10mm in the air and slowly walked down the hallway, carefully avoiding the long rope of intestines. "Hey, yo, Phons," he called out for his underboss. "You back here?"

Fat Petey was a couple of steps behind him. He was cautiously looking around the strip club, and his .45 was slightly aimed above Carmine's left shoulder.

Plrn.

"Damnit, Petey. Wouldja knock it off?"

"Carmy, I'm sorry."

When they approached the office, the door was slightly ajar. Carmine looked back at Fat Petey and whispered, "I'm gonna go low. You go high. Capisce?"

Carmine crouched down and Fat Petey hovered over him. "All right," Carmine continued whispering. "In three... Two... One." He pushed the door wide open with his left hand and aimed the .10mm with his right hand. Fat Petey was locked, loaded, and ready to blaze, but the office was empty.

"Carmy, there's nobody here."

Carmine stood erect and swung the .10mm from right to left. It was just like Fat Petey said, the office was empty. He looked at his desk and noticed that his leather swivel-chair was turned backwards. The lumpy, gray rope stretched across the floor and wrapped around the right side of his mahogany desk.

As they stepped inside of the office, the pungent odor of warm feces smacked them in the face. "Carmy, that ain't me," Fat Petey quickly pleaded his case. "The last time I fluted a toot was out in the hallway."

Carmine looked at the fat Italian like he wanted to smack the shit out of him. Fat Petey could sense his anger, so he took a step backwards and held up his hands in a defenseless posture. "Carmy, I'm just sayin'."

Slowly and apprehensively, the two mobsters approached the desk with their weapons aimed at the back of the swivel-chair. "Whoever's sittin' in that fuckin' chair, you better turn around," Carmine warned.

Silence.

Carmine motioned for Fat Petey to go around the left side of the desk as he walked around the right side. His .10 milli was ready to bark at the slightest movement, and he could actually feel his trigger finger itching. Slowly, he grabbed the arm of the chair with his left hand and spun it around.

"Oh, my God," Fat Petey blurted out, completely caught off guard.

Carmine jumped backwards and then doubled over, spewing out vomit. Nothing in the world could have prepared them for this. Alphonso was sitting in the swivel-chair with his torso ripped inside out. His rib-cage was cracked open and stretched wide, with his organs on full display. The long, fleshy rope that trailed in from the hallway ended up in the ball of intestines that covered his groin area. His lips and eyelids were stitched closed with black lace, and his head was cocked backwards, slightly facing the ceiling. A long gash covered the front of his neck, and where his Adam's apple should have been, his fat tongue dangled like a pink necktie.

"Carmy, look," Fat Petey said. He was pointing the barrel of his gun at the 50-inch plasma that hung on the wall adjacent to the desk.

Carmine wiped the vomit from his mouth with the back of his hand and then looked up at the television. A Mexican man was staring at him with a blank expression. His bald head and cleanly shaved face was covered in tattoos, and a pair of implants that resembled devil horns protruded from both sides of his forehead.

"Who the fuck are you?" Carmine asked, wondering how the man had managed to hack into his security system.

"Me?" The Mexican smiled at him. "I'm Diablo. The one who God sent to punish the world."

"Is this motherfucker serious?" Carmine said with a screwed-up face.

"I'm the punishment of God," Diablo continued. "And had you not committed great sins, God would not have sent a punishment like me upon you."

Carmine spat on the floor. "Gimmie a fuckin' break. A dead man, that's what the fuck you are. A fuckin' dead man."

Diablo chuckled. "You know, Carmine, at one point in time, you Italians had a lot of heart. But now," he picked up Alphonso's heart and held it in front of the camera, "you motherfuckers are helpless and weak." He crushed the heart in the palm of his hand and thick globs of blood oozed from in between his tattoo-covered fingers. "There's a cell phone where your compadre's heart used to be," he stated with emphasis. "*Use it!*"

The screen went black and Carmine returned his gaze to Alphonso's corpse. In the center of his rib-cage, slightly to the right, in the cavity where his heart had been eviscerated, his eyes locked on a blood-covered iPhone. Enraged, he looked at Fat Petey.

Plrrrrrnnnnn.

Chapter Three
Hidalgo County, Texas

Two miles north of the Mexican border, Chico Rivera was slipping in and out of consciousness. His 6' 8", 295-pound frame was dangling upside down from a wooden beam in the middle of a horse stable, and his legs were spread apart, just a tad bit wider than the width of his shoulders. The iron cuffs that locked around his ankles were connected to two thick chains, and each of the chains were attached to the railroad spikes that protruded from the wooden beam.

The horse stable was large and spacious. The twelve-foot-high walls were decorated with horseshoes, pitchforks, and a variety of gardening tools. The floor was covered in straw, and large bales of hay were scattered all around. There was a total of sixteen stables, eight to the left and eight to the right. They were ten feet high, five feet wide, and secured with a black iron gate. Each of the stables was occupied by a cinnamon-brown, Arabian horse. Their massive bodies were strong and stout, and their shiny brown coats were topped off with long tufts of silky black hair.

Dangling upside down and slowly swinging back and forth, Chico was dazed and disoriented. The last thing he remembered was being escorted to The Alverez Cattle Ranch in the Rio Grande Valley, where he was scheduled to meet Chatchi Alverez, the acting boss of the infamous Sinaloa Cartel. Unfortunately for Chico, things had gone drastically wrong.

Swoosh.

Whack.

"Ayyy," The large Mexican screamed when the leather bullwhip ripped the flesh from his bare back.

Swoosh.

Whack.

"Ay yi yi."

Chico should have known that things would end this way. A little over two months ago, he was given the task of accompanying Chatchi's nephew, Roberto Alverez, to Philadelphia. Acting as

Roberto's bodyguard, he was instructed to keep the young boxer out of trouble. But more importantly, at all cost, he was responsible for keeping Roberto safe. He failed.

Their first month in the City of Brotherly Love went according to plan. Roberto was focused and training hard for his American debut in the Welterweight division. Every morning, just before 3 a.m., he would awaken to a light breakfast of wheat toast, egg whites, Greek yogurt, and fresh fruit. Then after filling his gas tank with the proper nutrients, he would throw on his Under Armor sweat suit and jog a total of ten miles to the Executioners Boxing Gym. There, he would spend the remainder of his day working out with Philadelphia boxing legends, Bernard Hopkins and Danny Garcia.

Chico was extremely proud of the young boxer, but then seemingly out of nowhere Roberto began to change. Instead of his daily workout regimen, he developed the habit of sleeping all day and partying all night. He rented a Pepsi-blue Lamborghini and began hanging out with Carmine Gervino, the boss of The Gervino Crime Family.

One night, while leaving Carmine's strip club, Chico and Roberto were ambushed by three men. Chico was knocked unconscious and when he came to, Roberto was gone. Terrified, Chico searched high and low for Roberto, but he never found him. He failed to protect the boss' nephew, and now he had to pay... with his life.

Swoosh.

Whack.

"Ay yi yi," Chico cried out. The burning sensation of the bullwhip was hotter than fire. "Chatchi, please," he begged his tormentor. "It wasn't my fault, eh! Somebody set us up!"

Chatchi was standing behind him with the ten-foot-long bullwhip clutched in his right hand. As the acting boss of the Sinaloa Cartel, he was the most powerful man in the Rio Grande Valley, and arguably the most powerful man in North America. His drug cartel was responsible for smuggling forty tons of cocaine across the border every year, and his four-billion-dollar empire was the most notorious in all of Mexico. Rival drug crews, such as The Gulf

Cartel and Los Zetas, were close in stature, but nothing compared to the murderous, bloody Sinaloa.

Dressed in a fresh wife-beater, tan slacks, and black suede shoes, Chatchi circled the horse stable like a caged lion. His 5'6", 158-pound body was chiseled like a Roman statue, and beads of sweat glistened on his golden-brown Aztec skin. "I put my trust in you, homes. And you let me down."

Swoosh.

Whack.

"Ayyyy, Chatchi, please, homes. It wasn't my fault, eh."

"You don't get no sympathy from me, homes," Chatchi said in his Mexican accent. He was burning with rage, but his voice was calm and steady. "You don't deserve it. My mother and my sisters are back in Mexico crying their eyes out because somebody kidnapped and murdered my nephew. My brother, Joaquin, is sitting in a jail cell, furious and thirsty for revenge, and you got the nerve to beg for sympathy?"

He raised the bull-whip over his head, twirled it around like a lasso, and then let it rip.

Swoosh.

Whack.

"Ayyyy," Chico wailed from the pain. "Ay dios mio. Ay dios mio."

Chatchi looked at him and shook his head in disbelief. "I hear you calling on God, mijo, but not once did you ask Him for forgiveness. I trusted you with the safety of my nephew, but you fucked up, eh. You returned from Philadelphia in one piece, but my nephew," he paused for a brief moment, "he returned in pieces, mijo. In pieces."

Swoosh.

Whack.

Swoosh.

Whack.

"Whoever kidnapped him, they sent his tongue and his hands to my mother," Chatchi continued shouting. "His tongue and his fuckin' hands, mijo."

Swoosh.

Whack.

"I want answers, Chico. Now."

Swoosh.

Whack.

Chico was in a dark place, mentally, physically, and spiritually. He'd been receiving this torture for the past ten hours, and a numbing sensation was beginning to wash over him. Chatchi crouched down beside him and spoke to him in a low, condescending voice. "Talk to me, homes. Are you sure that Carmine didn't turn you against me? Are you sure that he didn't kidnap and murder my nephew?" he smacked Chico in the face. "Come on, mijo, tell me something."

"I can't say for sure," Chico whispered, "but Carmine, Carmine was okay. He didn't give us any problems."

"I'm not so sure about that," Chatchi said as he stood erect and wiped the sweat from his brow. He walked over to the first horse stable where a two-foot-long, stainless-steel machete was laying on top of a bale of hay. After dropping the bloody bull-whip on the floor, he picked up the machete and held it in front of his face. The Friday the Thirteenth knife was sharp and shiny. After admiring his weapon of choice, he rested the blade on his right shoulder and then stood in front of Chico.

"So, let's get this straight, mijo. Earlier you told me that Carmine invited you and my nephew to his strip club, correct?"

"Si, Chatchi. Si."

"And later that night when the two of you left his club, my nephew was kidnapped, right?"

"Si."

"But yet you claim that Carmine had nothing to do with this?"

Silence.

"Answer me!"

Silence.

Chico's body was completely limp. His eyes were closed and his tongue was hanging out of the side of his mouth like a dead dog. Chatchi looked at him with hatred and contempt. The two men had grown up together in Isla Mujerez, Mexico, but none of that mattered now. Chatchi raised the machete over his head and positioned his body for a devastating swing. His focus was on the base of Chico's rectum. It was there, precisely in that spot, where his grandfather taught him as a young child to gut his enemy from groin to sternum.

The front door of the stable swung open and Chatchi's twelve-year-old son, Gato, slipped inside with a cell phone clutched in his right hand. "Poppy, you left, you left your phone in the truck. Here," he extended the touch-screen device towards his father, completely disregarding the large man dangling from the ceiling. "Somebody's try'na call you. It's been ringing like crazy."

Chatchi lowered the machete and grabbed the phone from his son. Looking at the screen, he flexed his jaw muscles and gritted his teeth. It was the call he'd been waiting for. It was Carmine Gervino.

"Talk to me," Chatchi spoke into the phone.

"Who the fuck is this?" Carmine snapped.

"Your worst fucking nightmare," Chatchi replied in a cold voice, and then handed the machete to Gato.

"Motherfucker, do you know who I am?" Carmine continued his rant. "Do you have any idea of what I'm capable of?" His words were boss, but the shakiness in his voice didn't give them any credence.

Chatchi was on point, and just like an apex predator, he could smell the fear in his victim. *Typical American*, he thought to himself, *a pussy-made bitch in a tailor-made suit.*

"Did you hear what the fuck I said?" Carmine continued snapping.

Ignoring his hostility, Chatchi remained calm. "My nephew, Roberto, was kidnapped and murdered a couple of weeks ago when he left your club."

Upon hearing this, Carmine calmed down. His heart dropped into his stomach, and his stomach did a cartwheel. "Ch-Ch-Chatchi?"

"My nephew, Carmine. I want to know what happened to my nephew."

Carmine was bitching. "Ah—Ah—Ah all I know is that he came into the club that night, he partied a little bit, and then he left. That's all I know," he lied. He was well aware that Roberto was kidnapped because he watched it unfold on his security cameras. He never said anything, because just like everybody else, he assumed that Chatchi's arch enemies, The Gulf Cartel, were the ones who kidnaped him.

"How long have you known me, Carmine?"

"A little over ten years."

"Okay, so do you know what I'm capable of?" he asked, using Carmine's words against him. When Carmine didn't respond, Chatchi chuckled. "So, you do know what I'm capable of!"

"Listen, Chatchi, I'm tellin' the truth. My family didn't have anything to do with Roberto being kidnapped."

"I'm not so sure about that," Chatchi replied, shaking his head in disbelief. "This shit happened too close to home for you not to know anything. So therefore, that leads me to believe one of two things. Either you're responsible for what happened to my nephew, or you're protecting the person who's responsible. Both are unacceptable, mijo. So, I'll tell you what, you have twenty-four hours to bring me the heads of the motherfuckers who kidnapped and murdered my nephew."

"But, Chatchi…"

"But, nothing," Chatchi yelled into the phone. "This is not a debate. And just to show you how serious I am, I've got a banana clip with a couple of names on it. Now, go to the nearest funeral parlor and pick out some fucking caskets."

Click.

Placing the cell phone in his back pocket, Chatchi looked over at Gato. The little boy was standing behind Chico and audibly counting out the lashings on his back. "Gato," he addressed his son, "what are you doing over there, eh?"

"Poppy, are you going to kill Chico?" he asked with a mischievous grin on his face. "I like Chico. He's funny."

Chatchi sighed. He approached the little boy and retrieved the machete from his hands. "Mijo, do you remember the dog we had when you was a little baby? Bandito?"

Gato nodded his head. "Si, Poppy. Bandito was my first Pitbull. He was my best friend."

"He was a good dog, right?"

"Si, Poppy."

"But one day," Chatchi calmly held the stainless-steel blade in front of Gato's face, allowing him to see his reflection, "Bandito bit you."

Tears welled up in Gato's left eye as he examined his mutilated face. When he was three years old, for no apparent reason, Bandito bit down and locked on the right side of his face. His jaws were so powerful that he crushed the little boy's eye socket, damaging his right eyeball beyond repair.

Gently, Chatchi caressed the little boy's back as tears trickled from his left eye. "Ssshhhh. Settle down, mijo. It's okay."

Gato nodded his head and wiped away his tears with the back of his sleeve. After calming himself down, he pointed at Chico and said, "Poppy, did Chico bite you?"

"He did, mijo, in the worst way possible."

Gato nodded his understanding. "So, now you gotta put him down the same way you had to put down Bandito?"

Chatchi squinted his eyes and slowly shook his head. "No, mijo. This time around I want you to put the dog out of his misery." He handed the machete back to his son, and the little boy smiled.

***

Club Spontaneous

"Carmy, what did he say?" Fat Petey asked. He was standing across from Carmine and looking at him inquisitively.

"He's holdin' us responsible for the shit that happened to his nephew," Carmine replied as he darted out of the office.

"But we didn't have anything to do with that," Fat Petey complained. He was a couple of steps behind Carmine, following him to the front door. "You gotta call him back."

"For what?" Carmine asked as he stepped outside and headed towards his Infinity. "There's nothin' we can do. He's givin' us twenty-four hours to find out who done it."

"But what if we can't find out?"

"He's gonna fuckin' kill us. Now, come on." He climbed inside of the car and started the ignition. "We gotta get back to the neighborhood. I think they're gunnin' for my grandfather."

***

Back at the Aramingo Diner

When Sonny and Grip emerged from the diner, they cautiously glanced around the parking lot. Satisfied that everything was kosher, they motioned for Gangsta to come outside. His black fitted hat was pulled down over his eyes, shielding his face from any potential witnesses. His right hand was gripped around the handle of a large carry-on suitcase, and Clavenski's body was folded up inside. He quickly glanced around the parking lot, and then used the device on his key ring to pop the back doors on his SUV.

"So, Uncle G, what's the next move?" he asked while pulling the suitcase towards his truck. He picked it up and carefully sat it down in the cargo compartment. After covering the suitcase with a blanket, he locked the back doors, and then joined Sonny and Grip beside the Escalade.

Grip looked at Gangsta, and then glanced at his Rolex. "First and foremost, I need to fly back to Cuba in the morning. Obama's supposed to be lifting the embargo, so I need to make sure that this doesn't affect our asylum agreement. I paid Raul a shit load of money, and it's imperative that I take the necessary steps to protect our assets."

Grip looked at Sonny, who was once again texting on his iPhone. "Sontino, just lay low until I get back. You're too valuable to the family and we can't afford you running around the city like a mad man. I know you wanna take it to Carmine, but you have to be patient. For now, I just need you to lay low."

"More or less," Sonny replied while stuffing his phone back in his Ferragamo slacks. The brown folder that he got from Gangsta was tucked under his right arm, and he couldn't wait to get home so he could thoroughly go through its contents. "When you get back to the states, just holla at me."

"Most definitely," Grip assured him. "I should be back before the summer hits, sometime around June. On the Fourth of July, we're scheduled for a meeting with The Conglomerate, and that's when I'll introduce you as the new boss of the family." He blew into his hands and rubbed them together. "Do you need us to take you anywhere?"

"Naw, I'm good," Sonny replied. "My man's a couple of blocks away. He should be here any second now."

Sonny extended his right hand and Grip accepted the gesture with a firm handshake. As he repeated the process with Gangsta, a black Rolls-Royce Phantom pulled into the parking lot and flashed the high-beams.

"That's my peoples right there," Sonny said as he pointed at the Phantom. "And just so you know," he looked at Grip, "if I catch one of them pussies slippin', I'm puttin' my murda game down."

Grip didn't respond. He already knew that Sonny would do everything in his power to eradicate the Italians, and truth be told, that's exactly what he wanted him to do.

Sonny walked away from the Escalade and climbed in the passenger's side of the black Phantom. As he reclined back in the butter leather seat, he looked over at his silent partner. "First thing in the morning, I want you to get with your people and let 'em know we got $250,000 on Little Angolo and another $250,000 on Carmine. And when you get back to the office, I want you to dig up all the information you can on this organization called The Conglomerate."

Mario Savino nodded his head and then backed out of the parking lot, refusing to give Grip and Gangsta the opportunity to see his license plates.

"So, Uncle G, do you think we can trust him?" Gangsta asked as the black Phantom cruised up Aramingo Avenue.

"Only time will tell," Grip replied as he opened the passenger's side door. "Right now, I just wanna focus on Little Angolo. Did you instruct Murder and Malice to take care of business like I told you?"

"Absolutely," Gangsta nodded his head. "They left for South Philly right before y'all got here. They know what to do."

"All right, that's all I needed to hear," Grip said as he climbed inside of the Escalade. "Now, get rid of Clavenski, and then meet me back at the house."

"Fa'sho."

Grip closed the door and then pulled out his cell phone. He reached inside of the glove compartment and pulled out a white piece of paper with numbers scribbled on it. After dialing the numbers, he held the phone up to his ear.

Ring. Ring. Ring.

"You've reached 1-800-Crime-Stoppers," a feminine voice eased through the phone.

"I would like to report a crime," Grip said. "I think someone's about to be murdered."

"Excuse me, sir?"

"I think there's about to be a murder, and I'm trying to stop it before it happens," he clarified.

"Do you have a location, sir?"

"Yes, I'm in South Philadelphia, on the 600 block of East Wolf Street. I just came in the house from walking my dog, and I noticed that two women were parked in front of my neighbor's house in a dark-colored Dodge Challenger. I looked inside of their car, and they were loading up guns. I honestly believe that they're up to something."

"Okay, thank you for the tip, sir. I'm dispatching a couple of units to your location."

"Thank you."

After disconnecting the call, he motioned for Muhammad to pull off. It was time to clean house, and he didn't want to waste any more time.

Chapter Four
South Philadelphia

A two-toned, silver and black, Cadillac DTS was double-parked in the middle of Wolf Street, and Tony Bruno was sitting behind the steering wheel waiting on Little Angolo. Their plane to Miami was scheduled to take off in less than an hour, and Tony was looking forward to spending a couple of months in the Florida sunshine. The city of Philadelphia had become a war zone, and just like Little Angolo, fifty-seven-year-old Tony Bruno wanted nothing to do with it.

"Let Carmy and the younger guys deal with this shit." That's what Little Angolo had told him a few minutes ago when they were watching Grip and Sonny on the Channel 9 News. "We've already made our bones. It's time for these younger guys to do the same."

Tony fired up a Carrillo cigar and took a deep pull. As he released the smoke, he looked at the two-story row home that once belonged to the original don of South Philly, and his mind traveled back to a day that he'd never forget.

September 2, 1985

He arrived at the don's house just a little before nightfall and was greeted at the front door by Little Angolo, the don's son and the underboss of the family. Dressed in a three-piece Loro Piana suit and handmade Italian leather shoes, Tony felt like a superstar. The books in the Philadelphia mafia had been closed for the past twenty-three years, so for a young Tony Bruno, being "made" was definitely an honor, a rebirth, an unadulterated dedication to a life of crime. From that day forward, The Gervino Crime Family would come first. It would come before his mother, his father, his sisters and brothers, his wife, and his children. If he was called upon to kill his own brother, then that's what he had to do, because this "thing" would come first.

When he entered the finished basement, followed by Little Angolo, he immediately laid eyes on the boss of the family, Angolo 'Big Angolo' Gervino, and his consigliere, Marco 'The Wop' Ferrenga.

In full mafia regalia, the two men stood firm and fearless, calm and deadly. Positioned at the head of a rectangular-shaped, oak wood table, their dark Sicilian eyes were fixed on his. Their shoulders were squared, and their powerful hands were folded in front of their bodies, right over left.

Big Angolo, dressed in a tailor-made, soft-gray Brioni suit, was larger than life. A diamond ring the size of a walnut glistened on his right pinky, and a diamond encrusted Rolex was wrapped around his left wrist. His rich, olive complexion was smooth without blemish and his slicked back salt and pepper hair was barbered to perfection. To the American government, he was a blood-sucking vampire who preyed on the innocent, but to Tony Bruno, he was a stand-up guy, a man of respect, a fucking legend.

In the center of the oak wood table, lined up in a row, were the three elements that represented La Cosa Nostra, a pocket knife, a .45 semi-automatic handgun, and a prayer card of Saint Peter. The pocket knife was a symbol of the mafia's cutthroat tactics. The .45 represented their willingness to shed blood for the sake of the family. And the prayer card was a reminder that their souls would burn in hell for all of eternity if they ever betrayed their family and friends.

As Little Angolo locked the basement door and positioned himself on the don's right-hand side, Marco the Wop began the ceremony. Looking Tony square in the eyes, he slowly recited The Oath of Omerta (The Oath of Silence) in the Italian language, and Tony repeated its every word.

"Io, Anthony Bruno, voglio entrare in quest organizzazione per proteggere la mia famiglia e proteggere i miei amici." (I, Anthony Bruno, want to enter into this organization to protect my family and to protect all of my friends.)

Tony further conceded that death was the only way he could leave this sacred fraternity, and he promised Big Angolo that under no circumstances, would he ever betray the Gervino Borgata. Satisfied with Tony's promise, Big Angolo ordered him to cup his hands together and hold them over the table. He then picked up the pocketknife and said, "Show me your trigger finger."

Tony wiggled his right index finger and Big Angolo pricked his skin with the tip of the blade. Tony's warm blood dripped from the tip of his finger and dotted the prayer card of Saint Peter. Big Angolo laid the knife on the table and picked up the prayer card. After setting the card ablaze, he placed it in the palms of Tony's hands. The card coiled and burned, but Tony didn't flinch. On the contrary, he stuck out his chest and held his head up high. He now walked among the elite. He was a "made" man, a certified member of The Gervino Crime Family.

Back to December 2014

"Hmmm," Tony sighed as he sat there dealing with his nostalgic memories of the mafia's glory days. Things were different now. The standards that once applied had been long forgotten. The new generation of La Cosa Nostra was so "Americanized' that they didn't even speak the Italian language. No longer was honor and respect the backbone of their "thing". Nowadays, it was all about self-gratification and greed.

"It's a friggin' shame," Tony said aloud as he sat there shaking his head.

The screen door on the row home opened up wide and Little Angolo appeared in the threshold. His brown Berluti lamb-skin jacket was zipped all the way up, and a beige Gucci scarf was wrapped around his neck. He closed the front door behind him and descended the concrete steps. Halfway down, he noticed a weird movement in the alley across the street from his house. He stopped walking and leaned forward to get a better look. "Goddamnit," he mumbled to himself, surprised to see a masked gunman running towards him with a black assault rifle clutched in his hands.

Brrrrroc. Brrrrroc. Brrrrroc.

"What the fuck?" Tony shouted, completely caught off guard by the sounds of gunfire and bright muzzle flashes. He crouched down in the driver's seat and looked at the row home just in time to see the first round of bullets twisting Little Angolo in different directions. A bullet blazed through the old man's right shoulder and made him do a one hundred eighty-degree spin. Another bullet crashed into the back of his left leg, separating his knee cap from his shin bone. He slumped against the railing, but refused to go down. His adrenaline was in overdrive and his will to survive was unbending. Defiantly, he crawled up the steps and reached out for the front door.

Boc.

A .223 slug ripped through the back of his skull and splattered his dome like a smashed pumpkin.

Tony Bruno was terrified. Attempting to flee the scene, he threw the transmission in gear and mashed down on the gas pedal.

Vrooooom.

The engine roared like a caged tiger, but the Caddy didn't move. Everything was happening so fast that he didn't realize the transmission was stuck in neutral.

Vrooooom.

The masked gunman turned his attention to Tony Bruno. Swiftly, he ejected the spent magazine and replenished his weapon with a fully loaded banana-clip. After cocking a bullet into the chamber, he aimed the barrel at the Cadillac and peppered the driver's side door.

Brrrrroc. Brrrrroc. Brrrrroc.

Empty shell casings bounced off of the pavement and tumbled in the air before rolling into the gutter. The masked gunman was in the zone. He aimed at the driver's side window and let off a single round.

Boc.

Instantly, the window splintered like a jigsaw puzzle, with hundreds of pieces of broken glass shattered in place. A lemon-sized bullet hole decorated the center, and thin strands of gun smoke drifted from the surface.

The driver's side door popped open and Tony Bruno stumbled from the car with a black .9mm clutched in his right hand. His gray overcoat was drenched in blood, and his coke-bottle granny glasses hung from his face at an obtuse angle. His black hairpiece was cocked to the side like a Yankees fitted hat, and his still-smoldering cigar was dangling from the left side of his mouth. His chubby body slammed against the back fender and a deep guttural sound escaped his lips. Exasperated, he dropped the pistol and looked up at the dark, starless sky. The Angel of Death was upon him. His soul was required in hell.

Brrrrroc.

The old man twisted, turned, spun around, and bounced off of the back fender before melting to the ground.

A black, 2015 Navigator pulled up beside the masked gunman and stopped abruptly. He snatched open the passenger's side door and climbed inside. After removing his ski-mask and breaking down the AR-15, he looked into the back seat where Jorge Dominguez, a Sinaloa captain, was seated in silence. A burning Marlboro was wedged in between his right index and middle fingers, and his dark eyes were tucked behind his Ray Ban sunglasses.

Jorge nodded at the Mexican hitman and said, "You did good, Diablo, very good."

"Who's next?" Diablo asked.

Jorge glanced at his white-gold Maurice Lacroix wristwatch, and then returned his gaze to Diablo. "I spoke to Chatchi a couple of minutes ago, and he told us to keep an eye on Carmine. He's got twenty-four hours to give us a list of names. And if he doesn't, then you'll do what you have to do."

Up the block, sitting behind the tinted windows of a purple Dodge Challenger, Murder and Malice were staring at one another in disbelief. Gangsta had given them specific orders to put Little Angolo out of his misery. But when they pulled up on the block a couple of seconds ago, they quickly realized that someone else had beaten them to the punch. The muzzle flashes of the AR-15 reminded them of the Fourth of July in Las Vegas. They didn't know the shooter's identity, but whoever he was, they knew he was a force to be reckoned with. His stealthy attack had the military written all over it. But who the fuck was he working for? That was the billion-dollar question.

"Fuck it," Malice said aloud as she shrugged her shoulders and started the ignition. "At de end of de day, de job is done and we didn't even break a fingernail. I'm cool wit' dat."

Murder chuckled. She reached inside of her BCBG clutch-purse and pulled out her cell phone. After dialing Gangsta's number, she sat the phone on the center console and settled back in her seat.

Ring. Ring. Ring.

"Holla at me," Gangsta's voice boomed from the speaker.

"Poppy, we're here, but somebody else got to him first," Murder informed him. "Little Angolo and Tony Bruno, de both of dem are dead."

"Was it Sonny's people?"

"I don't think so, Poppy. De mutherfucker who killed dem hopped in a black Navigator wit' Texas license plates."

"Did you get the numbers from the license plate?" Gangsta asked.

"No, we didn't. We couldn't. When we pulled up on de block, de mutha'fucka was already shooting, so we pulled over and watched. Den as soon as de shooting stopped, de black Navigator drove right by us and stopped in front of de house. De shooter hopped inside, den dey drove away," she explained.

"All right, just get back to La Casa Moreno and wait for me."

Click.

Murder looked at Malice and gestured for her to pull off. As they slowly approached the crime scene, they heard the loud wails of oncoming police sirens, and seemingly out of nowhere, red and blue lights illuminated the dark block.

"Fuck," Malice shouted in frustration as she mashed down on the brake pedal, bringing the Challenger to a stop. Surrounded by cop cars, she looked at Murder and shook her head slowly. She didn't have to speak, her road dog was already cocking the lever on her Mack 11. They were wanted for murders in ten different states, but dying in prison wasn't a part of the plan. It was time to hold court in the streets.

***

When Carmine and Fat Petey arrived at the intersection of 6th and Wolf, they couldn't believe what was happening. His grandfather's street was blocked off and the PPD was everywhere. A purple Dodge Challenger was parked in the middle of the block, and the cops had the car surrounded.

"Get out of the car," they heard the officers shouting in unison.

As they hopped out of Carmine's Infinity and attempted to get closer to the drama, a middle-aged black man ordered for them to keep it moving.

"Who the fuck are you?" Carmine asked with a screwed-up face.

The black man pulled out a badge and shoved it in Carmine's grill. "My name's Detective Ronald Sullivan, and this is a murder investigation. Now, the two of you need to back up. It's either that, or go to jail."

Carmine grabbed his crotch and looked at Detective Sullivan with a smug expression. He was about to say something slick, but looked over Sullivan's shoulder and saw another detective that he knew from the neighborhood, Detective James McFarland.

"Hey, yo, Jimmy," he called out to the red-headed Irish man. "What the hell is goin' on ova here? Is my grandfather okay?"

The detective looked at Carmine and sighed. He approached Detective Sullivan and whispered something in his ear. Carmine couldn't hear what was being said, but Detective Sullivan was looking at him with a raised eye brow. He nodded his head a couple of times, and then whispered something back to Detective McFarland.

"I'll take care of it, you have my word," Detective McFarland said as Detective Sullivan was walking away.

"Jimmy, what the hell is goin' on?" Carmine repeated.

"It's your grandfather, Carmy. Him and Tony Bruno were just murdered," he stated in a compassionate voice. "I'm sorry."

Carmine pounded his fist against his hand and then looked at Fat Petey. "Damn it, Petey. I fuckin' knew it."

Fat Petey just stared at him and shook his head from side to side. There was absolutely nothing he could do or say.

Askari

"Well, who's in the car?" Carmine asked as he pointed down the block.

"The murder suspects," Detective McFarland informed him. "We received an anonymous tip from one of the neighbors. Apparently, the neighbor became suspicious when they saw the two women sitting in the car. I believe it was mentioned that one of the women had a gun. We tried to get here as fast as we could, but unfortunately, we didn't make it."

"Fuck." Carmine snapped. "Fuck. Fuck. Fuck."

"Hey, ah, Carmy," Detective McFarland whispered and then looked around to see if anyone was listening. "They wanna question you about the shit that happened in North Philly earlier. So just get lost for now, and I'll keep you posted.

Carmine nodded his understanding and shook the detective's hand. "All right, Jimmy, thanks." After jumping back in his car, he activated his Bluetooth and said, "Call Joey."

Malice cocked back the lever on her Mack 11 and took a deep breath. Looking over at Murder, she asked, "Mommy, you ready?"

Murder cocked her shit back and looked her sister square in the eyes. "Let's get it."

The officer who was standing at the driver's side door was locked and loaded. His Glock 19 was aimed at the tinted window and his trigger finger was itching. He was more than ready to earn his paycheck.

"Driver," the officer shouted. "This is your last warning. If you don't open the door, I'm gonna…"

Bdddddoc.

The tinted window exploded in his face as a succession of hollow-tips blew his cerebrum out the top of his melon. He dropped to his knees and slumped against the driver's side door, face first. It happened so fast that his fellow officers were stuck in the moment, and before they had a chance to react, Murder was already out of the car with a Mack 11 in both hands.

Bdddddoc. Bdddddoc. Bdddddoc.

The police returned fire.

Boc. Boc. Boc.

52

Boom. Boom. Boom.
Pop. Pop. Pop.
Malice attempted to climb out of the Challenger, but a hail of gunfire blazed through the left side of her face, killing her instantly. Murder was in the zone. Bullets were ravaging her body, but she refused to go down. Her trigger fingers were squeezing relentlessly, and even as she stumbled from side to side, she did everything in her power to make the police feel her pain.
Bdddddoc. Bdddddoc.
Unfortunately, her attempts to bring the drama was cut short when a .40 caliber slug ripped through the right side of her head and knocked her eyeball out of the socket. As she dropped the Mack 11s and reached for her dangling eye, another bullet blazed through her left ear and sent her brains out the other side of her face.

"Hold your fire," Detective Sullivan shouted, realizing the two women were no longer returning fire. "Goddamnit," he continued shouting with his hands raised in the air. "Hold your fire."

When the shooting stopped and strands of gun smoke hung in the air, a slew of police officers rushed to the side of their fallen comrade, and Detective Sullivan just stood there shaking his head. He never imagined that such violence could permeate a single city in one day. Philadelphia was falling apart by its seams and he knew that he had to do something to stop it.

Askari

Chapter Five
La Casa Moreno

Stepping inside of his home office, Grip removed his trench coat, hung it in the closet, and then loosened his necktie. His return to the United States had proved to be more beneficial than he'd ever anticipated. The Gervino Crime Family was on the brink of extinction, and he was months away from solely inheriting his father's seat as a chairman of The Conglomerate. The only thing he had to do now was keep Sonny in check. The younger Moreno was the glue that held everything together, and as the new boss of the family, Grip had a peace of mind knowing that his empire and legacy was in good hands.

"Damn, I'm good," he patted himself on the back, referring to the role he played in the ambush at Easy's funeral. He poured himself a double shot of Hennessey, and then plopped down in the leather swivel-chair behind his desk. The tide was finally turning in his favor. After two years of bad blood between him and Sonny, he relished in the fact that he had his grandson exactly where he wanted him, gassed up and propped on his lap like a ventriloquist puppet.

A soft knock sounded from the door. It slowly opened up wide as Muhammad appeared in the threshold. "Mr. Moreno, your nephew, Joey's here. Do you want me to send him up?"

Grip nodded his head in the affirmative. "Yes, Muhammad, send him up."

Joseph 'Skinny Joey' Gervino was Little Angolo's only son. A true gangster in every sense of the word, he was once considered to be South Philly's equivalent to John Gotti. He was flashy and flamboyant, heartless and calculating, but the thing about him that stood out the most was his charismatic nature.

In the mid to late nineties, Joey was arguably La Cosa Nostra's brightest star. He ran a crew of bank robbers that were known as 'The Young Turks', and with a disciplined precision, they ransacked every bank vault from South Philly to Bucks County. There wasn't a federal agent in the eastern region who didn't know that Joey and The Young Turks were behind the brazen chain of bank robberies, but they moved so tight that building a case against them was nearly impossible. And just to piss off the feds, Joey became a true to life Robin Hood, stealing from the rich and giving to the poor. Often, he would invite the local media to his charity events, forcing the authorities to stand by and watch as he selflessly gave away money and gifts. On Thanksgiving, he would hand out turkeys, and every Christmas he would dress up like Santa Clause and hand out gifts as the impoverished citizens of Philadelphia crowded around chanting his name. "Joey. Joey. Joey."

It was during one of these charity events that he met a young hustler named T. Hill. In more ways than one, the young hustler reminded Joey of himself. He publicly took T. Hill under his wing, making him the conduit between himself and North Philadelphia's lucrative drug trade. The Gangster and the Gangsta, that was the caption used by the local media whenever they covered one of Joey's and T. Hill's events. The mob bosses in New York and South Jersey didn't approve of their relationship, and would often tell Joey that blacks were not to be trusted. "Be careful, Joey. That moulie of yours, he's gettin' too close." Unfortunately, Joey didn't listen and it cost him dearly.

In 2001, an indictment came down, and T. Hill did the unthinkable. He cooperated with the federal government, and as a result of his testimony, Joey received a twelve-year sentence. And just like that, the mafia's brightest star was labeled an embarrassment, and quickly found himself at the bottom of the food chain. To make matters worse, when it was time for Little Angolo to select the family's next boss, he bypassed Joey and gave the position to Carmine. Joey was livid, and when he came home from the feds a couple of months ago, he was determined to settle the score. He linked up with Grip and they devised a plan that would devastate and ultimately dismantle The Gervino Crime Family.

Grip knocked down his double-shot of Henny, and then reached inside of his wooden cigar box and removed a Cohiba cigar. As he clipped off the ends of the stogie, Joey strolled inside of the office with a satisfying smile on his face. He was dressed in a black, Fendi embossed, alligator-skin jacket, a pair of Levis, and black alligator-skin boots. At 5'10", 185 pounds, he was the spitting image of a young Little Angolo. His dark brown eyes were wily and cunning, and the slight crook in his nose was a tell-tale sign of the twelve years he'd spent in prison. His slicked back hair was faded on the sides and connected to a neatly lined five o'clock shadow.

Grip stood to his feet and embraced his nephew with open arms. After giving him a warm hug and kissing both of his cheeks, he took a step backwards and admired Joey's gangster.

"You did a good fucking job, Joey. Real good," he praised him. "The shooters on the motorcycles were a classic move, and the bomb inside of the hearse was fucking priceless. I couldn't have done it better myself."

"Fugget about it," Joey replied, "It was nothin'."

"Modesty," Grip acknowledged while sparking up his Cohiba and taking a light pull. "I like that." He returned to his seat and motioned for Joey to take a seat by the door.

"So, what are we gonna do about the old man?" Joey asked. "You know he's gonna be pissed off, right?"

Grip lounged back in his swivel-chair and blew out a thick cloud of smoke. Slightly rocking back and forth, and gazing up at the ceiling, he imagined the look that would cover his father's face when he realized that his little black bastard from Cuba found a way to outsmart him and snatch the carpet from underneath his feet. Grip smiled, knowing that Big Angolo couldn't do anything to stop it. Aside from being locked up in a maximum-security federal prison, the ninety-eight-year-old man was weak and irrelevant. And the biggest mistake he ever made was going out of his way to make things right with his first-born son.

Two years ago, he relinquished half of his empire to Grip, making him and Little Angolo the inheritors of his seat as a chairman of The Conglomerate. Grip and Little Angolo were instructed to share his power in a 50/50 split, but neither was willing to concede. Stuck in a stale-mate, they decided to go behind Big Angolo's back and wage war on one another, with their grandsons doing all of the dirty work. If Carmine won the war, The Gervino Family would hold the power, but if Sonny won, The Moreno Family would reign supreme.

Grip had no intentions of losing this war, and with Sonny tucked away in his back pocket, he was destined to be the most powerful man in the country.

"My father won't be a problem," Grip said as he returned his gaze to Joey. "The board is already acknowledging me and Little Angolo as the inheritors of his seat, so basically there's nothing that my father can do at this point."

"All right, but what about Sontino?" Joey inquired. "Eventually, he's gonna figure out that Carmine had nothin' to do with his father gettin' whacked, and when he does..."

Grip chuckled and waved him off. "Don't worry about Sontino. I've got him right where I want him, trust me. Now, that fucking Carmine," he took another pull on his cigar and blew out the smoke, "he's the one we need to be concerned about. He's more powerful than he realizes, and if he ever learns about The Conglomerate and the position he inherited by your father making him the boss of the family, he could prove to be a major fucking problem."

"And that's the reason we put him and Sontino on a collision course. Sontino's gonna fuckin' crush him."

"Absolutely," Grip confirmed with a devilish grin. "And knowing my grandson, he's going to do it sooner rather than later. I told him to lay low for a few months and not to make a move against Carmine, but that was the battery in his back to make him do the exact opposite. In many ways, Sontino's a chip off the ol' block." Grip smiled and shrugged his shoulders. "You kill my dog and I'll murder your cat, that's the Moreno mentality, and Sontino has shown it time and time again when we had our problems in the past. So, you mark my words, the first opportunity he gets to take out Carmine, he's going to make the best of it."

Joey took a deep breath and sighed. "There's one thing, though."

"Oh, yeah, and what would that be?" Grip asked, looking at him sideways.

"The bomb that blew up Easy's hearse, that wasn't my work," he confessed.

"Huh?" Grip replied with a confused expression written across his face. "Well, if you didn't place the bomb inside of the hearse, who did?"

"I'm assuming it was the same mutherfuckers who whacked him," Joey submitted, shrugging his shoulders as the words left his mouth.

Silently, Grip searched his mind for a logical explanation. "I don't think that's possible. Everybody knows that Sheed was the one who murdered my son." He looked off into the distance and gently massaged his beard. "You know what, Joey, now that I really think about it, Rasheed wasn't capable of making such a hit. The use of explosives was a little out of his reach. Damn it." He banged his fist against the desktop, exuding his frustration. "How in the hell did I overlook such a critical detail? Whoever whacked Ervin, they stuffed him in the trunk of his car, and then blew the mutherfucker up."

Grip flexed his jaw muscles and cracked his knuckles one by one. "Maybe your father was one who whacked him."

"Not at all," Joey said while shaking his head from left to right. "Carmine was handlin' all of the business, and trust me, Sontino and Easy weren't even on his radar. He was too busy cleanin' house."

Grip looked at him for a few seconds and then lounged back in his swivel-chair. "Well, whoever it was, I'm going to make it my business to find out. I can't afford any fuck ups. It's too late in the game for that."

Simultaneously, they both received incoming calls. Grip's Samsung vibrated in his pants pocket, and Joey's iPhone vibrated in his jacket. They looked at one another skeptically, and then slowly reached for their smart phones, maintaining eye contact the entire time. Grip looked at his touch-screen and saw that the caller was Gangsta. He held up the phone allowing Joey to see the identity of his caller, and Joey did the same, showing him Carmine's contact information.

"Hello," they said in unison.

"Uncle G, I just received a call from Murder. She told me that somebody whacked Little Angolo before they could get to him. I'm assuming that the hit came from Sontino."

"All right, Gangsta. Thanks for keeping me updated."

Grip looked at Joey and noticed the smile on his face. He smiled back, knowing that the gist of Joey's phone call was the same as his, Little Angolo was a done deal.

Joey disconnected the call and placed the phone back in his jacket pocket. He was just about to tell Grip about the beef between Carmine and Chatchi, but he never got the chance. He noticed a slight movement in Grip's blue eyes, and then turned around to see what the old man was looking at.

Whack.

The wooden handle of a double-barrel shotgun crashed into his nose, knocking him out of the chair. His vision became blurred and his legs wobbled like spaghetti noodles. He tried to stand up straight, but another blow from the wooden handle knocked him to the floor.

As Muhammad continued to bash Joey in the head, Grip hopped up from his desk and unfastened his belt buckle. After pulling the leather belt from his waist, he jumped on top of Joey, and wrapped it around his neck. Joey kicked his feet and struggled to get free, but Grip's powerful tug on the leather belt was just too strong.

"Sssshhhh," Grip whispered in Joey's ear as he forcefully choked the life out of him. "Just let it go, my little nephew. Just let it go. It's all over now."

Joey's struggles became weaker by the second. His olive complexion became dark burgundy, and thick veins protruded from his forehead. Slowly, begrudgingly, inevitably, the man who was once the face of La Cosa Nostra dwindled off into the spirit world.

Satisfied, Grip looked at Muhammad and nodded his head. The second phase of his takeover was almost complete. The only thing left for him to do was kick his feet up and let Sonny deal with Carmine.

***

Back In South Philly

Detective Sullivan looked from right to left taking an assessment of the maximum carnage that surrounded him. The Crime Scene Unit was out in full force, working in groups of three. Expeditiously, they were taping off the crime scene with yellow police tape, taking photographs, and placing white markers on the ground to identify the hundreds of bullet fragments and empty shell casings. Little Angolo was sprawled out on the steps with half of his head missing, Tony Bruno was stretched out in the street with the top half of his body tucked under his Cadillac, and the two Cuban beauties, Malice and Murder, were covered in blood, slaughtered beyond recognition.

"Sully, what the hell happened?" a voice spoke up from behind.

He looked over his shoulder and saw his partner, Detective Sabastian Phoenix, walking towards him. The two detectives shook hands and approached the shot-up Dodge Challenger.

"A friggin' massacre," Detective Sullivan stated while shaking his head disdainfully. "That's what the hell happened."

"So, I'm assuming this was retaliation for the shooting at Ervin Moreno's funeral," Detective Phoenix reasoned.

"It appears that way," Detective Sullivan said as he pulled open the passenger's side door. He reached inside of his trench coat pocket and pulled out a small flashlight. He shined the light inside of the Challenger and moved it around the front seat.

"What's that?" Detective Phoenix asked. He was standing behind Detective Sullivan, pointing at the center console. "It looks like a cell phone."

Detective Sullivan shined the flashlight on the cell phone and then leaned forward to grab it. "Sabastian, I need an evidence bag. You got one?"

"No, I don't think so," Detective Phoenix answered while patting his pockets. "Let me check with the C.S.U. guys." As he walked away looking for an evidence bag, the Apple iPhone vibrated in Detective Sullivan's hand. He glanced at the screen and the caption read, "Gangsta (267) 555-2011." The name didn't ring any bells but the number was familiar. He accepted the call and held the phone to his ear.

"Hey, Murder," Gangsta's voice came through the phone. "It's gonna take me longer than I expected to get rid of this mutha'fucka, so when y'all get back to the house, just chill, and I'll be there as soon as I can."

Silence.

"Murder?"

Silence.

Detective Sullivan couldn't believe it. The caller was DEA Agent Terry Long. The number struck him as being familiar, but the second he heard the caller's voice, he didn't doubt for one second that Gangsta was Agent Long. He reached inside of his pants pocket and quickly removed his cell phone. After punching in the telephone number of the incoming call, the caption on his LED screen read, "Agent Long (267) 555-2011."

"You son of a bitch," he said to himself as he glanced back and forth from one screen to the other.

"Sully, I found an evidence bag," Detective Phoenix announced while walking up behind him with the plastic bag dangling from his right hand. He noticed the distant look on his partner's face and asked him, "Sully, what's wrong? What happened?"

Detective Sullivan was looking at Murder's cell phone, and noticed that the call ended a couple of seconds ago.

"Sully, what's wrong?"

Detective Sullivan showed him the last incoming call, and then held up his own phone to show him Agent Long's phone number. Detective Phoenix examined both of the screens, and then looked up at his partner. "Umm mmm mmm, and the plot thickens."

Detective Sullivan carefully placed the iPhone inside of the evidence bag and headed towards his unmarked car. "Come on, Sabastian, we need to get back to the station. It's time to start connecting the dots."

***
At a Landfill in Montgomery County

Gangsta was standing beside the five-foot ditch that he'd just finished digging to bury Clavenski's remains. A shovel was gripped in his right hand and his cell phone was clutched in his left. Confused by the silence on the other end of the phone, he said her name, "Murder?"

Silence.

What the fuck, he thought to himself as he listened closely, sifting through the noise in the background.

"Sully, I found an evidence bag," he heard someone say. He pulled the phone away from his ear and looked at it quizzically. He placed it back to his ear and realized that the voice belonged to Detective Phoenix, and the "Sully" he was talking to was Detective Sullivan.

Yo, how the fuck?

"Sully, what's wrong? What happened?" He heard Detective Phoenix say. He quickly disconnected the call and dialed Grip's number.

Ring. Ring. Ring.

"Hello," Grip answered in his deep voice.

"Uncle G, we've got a major fuckin' problem."

"Lemme guess, Murder and Malice, right?"

"Yeah," Gangsta replied with a raised eyebrow. "How did you know?"

"I'm looking at the news," Grip answered. "The cops killed them in front of Little Angolo's house."

"Hey, yo, Unc, they got Murder's cell phone. I just called her and Sullivan's freak ass was the one who answered. Not only did he hear my voice, he had to have seen my number pop up on her screen."

"Don't worry about it," Grip replied. "Just finish doing what you're doing and then get back to the house."

Click.

Askari

Chapter Six
Temple University Hospital

Beep. Beep. Beep.

Rahmello's heart monitor was calm and steady. His fiancée, Olivia Nunez, was standing beside his hospital bed nervously watching the green line bounce across the screen. Her mother, Marisol, was sitting in the wooden rocking chair beside the door, and directly outside of the room, posted in the hallway, were two of Grip's bodyguards. Initially, the tall, neatly dressed Muslim men wouldn't allow the two women inside of the room. But after they received a call from Sonny, the women were granted access.

Beep. Beep. Beep.

Olivia's petite body cringed with ever high-pitched beep. She was gently caressing Rahmello's hand and studying the heart monitor, praying that the green line continued to bounce up and down. She looked at Rahmello and broke down crying. Dressed in nothing but a white hospital gown, he was stretched out on the Craftmatic bed with his left leg propped up in a sling. The damage to his femoral artery was immense. He'd loss so much blood from the gunshot wound that according to his doctor, the odds of him waking up from his coma were 50/50 at best. And even if he did wake up, there was a slight chance that the lack of oxygen to his brain may have caused irreparable damage. The test results from his CAT scan were currently being examined by the hospital's neurologist and Olivia was anxiously waiting on the final determination.

Warm tears trickled down her beautiful face and dotted his hospital gown. The sight of him sent chills down her spine. An intravenous needle was stuffed in his left arm and the tubes that protruded from his nose were connected to the oxygen tank on the other side of his bed. His eyes were closed and his chest rose up and down with his every breath.

Long breath. Long breath. Long breath.

Olivia was devastated. There wasn't a doubt in her mind that her father was responsible for Rahmello's condition. It seemed as though whenever she found love, Poncho would somehow take it away. First, it was the man that she met two years ago while vacationing in Cancun, Mexico. His name was Roberto Alverez, but to the Mexican boxing world he was known as "La Rattan." The name was given to him for his unique boxing style. At a combined record of 41 wins and 0 losses, he won every single fight by trapping himself in a corner of the ring, and then just like a rat, ferociously fighting his way out, dismantling his opponents in the process. The fighter was Mexico's Welterweight Champion, and he quickly became the love of Olivia's life.

Unfortunately, when Poncho found out about their relationship, he demanded that Olivia break it off with the young Mexican. He also vowed that if Roberto ever came to the United States looking for her, he would have him killed. That was eight months ago, and in the process of dealing with her heartbreak, Olivia met and fell in love with Rahmello. He was loving. He was caring. He was passionate. He was strong. He was handsome. He was hers. And now, all because of her racist father, he was stretched out on a hospital bed fighting for his life.

"Baby, wake up," she encouraged him with a face full of tears.

Beep. Beep. Beep.

"I'm so sorry that this happened to you and your family," she continued in a soft voice as she continued to caress his left hand. "This is all my fault."

The beeping of the heart monitor intensified and his breathing became harder, faster.

"My Papi was the one who did this to you," she said while laying her head on his chest. "Him and my brother killed your father, and they shot up his funeral."

"Olivia," her mother protested. "Ju stop dat right now," she scolded her daughter in her thick Columbian accent.

"No, Mami. If I would have told him from the beginning that Papi was the one who killed his father, none of this would have ever happened."

"Escucha me?" Marisol questioned as she got up from the chair and folded her arms across her chest.

"Yes, Mami, I heard you. But I don't care anymore," Olivia continued to cry. "Fuck Papi."

Marisol screwed up her face and disrespectfully spat on the floor. Her daughter was betraying their family right before her very eyes. "Ju are no longer my daughter," she hissed, refusing to accept Olivia's treachery. "Ju are nothin' to me."

As Marisol stormed out of the hospital room, one of Grip's bodyguards appeared in the doorway. "Is everything okay in here?" he asked while looking around the room.

"Yes," Olivia answered his question with tears pouring from her hazel eyes. "Everything's fine."

The large bodyguard looked around the room once more, and then returned to his post.

Olivia returned her head to Rahmello's chest and wrapped her arms around him. "Baby, I'm so sorry. I should have told you about your dad, but I was too afraid."

Rahmello's body began to tremble and the bed shook violently. His breathing became erratic and his heart monitor beeped like crazy.

Beep. Beep. Beep. Beep. Beep. Beep. Beep.

Short breath. Short breath. Long Breath. Short breath. Long breath.

She lifted her head from his chest and looked him in the face. "Ay, dios mio," she blurted out, completely taken by surprise. She couldn't believe it. His blue eyes were fixed on hers.

It was 8:35 p.m. when Sonny walked through the front door of his mansion. As he stepped into the foyer, he noticed that Daphney was standing on the balcony of their grand dual-staircase. She was dressed in a black Victoria's Secret nightgown, and her curly black hair was pulled back into a single braid. A half empty glass of wine was grasped in her right hand, and her arms were folded across her chest.

Immediately, Sonny could sense that something was wrong. Aside from the fact she had a screwed-up face, her eyes appeared to be a little puffy as if she'd just finished crying.

"Babe, what's the matter?" he asked in a concerned voice. "Are the kids, okay?"

"They're okay," she replied with an agitated undertone.

"What about my mom and my grandmom? They good?"

"Umm hmm, they're good. They left about a half an hour ago."

"They left?" Sonny looked at her skeptically. "Whatchu mean they left? Where the fuck is the twins? I told 'em to keep everybody here until I got back."

"I don't know," she said with an attitude and shrugged her shoulders. "They left, and them nut ass twins been left."

"So, what's poppin'? Why you standin' there lookin' all mad?"

"This ain't about me," she said with the snap of her neck. "It's about you. So, what, you fuckin' with the enemy now?"

Her question caught him off guard. "Yo, Daph, whatchu talking 'bout?"

"Nigga, you know what I'm talking 'bout?" She quickly replied.

Sonny sighed. "Actually, I don't know, so what's up?"

"I'm talking 'bout Grip," she barked at him, then shifted her weight to her left hip. "After everything that mutherfucker put us through, you're gonna side with this nigga? Really?"

Damn, he thought to himself, *she must have seen us on the news*. By making it appear as though he was rocking out with Grip, he never even considered how the people around him would feel.

"So, what about Mook?" She continued to grind him up. "What about my daddy? He's doin' life behind that slimy mutherfucker, and you have the audacity to be makin' moves wit' him?"

"Hey, yo, Daph, I'm not in the mood for this shit right now. All I wanna do is get some rest."

His nonchalant attitude pissed her off even more. She downed the rest of her wine, and then looked at him with squinted eyes. "Nigga, you ain't self-made. Everything you have is because of Mook. And this is how you repay him, by siding with the mutherfucker who killed him? Nigga, you ain't shit."

"Yo, it's not even like that," he quickly shot back. He wanted to give her the full scoop, but in order for his plan to work, he had to keep his cards close to his chest.

"Oh, it's not like that?" She pointed at the diamond ring on his right pinky. "So, why the fuck are you wearin' his ring? And why the fuck are they callin' you the new boss of The Moreno Crime Family? Nigga, you must think I'm stupid," she shouted at him.

Sonny took a moment to calm himself down before replying to her outburst. The last thing he ever wanted to do was disrespect his wife, but she was really starting to cross the line. "Listen," he spoke in a calm voice. "I had a long day and I'm tired as shit. All I wanna do is get some rest."

"Well, you're gonna have to get it somewhere else," she vehemently stated. "Because your grimy ass isn't welcome here, you fuckin' traitor."

Sonny chuckled. He was madder than a mutha'fucka, but still he remained calm. "Ay, yo, dig right, stop playin' wit' me, Daphney. I had a long ass day and I'm really not in the mood for this shit."

As he stepped off and headed towards his man-cave in the basement, Daphney snapped out. She cocked back and threw her wine glass, missing his head by inches. "Pussy, ain't nobody playin'. I want you outta my fuckin' house."

Sonny lost it. He darted up the right side of the staircase and got up in her face. "Bitch, is you crazy?" He snapped at her, inadvertently spitting in her face. "Who the fuck you think you talkin' to?"

"Motherfucker, I'm talking to you," she fired back, refusing to be intimidated by his aggression. She slapped him in the face, and before Sonny knew it, both of his hands were wrapped around her neck, and he was squeezing tightly. He pushed her against the railing and the top half of her body was spilling over.

"Get the fuck off of me, Sontino." She tagged him in the head and shoulders with wild punches, and continued shouting. "Get off of me."

Their Rottweiler, Rocko, ran up to the banister and began to bark and growl at Sonny. *Roof. Roof. Urrrr. Roof. Roof. Urrrr.*

"Rocko, shut ya stupid ass up," Sonny shouted at him. He kicked Rocko in the nose, and the large dog scampered away whimpering.

"Sontino, I'm not playing," Daphney shouted. "You better get the fuck off of me."

He yanked her away from the railing and tossed her to the floor. In the corner of his eye, he saw Dayshon running towards Daphney, and Keyonti crawling up the hallway. Both of his babies were crying, and when they reached their mother, they wrapped their arms around her.

Embarrassed and disappointed in himself, Sonny tried to console his family, but Daphney pushed him away and jumped to her feet. Like a woman possessed, she rushed him and threw punches at his face and shoulders nonstop. "Get the fuck outta my goddamned house."

Keyonti looked up at her parents and screamed at the top of her lungs. "Mama. Dada. No fight-fight."

Daphney caught him with a nice blow to the side of his head, and he backed away before things went any further. While shaking his head from side to side, he back-pedaled towards the end of the balcony, and walked down the stairs. After storming out of the house, he climbed inside of his Porsche Spyder and banged his fist against the steering wheel. "Fuck." He released his frustration. Everything that he loved and worked so hard for was slowly slipping away from him.

"What the fuck is goin' on?" he asked himself, looking at his reflection in the rear-view mirror. As he reached under the driver's seat to grab his car keys, his iPhone vibrated in his pants pocket.

Vrrrrrm. Vrrrrrm. Vrrrrrm.

"Yo, who the fuck is this?" he snapped into the phone, not recognizing the number.

"Sontino, it's Oli."

"Oli," he stated in a nervous voice. "What's wrong? Did somethin' happen wit' Mello?" His heart was racing and the last thing he needed was bad news stating that his little brother's conditioned had worsened.

"You need to get back to the hospital," Olivia stated with urgency. "It's Mello. He woke up from his coma and he's snapping the fuck out."

"A'ight, Oli, I'm on my way."

***

"Agh, shit," Rahmello shrieked when he tried to stand up on his injured leg. The last thing he remembered was the ambush at Easy's funeral. Images of his family crouched down in the bullet-proof Sprinter Van flooded his mind, and his blood began to boil. It was all coming back to him. His grandmother and step-mother were calling out for God. Daphney was down on the floor consoling his crying nephew and niece. And his team was fresh out of bullets.

"Sonny," he shouted. "Where the fuck is my brother?" He snatched the oxygen tubes out of his nose and ripped the intravenous needle out of his left arm.

"Baby, calm down," Olivia pleaded in a soothing voice. "Just calm down."

Confused, he looked at his fiancé, and then looked around the hospital room. "Yo, where the fuck is my family?" he continued snapping. "And who the fuck is these niggas?" He pointed at the large bodyguards, giving them the look of death.

"Your grandfather sent them to watch over you," Olivia quickly explained. Tears were dripping down her face and it was killing her to see him like this. He was confused and disoriented, and she didn't know what to say or do. She looked at the bodyguards and shouted, "Don't just stand there. Do something."

The bigger of the two bodyguards approached Rahmello's hospital bed and spoke to him in a calm voice. "Just relax, Little Brother. Your grandfather sent us here to protect you."

"My grandfather?" Rahmello asked. He was sitting on the edge of the bed with a scowl on his face. "Hold up, you mean Grip?"

"Yes," the bodyguard confirmed. "Mr. Moreno gave us specific orders to guard you with our lives."

Rahmello picked up the heart monitor and threw the large device at the man's head, causing him to duck and run out of the room. "Yo, where the fuck is my brother?" he asked Olivia.

"He's comin'," Olivia cried. "I just talked to him and he's on the way."

"Yo, we gotta get up outta here." He scooted off of the bed and wrapped his left arm around Olivia's shoulders. She tried her best to support his weight, but when he planted his left foot on the floor, his leg buckled under the pressure and he fell down. "Ummm fuck," he winced from the sharp pain that shot up his leg. "Yo, this shit hurt like a mutha'fucka."

Olivia reached down to help him up, and as she placed his left arm back around her shoulders, three security guards rushed inside of the room with two doctors right behind them.

"Sir, you need to calm down," one of the security guards warned Rahmello as he grabbed Olivia by the arm and pulled her away. His two colleagues positioned themselves around Rahmello, and watched him closely as the first security guard escorted Olivia towards the door.

"Rahmello, just calm down, baby, please," Olivia advised him as the security guard pulled her out into the hallway.

"Fuck that," Rahmello yelled at her. "Go get my fuckin' brother." He tried to stand on his feet but the security guards tackled him back to the floor. As they struggled to restrain him, Dr. Levy looked at his understudy and gestured for the rookie to hand him a sedative. The young doctor reached inside of his pocket and quickly removed a needle that was halfway filled with Thorazine. He removed the cap and handed the needle to Dr. Levy.

"All right, now hold him steady," Dr. Levy instructed the security guards as he gently pressed down on the dropper, causing a drop of Thorazine to trickle from the tip of the needle. The overweight black men adhered to the doctor's order. The older one held Rahmello's legs together, and the younger one placed his knees on Rahmello's back and then forcefully pinned down his left arm.

"Get the fuck off me," Rahmello shouted as he struggled to break free.

Dr. Levy approached them slowly, and then leaned forward to administer the shot. He buried the needle deep in Rahmello's left arm and gently pressed his thumb on the dropper. Rahmello continued to struggle, and then suddenly calmed down as the Thorazine shot throughout his bloodstream like a ten-dollar bag of heroin.

***

Police Headquarters

Police Commissioner, Monroe Jackson, was flaming mad. His phone lines were ringing non-stop, and every government official from the Governor on down had a few choice words for the top dawg of the PPD. The chain of murders in the last couple of weeks had attracted national attention, and the Commissioner was feeling the heat from all angles.

Sitting behind his desk with his face in his hands, he was pissed off, to say the least. About twenty minutes ago, his son-in-law, Detective Ronald Sullivan, sent him a text message claiming that he'd made a break in the case and that he was on his way to pay him a visit. Unfortunately for Detective Sullivan, he was walking face first into a shit storm. Like most organizations that operated through a chain of command, shit rolled downhill, and son-in-law or not, Commissioner Jackson was more than ready to tear him a new asshole.

A knock sounded from the door and Commissioner Jackson lifted up his head. "Come in."

Detective Sullivan stepped inside of the office with Detective Phoenix close behind. He approached the Commissioner's desk with the evidence bag clutched in his right hand. Looking at him, he shook his head from side to side, and said, "Dad, you won't believe this shit."

The Commissioner leaped out of his chair, leaned across the desk, and grabbed Detective Sullivan by the collar of his trench coat. "Do you have any idea what these sons-of-bitches are try'na do to me?" he shouted in Sullivan's face. "Do you?"

Detective Sullivan was like a deer caught in the middle of on-coming traffic lights, stuck on stupid. He looked at his partner with pleading eyes, but Detective Phoenix lowered his head and took a step backwards.

"These motherfuckers are coming for my goddamned pension," the Commissioner continued shouting. "The entire city has run amuck and they're blaming me, Ronald. The Governor's been coming down on the mayor. The mayor's been coming down on the goddamned District Attorney. And now that cock-smoking son-of-a-bitch is coming down on me."

"D—D—Dad, just cool out for a second and hear me out," Detective Sullivan said with his hands held up in a defenseless posture. He'd always known that his father-in-law had a propensity to get goofy, but he never imagined that the commissioner would put his hands on him.

The commissioner pushed Detective Sullivan backwards, and then looked back and forth between him and detective Phoenix. He pointed at the evidence bag and ordered Sullivan to hand it over. "What the fuck is this?" he asked while examining the cell phone.

"It's the break in the case that we've been looking for," Detective Sullivan stated as he straightened out his collar. "While searching the suspect's vehicle, Sabastian spotted the phone laying on the center console. I picked it up, and by happenstance, we received an incoming call. The caption on the screen indicated the name 'Gangsta', and right below the name, there was a telephone number that I partially recognized. Initially, I couldn't put the pieces together, but when I answered the incoming call and heard the caller's voice, I immediately knew who it was."

"And who the hell was it?" the commissioner inquired with a scowl on his face.

"It was Terrance Long. He's an agent with the DEA."

The Commissioner gave him a funny look. "The DEA? Are you sure about this, Ronald?"

"A hundred and ten percent," Detective Sullivan replied, nodding his head in the affirmative. He reached inside of his trench coat pocket and pulled out his personal phone. After scrolling through his rolodex and bringing up Agent Long's contact information, he handed the phone to the commissioner. "The second I heard the caller's voice, I compared the contact information from the suspect's phone with the information in my phone, and the numbers were a match. Apparently, and this is solely based on the call log, Agent Long is somehow involved with this incident. As you can see, he was contacting the suspects prior to, and immediately after these murders."

The commissioner rubbed his chin and sighed. Things were becoming more and more complicated by the second. "First thing in the morning, I want you to do a little fishing and have a conversation with this Agent Long. In the meantime, I'm going to get a subpoena for these phone records." He placed the cell phone back in the evidence bag, and then slowly shook his head from side to side. "I need a goddamned drink."

Askari

Chapter Seven
An Hour Later

After stopping by his house on Reese Street to take a quick shower and throw on some fresh clothes, Sonny returned to the hospital to see about Rahmello. Carefully avoiding any unwanted attention, he parked his Porsche across the street from the hospital, right in front of the deli on Old York Road. After climbing out the coupe with the fox-fur hood on his Sean John coat covering most of his face, he locked the doors, and cautiously walked towards the emergency room entrance with his left hand gripping the .10mm in his coat pocket.

When he stepped inside of the lobby, he was relieved to see that the media circus from earlier was long gone. There were no cameras, no bright ass lights, and most importantly, no nosey ass news reporters. Approaching the receptionist's desk, he pulled down his fox-fur hood and politely addressed the red-head white woman who was sitting behind the desk, typing on her computer.

"Excuse me, my name's Sontino Moreno. I'm here to see my brother, Rahmello Moreno."

The receptionist gave him a weird look. The Moreno Crime Family was the trending topic throughout the hospital, and ever since the beginning of her shift, she'd been hearing stories about a federal agent being blown to pieces by a car bomb and a two-minute-long shootout in the middle of Broad Street. The stories were almost surreal. But the second she laid eyes on the two bodyguards posted up in front of Rahmello's room, she realized that The Moreno Crime Family was from an urban legend.

Immediately, Sonny could see that he was making the woman uncomfortable. He expected as much. The woman began to speak, but he held his right index finger up to his lips, signaling for her to keep quiet. "Sshh." He then reached inside of his pants pocket and pulled out a white envelope. "Here," he slid the envelope across the counter and looked at her attentively. "It's five thousand dollars inside of this envelope. Please don't call any news reporters or alert anyone else to my presence."

Intrigued, the white woman just sat there shaking her head. In a weird way, it felt as though she were playing a minor role in their crime syndicate and her pussy muscles clenched together. "All I need you to do is page Dr. Levy, and tell him I'm here. He's expecting me."

"Right away, Mr. Moreno." She picked up the telephone receiver, hit a button on the keypad, and her voice boomed over the intercom. "Dr. Levy to the emergency room receptionist's stand. Dr. Levy to the emergency room receptionist's stand."

"Thank you," he mouthed the words and then took a seat in the first row of chairs.

Damn, Grip wasn't bullshittin', he thought to himself, referring to the news break that came across the radio while he was driving to the hospital. According to Power 99, Little Angolo and his capo, Tony Bruno, were executed in front of his South Philly row home. The radio station also mentioned that two Spanish women, who were believed to be the shooters, were killed by the police as they attempted to flee the scene. *Yo, that had to be Murder and Malice they was talking 'bout. Damn, after everything we went through, this nigga's really out there ridin' wit' me.*

The double-doors that led to the back of the emergency room swung open and Dr. Levy strolled into the lobby with a cup of coffee in his right hand. Sonny stood to his feet and waved him over.

"Yo, doc, I got the word from my brother's lady. What's good? She told me that Mello came up outta that thing."

"He did," Dr. Levy said with a smile. "Come on, I'll take you to him."

He led Sonny down the hallway and up to the third floor where Rahmello's room was located. "We had to sedate him, so technically, he's knocked back out. But he should wake up in another hour or so."

"A'ight," Sonny replied while taking in his surroundings. The walls were a bright white and the checkered linoleum floor had a polished glow. The atmosphere was nice and cool, and the aroma of fresh disinfect permeated the air. As they continued walking down the long hallway, Sonny couldn't help but to peek inside of the rooms as they passed by. Up ahead, he spotted two of the body-guards from earlier. They were standing in front of a room that he assumed was Rahmello's. When they saw him approaching, they nodded their heads respectfully, and he returned the gesture.

When they finally reached the room, Olivia got up from the rocking-chair and wrapped her arms around Sonny.

"Sontino, he woke up and went crazy," she told him. "He ripped the heart monitor out of the wall and threw it at the bodyguards, and the doctors had to give him a needle to calm him down."

"Yeah, Sontino, it was bad," Dr. Levy added as he approached Rahmello's Craftmatic bed. "We actually had to move him into another room."

"A'ight," Sonny said with his arm wrapped around Olivia's shoulder, "but other than that, everything's good?"

"It certainly appears that way," Dr. Levy replied. He picked up the chart from the foot of Rahmello's bed and flipped it open. "Based on the report from the neurologist, he didn't suffer any brain damage, so he should be up and running in no time at all."

"Brain damage?" Sonny asked. "Why would he have brain damage?"

"Well, that would have been a result of his severe blood loss. The femoral artery is responsible for a large percentage of the body's blood flow, and as we all know, the body's blood flow carries oxygen to the brain. Rahmello was quite lucky. Usually, when a patient has suffered from severe blood loss, the result is minor brain damage. Actually, in some cases the damage is major," Dr. Levy explained. He closed the chart and returned it to its holder.

"So, my brother's good, then?"

"Yes, Sontino, your brother's going to be fine."

Upon hearing this, Olivia broke down crying and rushed to Rahmello's side.

Sonny shook the doctor's hand and said, "Thanks for everything, doc."

"Just doing my job," Dr. Levy replied with a smile. He started to leave the room, but stopped when Sonny called him.

"Hey, yo, doc, is there a time frame as to when I can get him out of here?"

Dr. Levy glanced at his watch, and then looked at Rahmello. "We'll probably be releasing him in the morning. His condition is stable, so there's really no need for him to hang around."

"Well, what if I wanted to get him out of here tonight?" Sonny asked with a pleading undertone.

"Ah, that wouldn't really be a problem, but hospital protocol mandates that we keep him for at least twenty-four hours."

"A'ight, doc, thanks."

As soon as Dr. Levy left the room, Sonny got the attention of the two bodyguards. "You," he pointed at the tall light skinned man, "get my grandfather on the phone. And you," he directed his attention to the dark-skinned man, "I need you to help me carry my little brother out to the car."

***

La Casa Moreno

Grip was seated at the marble island in the center of his kitchen. The roasted lamb that he was feasting on tasted like butter, and was topped off with wild rice and beans. It was a meal fit for a king. A tall glass of iced tea with lemon was cradled in his left hand and his cell phone was loosely positioned in his right.

"So, what time is your flight leaving for Cuba?" his personal advisor and best friend, Judge Gregory Johnson, asked him.

Grip swallowed the piece of lamb he was chewing and then took a sip of his iced tea. "Four a.m.," he replied before wolfing down another forkful of lamb shoulder. "Heldga's upstairs packing our luggage. I've decided to bring Muhammad and Gangsta along for the trip," he continued with a mouth full of food.

"All right, Gervin, now please don't take this the wrong way," Judge Johnson cautioned. "Do you really think we can trust Sontino?"

Grip dropped his fork and then knocked down the rest of his iced tea. "Come again."

"Do you think we can trust him?" Judge Johnson repeated his question. "You know, after everything that's happened between you two."

Grip tossed the question around in his mind, sifting through the pros and cons. "Trust will come later," he said. "It might be a little rocky at first, but he'll come around eventually."

"But, what if he doesn't?" Judge Johnson countered.

"He will," Grip replied, raising his voice a few octaves. "He has to."

Judge Johnson sighed. "Listen, my brother, all I ask is that you think it over a little more. By investing everything into Sontino's acquiescing to his new role as the boss of the family, you're neglecting the two things that made you the biggest boss that Philadelphia has ever seen."

"Oh, yeah, and what would that be?" Grip asked with a slight attitude.

"Your ability to anticipate future problems, and making the necessary adjustments to have them obliterated before they even materialize."

Grip flexed his jaw muscles. He knew that his old friend had spoken the truth, but so much was already invested in Sonny. There was absolutely no way he could move forward without his grandson at the helm.

An incoming call illuminated his touch-screen. "G.J., I've got an incoming call. It's Brother Aziz. Him and Brother Shabazz are at the hospital with Rahmello."

Rahmello. Rahmello. Rahmello.

The name bounced around his brain like a loud scream in a dark deserted cave. *Rahmello. That's it.* Instantly, he realized that his younger grandson was a much better candidate than his older brother. There wasn't any bad blood between them and, therefore, he didn't have to worry about any future retaliation.

"Grip?" Judge Johnson's voice boomed through the phone, interrupting his thoughts. "You still there?"

"Yes, G.J., I'm still here. But I really need to take this call."

"All right, my brother. Just make sure you give me a call when you touch down in Cuba," Judge Johnson said before disconnecting the call.

Grip swiped his right index finger across the screen, accepting Brother Aziz's call. "As salaamu alaikum," he gave the Islamic greeting. "May peace be upon you, my brother?"

"Wa alaikum salaam," Brother Aziz returned the greeting.

"How's my grandson?" Grip quickly inquired.

"All praises are due to Allah. The little brother has awakened from his coma."

"Is he with you right now?" Grip asked. "Does he know what's going on?"

"It was rocky at first," Brother Aziz informed him. "When he awakened, he completely lost it. He was screaming for Sontino, and when me and Brother Shabazz tried to calm him down, he yanked his heart monitor out of the wall and threw it at us. It got so crazy that the doctors had to sedate him."

"Has anyone contacted Sontino?"

"Yes," Brother Aziz confirmed. "Rahmello's fiancée, the little Columbian sister, she was the one who called him."

"And what happened?"

"He arrived a couple of minutes ago. He spoke to the doctor, then the next thing I know, he told me to get you on the phone, and he told Brother Shabazz to help him carry Rahmello outside to his car. And Brother Gervin," he continued in a voice that was all business, "you made an excellent decision. Everything about that little brother is boss."

"Where is he now?"

"He just finished strapping Rahmello in the back of Brother Shabazz's Tahoe. Hold on, lemme call him over."

Brother Aziz honked the horn and waved Sonny over to his Suburban. "Here he comes," he spoke into the phone before handing it to Sonny through the passenger's side window.

"The doctor said that Rahmello's going to be fine," Sonny informed his grandfather. It didn't make any sense for me to leave him here, so I snuck him out."

"Okay," Grip replied. "And where do you plan on taking him?"

"Back to my block," Sonny said. "I'ma be in the hood for a little while."

"In the hood? What about your estate?"

"My estate?" Sonny asked with a raised eyebrow, wondering how Grip knew about his house. "Yo, who the fuck told you about my crib?"

"I own it," Grip revealed.

Sonny went dead quiet.

"I think it would be best if you came to see me," Grip continued in his deep voice. "Tell Brother Aziz I said to bring you to me."

Click.

***

Back At Club Spontaneous

"We're fuckin' closed tonight," Fat Petey shouted at the crowd of exotic dancers. He was posted in front of the entrance with his flabby arms folded across his chest.

"But, Carmine said that I could work in V.I.P. tonight," a beautiful Persian woman complained.

"That ain't my problem," Fat Petey shot back.

"Petey, y'all on that bullshit," a curvy Latina in a black waist-length mink snarled at him.

"Yeah, yeah, yeah. Keep it movin', toots."

Jonathan *Jon-Jon* Veasy pulled up in a white Ram truck and hopped out looking like the stereotypical white rapper that he was. His Gucci parka was unzipped and the diamond pendent that hung from his platinum chain was swinging back and forth with his every step.

"Yo, Petey, what's good?" he asked with his arms stretched out wide. "My party's tonight and everybody's textin' me sayin' that you won't let 'em inside. Yo, what's up wit' dat?"

Fat Petey shot him a look that said, *Who gives a fuck?* Jon-Jon was connected to the family, but he wasn't a "made" man, and therefore Fat Petey couldn't have cared less.

"Well, whoever told you that, they were tellin' the truth," Fat Petey told him flat out. "We're closed for the weekend, so call Carmy and reschedule."

Jon-Jon looked around the parking lot and was vexed to see everyone leaving. "Yo, Petey, this is bullshit. Straight up."

Fat Petey scowled at the fake ass Paulie D, and then smacked the dog shit out of him. "I said we're fuckin' closed," he snapped at him. "Now, get your Jersey Shore lookin' ass outta here."

After the crowd of strippers and patrons left, Fat Petey stepped inside of the club and locked the door behind him. Michael "Little Mikey" Castello and Peter "Pap-Pap" Clamenza were down on their hands and knees cleaning the blood off of the floor. And Fat Petey's nephew, Anthony Deluca, was down in the basement chopping up Alphonso's body.

"We gotta get rid of him," Carmine had said when they'd returned to the club. "The last thing we need is the fuckin' cops snoopin' around."

As he approached the door to Carmine's office, he knocked softly and said, "Carmy, you okay?"

The door opened and Carmine ushered him inside. Fat Petey could tell that Carmine had just finished crying, but he didn't say anything about it. Instead, he closed the door behind him and looked around the office.

"Little Mikey and Pap-Pap did a good job of cleanin' the place up, huh, Carmy?"

"Yeah, they did alright," Carmine replied in a low voice. He positioned himself in front of the television and aimed his remote control at the Blue Ray machine. Pressing the *rewind* button, he looked at Fat Petey and said, "I was watching the footage from the night Roberto went missin' and I got the three motherfuckers on camera who did it." He released his finger from the *rewind* button and pressed *play.*

The video didn't have any audio, but the picture was crystal clear. Chico was carrying Roberto back to his Lamborghini when a dark-skinned black man with shoulder-length dreads approached them from behind. Chico spun around as if the dark-skinned man said something to get his attention. As the dark-skinned man got closer to Chico and Roberto, he pulled out a stun-gun and shot Chico, causing the large man to drop Roberto. As Chico staggered towards his attacker, reaching out to snatch away the stun-gun, another black man with shoulder-length dreads emerged from the black Hummer that was parked beside Roberto's Lamborghini, and jumped on Chico's back. Chico slammed him into the chrome grill of the Hummer, and then another black man climbed out of the SUV. He whipped out a gun and aimed it at the back of Chico's head. But before he had the chance to let off a shot, the hydrodynamics of the stun-gun took its toll and Chico crashed to the pavement. When all was said and done, Chico was stretched out in the parking lot, and Roberto was handcuffed and tossed in the back of the Hummer.

"Petey, have you seen these niggers before?" Carmine asked while pressing the *stop* button.

"No," Fat Petey said, shaking his head from side to side. "But rewind the footage back a little further. It looks like the first kid, the one who crept up behind them." He pointed at the screen. "There, him right there. It looks like he followed them out of the club."

Carmine checked the time of the video, then switched over to the security cameras that covered the stage, bar, and dance floor. He punched in the date and time, and then pressed the *rewind* button for a couple of seconds.

"Hold up," Fat Petey blurted. "Right there," he pointed at the bottom of the screen. "Press the *zoom* button."

The camera zoomed in on a dark-skinned man sitting at the bar. He was sipping on a Corona and watching Roberto like a hawk. A petite, light skinned woman in a baby-blue thong walked by, and he grabbed her by the arm. After talking for a couple of minutes, he pulled out a wad of money and tried to hand her a few bills, but she turned him down.

"Hey, Petey, isn't that the Asian-lookin' broad that you was stickin' the sausage to?" asked Carmine.

"Yeah," Fat Petey confirmed. "That's Jasmyn. I been bangin' the broad for a while now."

"Doesn't it seem like the two of them know one another?"

"Yeah, it does," Fat Petey nodded his head. "It's possible, anyway."

Carmine pressed the *pause* button. "I want you to print out this screen-shot, and show it to her. This broad knows somethin', and whatever it is, you's better get it out of her. Capisce?"

"I'm on it, Carmy."

"All right, now leave me alone for a while. I need to call my great-grandfather."

Fat Petey nodded his understanding, and then headed for the door. As he gripped the door knob, he looked back at Carmine. "Hey, Carmy, I'm sorry about what happened to your grandfather."

Carmine sighed, "Thanks, Petey."

As Fat Petey left the office, he pulled out his cell phone and called the original don of South Philly, his great-grandfather, Angolo *Big Angolo* Gervino.

Chapter Eight

"This nigga owns my house?" Sonny questioned himself as he followed behind the two SUVs. Their destination was Grip's estate in Bala Cynwyd, Pennsylvania. Brother Aziz was leading the convoy in his black, 2015 Chevy Suburban, and Brother Shabazz was right behind him in a forest-green Tahoe, with Rahmello and Olivia safely strapped in the back seat. As they drove up City Line Avenue, Sonny activated his Bluetooth and said, "Call Daphney."

The phone rang about ten times and then went to voicemail. Frustrated, he repeated the process for two minutes straight, and the same thing happened every time, no answer. "Yo, this some nut ass shit," he complained aloud. As far as he knew, the mansion, the house in Cheltenham, the nightclub and sports bar was owned by M&R Real Estate, the company that Alvin left to Daphney. So, what the fuck was Grip talking about?

Brother Aziz turned off of City Line Avenue and led the convoy down a long hilly road that cut through a grove of willow trees. The naturally dark road was fairly lit by towering light posts, and up ahead, atop a steep hill, Sonny could see a wide range of burgundy shingles. Elegantly placed, the large shingles were layered down the slopes of a cream-colored roof. As they ascended the steep hill and slowly cruised down the other side, Sonny was blown away by the sight of Grip's mansion. It was hands down the most beautiful piece of property that he had ever seen. Surrounded by a ten-foot-high, Roman stonewall, the 25,000 square foot mansion was more akin to a small gated community rather than a single house.

When the three-vehicle convoy reached the bottom of the hill, they slowly approached a black, eight-foot-high, iron gate with "La Casa Moreno" written across in large solid gold letters. A small security booth was positioned to the left, and a uniformed security guard was standing beside it. The older black man nodded at Brother Aziz, and then activated his walkie-talkie. After receiving permission from Muhammad, he stepped inside of the booth and hit the button that opened up the gate.

One by one, the three vehicles drove through the open gate and coasted up the cobble-stone driveway. A succession of in-ground lanterns was lined up along the sides of the driveway, and the cobble-stone road led to a large loop that wrapped around a large water fountain. The fountain's icy blue water was illuminated by built-in halogenic lights, and the statue of a life-sized lion was prominently positioned in the center. The large beast was standing on all fours and facing the driveway. His muscular chest and full-grown mane were proudly on display, and his facial expression was Grip's silent warning, "Fuck around if you want to."

As Brother Aziz pressed down on the brake pad and brought the convoy to a stop, the mansion's double-doors opened up wide and Grip was standing in the threshold with an old white woman standing beside him. Brother Shabazz hopped out of his truck and then opened the back door for Olivia. He then motioned for Brother Aziz to help him carry Rahmello into the house.

Sonny reached down and grabbed the Glock .40 that was stashed under his driver's seat. Placing the pistol in his left jacket pocket, he killed the ignition, and then climbed out of the Porsche. He looked to his right and saw the two bodyguards carrying Rahmello. Olivia was a couple of steps behind them, and he could see that she was still crying.

"As salaamu alaikum," Grip greeted his soldiers.

"Wa alaikum salaam," they replied in unison.

"Heldga," Grip addressed his housekeeper. "This is my grandson, Rahmello. He's hurt very bad and I need you to look after him, you hear?"

The elderly Armenian woman looked at him and nodded her understanding. She hardly spoke the English language, and therefore she only spoke when necessary.

"Very well," Grip smiled at her. "Take them to the first guest room on the second floor."

Again, she nodded her understanding. She looked back and forth between Brother Shabazz and Brother Aziz, and then gestured for them to follow her into the house.

As Grip stepped aside, he looked at Sonny and sighed. "Welcome to La Casa Moreno," he greeted his grandson. Sizing him up, he noticed the bulge in his fox-fur coat. "It's freezing out here. Why don't you come inside?" He spun around and began walking towards his office. "Follow me," he said over his right shoulder. "I need to show you something."

Sonny stepped inside of the house and closed the double-doors behind him. The grandeur of Grip's mansion was utterly breathtaking. The twenty-foot-high ceiling was supported by large white columns, reminding him of the lavish middle-eastern masjids that he'd seen on television. The walls were painted a soft mint-green, perfectly matching the money-green marble that covered the floor, and as he followed Grip down the hallway, he couldn't take his eyes off of the million-dollar Pablo Picassos that decorated the foyer.

Damn, he thought to himself. *This nigga's caked up fa'real.* He was accustomed to being around money, but his grandfather was on a different stratosphere. Fuck the mansion, his art collection alone was worth more than Sonny's empire. *Damn.*

He followed Grip into his office and took a look around. The first thing he noticed was the picture on the wall behind Grip's desk. It was a black and white picture of Grip infused with the Philadelphia skyline. Towering over the city, he was dressed in a black tuxedo and his Bossalini hat was slightly cocked to the right. He was puffing on a Cohiba cigar and his cold blue eyes were looking down on the streets of Philly.

Taking his eyes off of the picture, Sonny looked at the mahogany desk. A gold lamp was positioned beside a 19" computer monitor, and off to the right, he noticed the security monitors that were built into the wall. There was a total of ten monitors, and each monitor showed a different section of the mansion. On the left side of the desk, he spotted a fully stocked book shelf with damn near every title from *The Art of War* to *The Qur'an*, and in the far-right corner, he saw a wooden coat rack and a file cabinet. A 60-inch plasma was built into the far wall, and two leather swivel-chairs were positioned in front of his desk.

"Have a seat," Grip instructed him, gesturing towards the two swivel-chairs. He approached his file cabinet, opened the top drawer, and extracted a red folder. He sat down behind his desk and opened the folder. He pulled out a five-page document and sat it down on the desk.

"About your estate in Upper Dublin," he said, looking Sonny square in the eyes. "It's owned by M&R Real Estate. Your house in Cheltenham, your nightclub on Broad Street, and your sports bar on Spring Garden Avenue are all owned by M&R, correct?"

"Yeah," Sonny said while nodding his head. His left hand was still wrapped around the handle of his Glock .40 and he wouldn't hesitate to use it if he felt that he had to.

"Well, guess who owns M&R Real Estate?"

"You."

"Absolutely," Grip said with a smile. He flipped to the last page of the document and picked up his gold ink pen. After signing his name at the bottom of the page, he laid the pen on top of the paper and slid it over to Sonny. "All you have to do is add your signature, and M&R Real Estate belongs to you."

The look on Sonny's face exuded his frustration and confusion. "I need you to explain how you own M&R because, as far as I know, Alvin Rines left the company to my wife when she was a little girl."

"He did," Grip confirmed. "But he only owned ten percent of the company. You see, Alvin was my number one soldier before he went to the can. Clavenski created a bullshit case against Alvin, hoping that Alvin would turn state's evidence against me, but he didn't. He remained strong, even in the face of a life sentence. His loyalty was immensely appreciated, and to compensate him for his sacrifice, I relinquished ten percent of my company, making him a minority owner. At the time, Moreno Real Estate was worth forty million dollars. Today, it's worth one hundred fifty million dollars."

"Yo, hold up," Sonny said with a screwed-up face. "So, what, you're tellin' me that you know my wife?"

"No, not personally," Grip clarified. "But on the strength of Alvin, I've been taking care of Daphney since she was five years old."

"Well, does she know about you?"

"Not that I'm aware of," Grip stated. "In 1992, the same year that Alvin went to prison, I changed the company's name from Moreno Real Estate to M&R Real Estate, and the company went public. Alvin retained his ten shares of the company and signed them over to his daughter, your wife, Daphney. Now, me on the other hand, I sold thirty-nine of my ninety shares on the open market. And as of right now, M&R Real Estate has a total of thirteen owners. However, by retaining fifty-one of the shares, I'm the majority shareholder, which means that I'm still the boss. Now, my twelve co-owners, including Daphney, can make suggestions, but ultimately I'm the one calling the shots."

"I'm sayin', though, based on everything that I've seen, Daph's the one running the show."

"And she's supposed to," Grip nodded his head. "Aside from owning ten percent of the company, she's also the Chief Executive Officer, and therefore she's responsible for the day-to-day operations. But even then, she doesn't call the shots. The most she can do is make suggestions pertaining to the daily operations."

"A'ight," Sonny replied. "Let's say I choose to sign this document, then what?"

Grip smiled at him. "You'll be the majority shareholder, claiming ownership of numerous properties. And that's including La Casa Moreno, your Upper Dublin estate, and the two businesses you thought you owned."

Sonny looked at the documents, and then returned his gaze to Grip. "Yo, cut the bullshit. What's your angle? After all the shit we been through, why the fuck is you goin' outta ya way to do all of this for me?" He removed the Glock .40 from his coat pocket and sat it down on top of the paperwork. "What makes you think you can trust me?"

Grip smiled at him, and then cleared his throat. "Ah em."

Before Sonny even peeped what was happening, Muhammad was standing beside him with a sawed-off shotgun clutched in his hands. Sonny was unmoved. He didn't even flinch. Instead, he just looked at Muhammad and dismissed him with the wave of his left hand.

Like a proud grandfather, Grip chuckled and clapped his hands together. "That's the reason I trust you, Sontino. You're just like me, solid. You fear nothing. You're a great leader, and a strategic thinker, a little rough around the edges, but strategic nonetheless. And most of all, you've got a good head on your shoulders, and you know what side of the toast that your bread is buttered on." He looked at Muhammad, nodded his head, and the lanky old man left the office without saying a word.

"Yo, Grip, you mind if I put somethin' in the air?" Sonny asked, holding up a neatly rolled Backwood.

"Not at all," Grip said. "You're the boss now. You get to do whatever the hell you want."

Sonny shrugged his shoulders. "More or less." He placed the Backwood between his lips, sparked it up, and took a long, hard pull. While exhaling a cloud of smoke, he asked, "So, what about my nigga, Mook? I'm 'posed to just let that ride?"

Grip fired up a Cohiba and took a nice pull. "No disrespect, Sontino, but fuck Mook. That mutha'fucka wasn't doing nothing but holding you back," he spoke through a thick cloud of cigar smoke.

"But Mook was my Big Homie," Sonny countered. "When my pops was gettin' high back in the day, Mook stepped up to the plate and held me down. That nigga practically raised me."

"Your Big Homie?" Grip repeated his claim. "He wasn't your Big Homie, he was your goddamned boss, and Morenos don't have bosses. We are the bosses," he declared, raising his voice a few octaves. The thought of his bloodline working for another motherfucker was pissing him off, but he quickly calmed himself down. "Listen, Sontino," he said in a softer tone of voice. "Mook wasn't nothing but a crutch, and the only way I could get you from underneath him and put you in a position to stand on your own two feet, was to get him out of the way. And I can understand that you had love for him. But in the life we live, sometimes you have to do what's necessary." He took another pull on his Cohiba and released the smoke.

92

"Like when you left my grandmoms for dead when the Italians kidnapped her?" Sonny asked, laying all of his grievances on the table.

"It was a rough decision," Grip admitted, thinking about the hardest decision that he ever had to make. "And did I make the wrong decision? Yes. But if I had to do it all over again, I wouldn't change a goddamned thing." He took another pull on his cigar, and then plucked the ashes in the ashtray. "It's just like I told you," he released a cloud of smoke, "sometimes you've gotta do what's necessary."

Sonny took another pull on his Backwood, and then stubbed it out in the ashtray. "I'm sayin', though, that was your wife and unborn child. If you'll cross them, what's to say that you won't cross me?"

"It was a bluff," Grip explained with a smile on his face.

"A bluff?" Sonny asked with a raised eyebrow. "On whose end, yours or theirs?"

"On theirs," Grip replied while lounging back in his swivel-chair and locking his fingers together. "You've gotta remember, Sontino, I was raised by the mafia. And up until the age of thirteen, I was indoctrinated into their way of life. Aside from their Oath of Silence, they have two specific rules when it comes to doing business, they can't touch government officials, and they can't harm innocent women and children. So, when they kidnapped your grandmother and threatened to kill her, I knew it was bullshit."

Sonny thought about his grandfather's explanation, and strangely it made sense. "So, basically, by refusing to pay the ransom, you called their bluff and solidified your gangsta at the same time."

"Absolutely," Grip confirmed. "I showed the city that nothing or nobody would stop my movement, and that I was willing to do whatever it took to maintain my position. In the process, I put fear in the hearts of the heartless, and at the same time, cast a shadow of ignominy over my father and his family." He smiled and raised his hands in victory. "Checkmate, the Morenos win."

Sonny laughed at him. "Damn, man, I'm really glad we had the chance to sit down and talk. 'Cause on some trill shit, I was definitely thinking 'bout killin' you."

Grip joined him in laughter. "And I was thinking the same shit about you."

The laughing stopped and they looked at one another in admiration. "So, we cool?" Grip asked as he extended his right hand.

"Yeah," Sonny nodded his head and accepted Grip's gesture. "We cool."

"Good. Now, sign these papers so I can officially retire."

Chapter Nine
ADX Florence Correctional Facility in Florence, Colorado

Alcatraz in the Rocky Mountains, that's what the federal inmates who resided at ADX Florence called the super-max prison. A bonafide hell on earth, it was the final abode for some of America's most dangerous criminals, and Angolo "Big Angolo" Gervino was one of them. Housed in a small six by eight-foot cell with nothing but a stainless-steel sink, a stainless-steel toilet, and a concrete slab with a three-inch mattress, the ninety-eight-year-old mafia don was teetering on the brink of his twilight. Inflicted with pancreatic cancer, the original don of South Philadelphia was fragile and weak. But that didn't stop him from engaging in his favorite pastime, a nice game of chess.

Sitting on his bed in complete silence, the old man was contemplating his next move. Notoriously known for being the best chess player on the compound, for a thousand dollars a game, he willingly accepted any and all challengers. His makeshift chessboard was laid across the foot of his mattress. Designed from the cardboard backs of two legal pads, its rectangular-shaped boxes were numbered from one to sixty-four, and shaded in with the black ink from his flexible security pen. His green and white chess pieces were expertly carved from bars of soap, and with his droopy eyes looking at the pieces from every angle, he was silently anticipating the impending fate of his opponent.

The entire cell block was quiet, extremely quiet. It was the unified silence of a hundred and fifty-seven inmates propped against their cell doors, patiently waiting for Big Angolo to announce his next move.

"My Queen on thirty-seven takes your Rook on sixty-four. Check," Big Angolo shouted in a raspy voice, eliciting "oohs" and "ahhs" from his spectators. Every inmate was attentively watching the game play out on their individual chessboards, and every time Big Angolo or his opponent announced their move, the inmates would move the pieces on their individual boards, essentially seeing the game first hand.

95

His opponent, Omar Yusef, a convicted terrorist, chuckled and rubbed his hands together. This was the first time in over twenty years that Big Angolo made a mistake of this magnitude. The mafia don appeared to be so focused on his offense, that he uncharacteristically overlooked his defense. "My Knight on fifty-four takes your Queen," Omar shouted in a thick Iranian accent. "The check is cleared."

"Ohhhh," the spectators exclaimed, surprised by the fact that Big Angolo had lost his Queen so early in the game.

Big Angolo cackled like a hyena, astonished that Omar took the bait. By moving his Knight from the fifty-fourth square to take his Queen, he left his King completely vulnerable. "My Rook on three moves to four. Checkmate."

Utterly stunned, Omar shook his head from left to right, realizing that the game was indeed over. The entire cell block went crazy. Many of the inmates were working side-bets and they wasted no time collecting their winnings. A plethora of fishing lines covered the tier and in a matter of minutes, every commissary item from toothpaste to cupcakes was being transported from one cell to the other.

"Scooby Doo on the move," Vladamire Melnik, a convicted Soviet spy shouted, alerting his fellow prisoners that a U.S. Marshal was patrolling the tier. Instantly, the fishing lines disappeared and a deathly silence washed over the cell block.

The U.S. Marshal walked down the tier with a manila envelope tucked under his left arm. He stopped in front of Big Angolo's cell and opened up his tray slot. "Mr. Gervino, you have a legal package that was sent to you by way of certified mail. I need you to inventory the contents, sign the receipt, and then slide the empty envelope back through the tray slot."

"Thanks, Mitchie," Big Angolo smiled at him, knowing that the legal package was just a decoy for the U.S. Marshal to hand him his cell phone. For two thousand dollars a month, the young Marshal would bring him his cell phone whenever he had an incoming call, or needed to make an outgoing call. He grabbed the manila envelope and carried it over to his bed. After removing his Samsung, he stood beside his window to get the best reception possible. He placed the phone up to his ear and said, "Hello."

"Poppo?" Carmine questioned.

"Yeah, Carmy, it's me. How's everything going?"

"Poppo, things are bad, very bad."

"Like what, Carmy? Talk to me."

"It's Gramps," Carmine sighed heavily. "Him and Tony Bruno got whacked."

"What? How? Who done it?" Big Angolo asked in a shaky voice. "Please tell me that it wasn't Gervin."

"No, Poppo, it wasn't Grip."

"Well, who in the hell was it?" Big Angolo pried, raising his voice a few octaves.

"It was the Mexicans," Carmine revealed. "A situation happened outside of my club a couple of weeks ago. Chatchi's nephew was kidnapped and murdered. We assumed that it had something to do with the beef between Chatchi and El Gallo, so initially we didn't pay it any mind. But now, that fuckin' Chatchi's holdin' us responsible, and he's pickin' us apart left and right. First, he whacked Alphonso, then he whacked Gramps and Tony Bruno. And to make matters worse, he's givin' me twenty-four hours to hand over the mutherfuckers responsible for kidnappin' his nephew."

Big Angolo was crushed. He never trusted the Mexicans and he stated as much time and time again. He also advised Carmine and Little Angolo to keep away from the drugs, but they wouldn't listen. Now, they had to deal with the consequences and there was nothing he could do about it.

"Poppo," Carmine sobbed. "You still there?"

"Yeah, Carmy, I'm here."

"I don't know what to do, Poppo. You gotta tell me what to do."

"Listen, Carmy, you need to go see Gervin. I'm pretty sure that the two of yous can figure this shit out."

"Grip? Are you friggin' kiddin' me? We're basically goin' to war with the Morenos, and you want me to ask him for help?"

"A war?" Big Angolo questioned. As far as he knew, Grip and Little Angolo were playing for the same team. That was the stipulation they agreed to when he left them his position in The Conglomerate. He made it pellucid that his two sons had to bury the hatchet and come together as one family.

"Yeah, Poppo, for the past couple of weeks, we've been havin' some serious issues. Grip returned from Cuba and whacked one of my soldiers. I told Gramps about it and he told me to put the son-of-a-bitch outta his misery. I thought you knew about this."

"Absolutely not," Big Angolo snarled through the phone. "What about The Conglomerate? Those degenerate fucks were supposed to be managing my seat, together as one."

"The Conglomerate? Your seat? Poppo, what the hell are you talking about?"

"You mean they never told you about The Conglomerate? They never told you about their inheritance?"

"They? Who's they?"

"Your grandfather and your uncle."

"Uncle Joey?"

"No, you nitwit. I'm talkin' about Gervin. My son. Your goddamned uncle," Big Angolo snapped. "I left those sons-of-bitches my seat and they promised to merge our families. The Gervinos and Morenos!"

"Poppo, I'm lost."

Big Angolo needed some time to calm down. He laid the phone at the foot of his bed, and then went to his sink for a drink of water. Frustrated, he splashed his face with two handfuls of warm water, and then returned to his phone call.

"Carmy," he said after picking up the phone. "I'm talking about the two families that sprang from my loins, The Gervino Family and The Moreno Family. Me, myself, I'm the progeny of Charlie 'Lucky' Luciano. Lucky was my boss, and in 1937, he gave his blessing to branch out and start my own family in Philadelphia. I had two sons, Gervin and Angolo Junior. Your grandfather became the boss of my family, and Gervin did his own thing. But nevertheless, they both came from me. This is my bloodline. This is my legacy."

"Poppo, I understand that much, but what about The Conglomerate?" Carmine asked. "What's that?"

"In 1952, Mr. Luciano started The Conglomerate. It was meant to be the biggest crime syndicate in the world. La Cosa Nostra was specifically designated for the Italians, but The Conglomerate was something much bigger. At the time, Mr. Luciano was in exile, deported back to Naples, Italy. He handpicked ten different bosses from ten different countries, and I was selected to represent the United States. Together, me and the other nine bosses became The Conglomerate. Your grandfather was supposed to have talked to you about this. As the boss of my family, you're next in line, and now that he's gone, you automatically inherit half of my seat."

Carmine was silent. None of what Big Angolo was saying made any sense to him. If this so-called "Conglomerate" was so important, why didn't Big Angolo tell him about it? "So Poppo, how do I get in touch with these other bosses? And what am I supposed to do about Chatchi?"

"As far as the other bosses, you let me worry about that. Now, as far as the Mexicans, they also have representation in The Conglomerate. Chatchi's brother Joaquin holds a seat. He's currently locked away in a Mexican prison camp, but he's still a chairman of The Conglomerate. I'm gonna reach out to him and hopefully I can fix this shit before it goes any further."

"All right, now what about Grip? How am I supposed to reach out to him when he's gunnin' for me?"

"Don't worry about Gervin," Big Angolo assured him. "I'm gonna fix that as well. But for now, just lay low and keep your eyes open. And unless I tell you otherwise, trust no one, absolutely no one."

"All right, Poppo."

Click.

"Mr. Gervino," the U.S. Marshal whispered into his cell and held up his watch. "We're cuttin' this thing kinda close."

"Just gimmie a couple of more minutes, Mitchie. There's another call I gotta make."

The U.S. Marshal looked up and down the tier, making sure that none of his fellow Marshals were coming. Satisfied that the coast was clear, he pressed his face against the gated window and said, "All right, Mr. Gervino, but make it quick."

Big Angolo reached inside of his shirt pocket and pulled out his miniature-sized Bible. He flipped it open to the first book of Psalms and removed the small piece of paper that he used as a book mark. He unfolded the piece of paper and then carefully dialed the numbers that were scribbled on the inside.

Ring. Ring. Ring.

***

Back at La Casa Moreno

Grip and Sonny were discussing his trip to Cuba when Gangsta stormed into the office with a crazed look on his face. "I've gotta kill this mutha'fucka," he stated to no one in particular. "He's too close. He could fuck around and ruin everything!"

"Yo, who are you talking 'bout?" Sonny asked him.

"Sullivan, that nut ass detective bul," Gangsta replied with his arms stretched out wide. He took a deep breath, and then slowly paced back in forth.

"Gangsta, will you sit your black ass down," Grip commanded with a voice full of agitation. "Just cool out and sit the hell down somewhere. Damn."

"Uncle G, this shit is real. They got Murder's cell phone. All they gotta do is subpoena the phone records and I'm done. Everything we've been workin' on would have all been for nothin'. I'm tellin' you, we've gotta kill this mutha'fucka before it's too late."

"It doesn't matter," Grip replied while leaning back in his swivel-chair. "I've decided to take you to Cuba with me. Your work here is done."

Gangsta sighed. "But I'm sayin', though, Murder and Malice are dead. How the fuck did the cops know about the hit on Little Angolo in the first place?"

"It's a new day, my little nephew, a new day, a new time, a new generation, and a new regime. My number one priority is Sontino, and to make his transition as comfortable as possible, it was imperative that I clean house. Murder and Malice had to go, and the same rules applied to Joey."

"Clean house?" Gangsta looked at him like he was crazy. "That was your work? You're the one who lined them up?"

Grip scowled at him with a deadly expression, and his silence spoke volumes.

"Yo, that's crazy," Gangsta protested. "Murder and Malice was like family. They've been ridin' wit' us for years, and that's how you do 'em?"

"Boy, you better watch it," Grip cautioned with a raised eyebrow. "My decision was my decision, and that's the end of it, you understand?"

Disgusted, Gangsta shook his head and stormed out of the office. Sonny was speechless. Being from the streets, he'd never saw the police as a means of waging war. But in the same vein, he realized that his grandfather was conducting business on an entirely different level, a level in which politicians, federal judges, and worldwide crime figures came together for one common cause, that almighty dollar.

Vrrrrrm. Vrrrrrm. Vrrrrrm.

Grip's cell phone vibrated on his desktop, breaking the silence. He picked it up, glanced at the screen, and then looked at Sonny. "Excuse me, Sontino, I need to take this in private."

"More or less," Sonny said while standing to his feet. As he headed towards the door, he held up the documents for M&R Real Estate, and looked at Grip with a quizzical expression.

"They're already signed," Grip stated. "Just add your signature and the company's yours."

"More or less." Sonny nodded his head and then left the office.

When the door closed behind him, Grip accepted the incoming call. "Old timer," he addressed his father. "You finally got around to callin' me, huh?"

"Cut the shit, Gervin. What the hell is going on out there?" Big Angolo barked at him.

"I don't know father," Grip said with a sarcastic undertone. "Enlighten me."

"The goddamn Mexicans whacked your brother."

"That's not my problem," Grip replied in a nonchalant manner, even though he was intrigued by the new information.

"That's not your problem? What do you mean that's not your problem?" Big Angolo retorted. "I told the two of yous to come together for the sake of the family. You need to live up to your end of the deal."

"Is that right?"

"Abso-fuckin-lutely. And I just got off the phone with Carmine. He told me that you and Little Angolo were takin' shots at one another. Why?"

Grip chuckled. "You're a wise man. I'm sure you can figure it out."

"Gervin," Big Angolo stated with authority, "stop fuckin' around. This is serious. The Mexicans whacked your brother and you have to respond. It's the only way. Nobody, and I mean nobody, gets away with bringing harm to my family."

"That's your family," Grip shouted into the phone. "Not mine. Me, my mother, and my little sister, we were your family, and look at the way you treated us. You abandoned us, you son-of-a-bitch. You brought us to America and then turned your goddamned back. So, don't you ever talk to me about family."

Big Angolo sighed. "Gervin," he stated in a pleading voice, "please, I'm beggin' you, do not force my hand."

Grip laughed at him. "Force your hand? You have no hands. They belong to me now. Everything that you ever had belongs to me. Now, lay down on your fucking bunk and stare up at the ceiling, knowing that the bastard son that you threw away like yesterday's trash was the same one who defeated you."

Chapter Ten
The Creek Side Apartments in Bensalem, Pennsylvania

Jasmyn was stretched out, sound asleep on her living room floor. After watching the six o'clock news and learning that Sheed was one of the victims in what they referred to as "The Broad Street Massacre," she broke down crying, devastated from heartbreak. Four hours later, there she was sprawled out in nothing but a wife-beater and a pair of pink boy shorts.

Chrrrrrn. Chrrrrrn. Chrrrrrn.

Sluggishly, she lifted her head from the carpet and looked around the room skeptically. She was so caught up in her grief that she didn't even realize she fell asleep on the floor.

Chrrrrrn. Chrrrrrn. Chrrrrrn.

The intercom box that was positioned on the wall beside her front door was ringing non-stop. Irritated, she hopped off of the floor and ran towards it. "Who the fuck is this?" she shouted after snatching up the receiver. "And why the fuck are you blowin' up my goddamned intercom?"

"Whoa, toots. Calm down, it's just me," Fat Petey announced his presence. He was standing outside of her building, cautiously looking around the parking lot. "Lemme up, I need to talk to you."

"Now's not a good time, Pete. I'm sorta goin' through some-thin'," Jasmyn stated in a voice that was much calmer.

"Goin' through somethin'? Is that a polite way of tellin' me you have company?"

"No, it's nothing like that," she clarified. "A close friend of mines was murdered today, and I'm really fucked up about it."

"Damn, toots, I'm sorry to hear that," Fat Petey said in a compassionate voice. "But I really need to talk to you. It'll only take a couple of minutes. I'm hopin' you can help me out wit' somethin'."

Jasmyn took a deep breath and exhaled. As bad as she wanted to turn him away, she couldn't. For the past year, Fat Petey had done so much for her and her daughter. He even gave her the deposit money to put down on her apartment. "All right, Pete, but no funny business."

After buzzing him inside of the building, she cracked the door, and then plopped down on her suede love seat. A couple of minutes later, Fat Petey appeared in the doorway. He was breathing heavy and beads of sweat were glistening on his forehead.

"Goddamnit," he said after finally catching his breath. "Those two flights of stairs was like climbing up the Statue of friggin' Liberty. Damn."

Jasmyn smiled at his witty remark, but deep inside she was hurting. To keep him from getting any ideas, she pulled the bottom of her wife-beater over her knees, covering her pink boy shorts.

Fat Petey closed the door and locked it. Unzipping his coat, he approached the love seat and sat down beside her.

"All right, Pete, what's good?" She scooted over so he could have enough room on the love seat and looked him square in the eyes.

"We had a little problem at the club a couple of weeks ago, and I was hopin' that you could shed some light on the situation." He reached in his coat pocket and pulled out his cell phone.

"A problem like what?" she asked nervously. Her eyes were moving back and forth between his face and his iPhone, and her body temperature was steadily rising. Although they were friends with benefits, Fat Petey was a made man, and she knew firsthand how dangerous the mob could be. "I didn't steal anything," she quickly declared. "So, if something's missing, I swear to God it wasn't me."

"Calm down, toots. There's nothin' missin'." He pulled up the video footage and then handed her the phone. "Who's he? I need to know his name and whatever else you can tell me about him."

Jasmyn looked at the screen and squinted her eyes. The footage was a little dark, but it didn't stop her from seeing herself standing in front of Egypt. They were posted up in front of the bar talking.

"Obviously, the two of yous know one another, so who is he?"

She looked at him skeptically, deciding whether or not to answer his question. "Why? What did he do?"

"What did he do?" Fat Petey replied in a sarcastic voice. "He butt-fucked a couple of nuns. What do you friggin' care? Do you know him or not?"

She sucked her teeth and rolled her eyes. "Yeah, I know him, but I don't appreciate your attitude."

"Yeah, yeah, yeah," he waved her off. "Just tell me his friggin' name."

"His name's Egypt."

"And what do you know about him?"

"He's from North Philly."

"And?"

"He's a major dude in the city."

"All right, now this is where I really need you to help me," he said condescendingly. "Who does he work for?"

"The bul, Sonny. Egypt and his twin brother Zaire, they both work for Sonny."

"Sonny?" Fat Petey screwed up his face. "Who the fuck is Sonny?"

"You know, the Moreno bul. The one who's been on the news all day. His grandpop is supposed to be the boss of The Black Mafia. Matter of fact," she perked up, "now that I think about it, Egypt probably had somethin' to do with my friend gettin' killed. Shit, I hope y'all murder his black ass."

Fat Petey looked at her like she was crazy. "Hold on, wait a minute. I never said nothin' about whackin' him. I only wanna talk to him."

"Umm hmm, is that what y'all call it these days," she used her index fingers to indicate quotation marks, "talk to him?"

Fat Petey laughed at her as he stood to his feet. "You're funny, Jas, real fuckin' funny. You shoulda been a comedian. But look, do you have somethin' to drink? I'm a little thirsty from climbin' up all those steps."

"I think there's some soda in the fridge, want some?"

"Yeah, that sounds pretty good right about now."

Jasmyn got up from the love seat and walked into the kitchen with Fat Petey a couple of steps behind her. As she opened the refrigerator door and leaned forward to grab the bottle of soda, Fat Petey reached inside of his coat and pulled out a .45 semi-automatic that was equipped with a three-inch silencer.

Jasmyn paused and an awkward feeling spread throughout her body. She glanced over her right shoulder just in time to see Fat Petey aiming the pistol. "What the…"

Pfft. Pfft.

The hollow tips erupted from the barrel and blazed through both of her cheeks. Her little body slammed against the refrigerator door and she dropped the bottle of Pepsi that was clutched in her right hand. Dazed and disoriented, she attempted to crawl away but another bullet crashed into her left shoulder and she fell back into the refrigerator. Blood was pouring from the gunshot wounds to her face, and her left arm was completely numb. Crying and begging for her life, she looked into the silencer's little black hole.

Pfft. Pfft. Pfft.

***

Back At La Casa Moreno

Rahmello opened his eyes and smiled when he saw Olivia. She was lying on the bed beside him and gently wiping the sweat from his brow with a warm rag. "Oli," he said just above a whisper. "Where's my brother?"

"He's downstairs," she said with a smile, and then softly covered his face with kisses.

"Where are we?" He asked while looking around the large room. The large California king-size bed that they were laying on was positioned in the center of the room, elegantly placed on a platform with a two-step drop. Polished mahogany furniture decorated the room. The walls were painted a crispy white, and a gold fan equipped with a crystal bulb was dangling from the ceiling. "Whose house is this?"

"This is your grandfather's house. Sontino brought us here."

"Where's the rest of my family? Are they okay?"

"As far as I know everyone's safe," she told him, then gently kissed his bottom lip.

Releasing a sigh of relief, he looked Olivia square in the eyes and said, "Oli, is it true what you said about my pops? Did your dad really kill him?"

Shamefully, she nodded her head in the affirmative. "It was Papi, my brother Estaban, and Chee-Chee."

"Chee-Chee?" Rahmello asked with a screwed up face. "You talking 'bout the lil' scruffy looking mutha'fucka who was at the bodega the last time we copped from your dad?"

Again, she nodded her head.

"Yo, how do you know all of this?"

"I was... I was there when it happened," she managed to say as tears began to run down the sides of her beautiful face. "It happened in Papi's office."

"I'm sayin', though, what the fuck they kill him for? What did he do?"

"My brother, Angelo, was killed a couple of years ago on 4th and Indy. Estaban was there when it happened, and I heard him tell Papi that your dad was the one who killed Angelo."

Gently, Rahmello wiped away her tears. Aside from his family, he loved Olivia more than anything, and he hated to see her upset. "I need you to tell me how to find 'em."

"I can't," she said. "They went back to Columbia. After everything that happened at the funeral, they panicked when they heard that a cop got killed. And my Uncle Juan took them back to Columbia."

"Damn, Oli, why ain't you tell me this shit sooner?"

"I wanted to, but I couldn't," she responded with a face full of tears. She sat up and looked at everything in the room except for his eyes.

"Oli, look at me."

Defiantly, she continued to look away.

"Look at me, I said."

When she finally looked into his blue eyes, he wrapped his arms around her and kissed her on the forehead. "You should've told me, ma. My brother and his right-hand man went to war behind this shit and a lot of people died."

"Baby, I wanted to tell you, but I was too afraid," she sobbed.

"Afraid?" He looked at her with a creased brow. "Afraid of what?"

"I was afraid of what would have happened to you if you tried to retaliate. My Papi would have killed your entire family, and I couldn't stand the thought of losing you."

"A'ight, but if that's the case, then why are you tellin' me this shit now?"

"I don't know," she shrugged her shoulders and sighed. "After everything that happened today at your father's funeral, I knew that my Papi was comin' for you. So, basically, I had two options, either tell you who your enemy was, or just sit back and watch you get picked apart."

"Damn," Mello sighed. He was thinking about Sonny and the vow they made when Easy was first murdered. They promised one another that not only would they kill the motherfuckers responsible, they would body their entire family. "Oli, did you tell my brother about this?"

"No," she quickly replied and vigorously shook her head. "The only person I told was you."

"A'ight, you gotta keep it like that," he instructed. "Because if Sonny finds out..."

Subconsciously, she placed her hands on her stomach and looked at him with a concerned expression. "Do you think he'll try to hurt me? Or my Mami maybe?"

Rahmello took a deep breath and sighed. "I don't know, ma. For now, just keep that shit under wraps and gimme some time to figure things out."

The door opened slowly and Sonny stuck his head into the room. "Mello," he smiled at his little brother, happy to see him sitting up with his back propped against the padded headboard. "I see you back, Babyboy!"

Rahmello returned his smile. "Come on, bro, you know a nigga built Ford tough." He returned his gaze to Olivia and wiped away her tears. "Babe, can you step outside for a minute? I need to holla at my brother."

She nodded her head and then carefully climbed off of the California King. "I'll be out in the hallway." She walked past Sonny and when he looked at her, she lowered her head to avoid eye contact.

As the door closed behind her, Sonny looked at the wooden frame, and then returned his attention to Rahmello. "What was that all about?" he asked, immediately picking up on the weird energy.

"She's a'ight," Rahmello assured him. He re-positioned his body and winced from the pain that shot up his left leg.

"Damn, bro, you gotta take it easy," Sonny advised him. "Them bitch ass niggas is gettin' mopped up behind this shit, you feel me?"

"Yeah, I feel you," Rahmello said. "But you know what I'm about to ask you, right?"

Sonny chuckled. "Grip?"

"Nigga, you already know. This nigga was public enemy number one, and now we lampin' up in his fuckin' house. Yo, what the fuck is goin' on?"

"Life is too short, bro, and family's everything," Sonny said while plopping down on the leather recliner that was positioned beside the bed. "Blood is thicker than water, and at the end of the day, Grip is our grandfather. We had our issues in the past, but we agreed to put that shit behind us."

"Yo, Sonny, this shit is fucked up, bro. Niggas really tried to park us some crazy shit. Matter of fact, what's up wit' the fam? Please tell me that everybody's straight."

"Everybody's good, my nigga. We're just waitin' for you to hurry up and get better."

"I'm sayin', though," Rahmello looked at him skeptically, "why we over here? Why ain't you take me back to your house?"

"Me and Daph is beefin' right now, so I'm givin' her some time to cool off," Sonny explained.

"Cool off? From what?"

"From all of the shit that's goin' on wit' me and Grip. My nigga Mook was like her big brother, and she's mad at me for fuckin' wit' Grip. She had me mad as shit, bro. I damn near had to put my hands on shorty, and I don't even get down like that."

"Damn, bro, that's crazy," Rahmello replied, feeling sorry for him. "But I'm sayin', though, if the ol' head ain't come through when he did, them niggas would have parked us."

"Who you tellin'," Sonny said, looking at him knowingly. "But Daph's gonna come around eventually. I just gotta give her some time."

"A'ight, so now that Sheed's outta the way, everything's good, right?"

"Nizzaw," Sonny shook his head. "We caught up in some real shit, but we gon' hold it accordingly."

Rahmello was stuck, automatically thinking that Sonny was referring to Poncho and the Columbians.

"Damn, nigga, whatchu seen a ghost?" Sonny smiled at him, noticing the distant look on his face.

"Naw, I just assumed that with Sheed being dead, everything was settled."

"I wish it was, but it's not. We goin' through it wit' the Italians, them fake ass mob niggas from South Philly."

"The Italians?" Rahmello asked with a raised eyebrow. "What's that about?"

"They're the ones who killed pops," Sonny said.

Shamefully, Rahmello lowered his head. He wanted so badly to tell Sonny that Poncho was the one who killed their father, but to do so would be a death sentence for Olivia. "I'm sayin', though... how you know the Italians were the ones who killed pops?"

Sonny reached in his pants pocket and pulled out a pack of Newports. After extracting one from the pack, he sparked it up and took a deep pull. "It all started in Cuba..."

***

Back In North Philly

Egypt was parked in front of his trap house on Marshal Street. A burning Backwood was dangling from his lips and his eyes were glued to his iPhone. Facebook and Instagram were flooded with images of Sonny and Grip, and he couldn't stand it.

"Nut ass nigga," he said aloud, and then exhaled a thick cloud of Haze smoke. He glanced at his Cartier and saw that the time was 10:25 p.m. "Yo, where the fuck is this nigga at?" he asked himself, referring to his man, Chino. The eighteen ounces of coke that he had for him was stashed under the passenger's seat in a brown paper bag, and the faster Chino came to pick it up, the faster he could get back to playing in some pussy. He plucked the ashes off of the Backwood, and then took another pull. "Yo, this nigga better hurry the fuck up 'fore I bounce back to Jersey." The thought of his young jawn deep-throating his dick was making him anxious, and he was dying to get back to her.

A brown, late model, Ford Bronco turned off of Montgomery Avenue and pulled up behind Egypt's Panamera. He looked in the rear-view mirror and saw Chino hopping out of the driver's side. The skinny Puerto Rican was dressed in a black skully hat, a black North Face, blue jeans, and black Timbs. Chino opened the passenger's side door, hopped inside, and reclined back in the butter leather seat.

"Goddamn, nigga, about time," Egypt said. "You had me sittin' out here for damn near a half an hour."

"Aww, come on, Papi," Chino replied with a silly smile, showing off the diamond grill on his bottom row of teeth. "Niggas was blowin' up my jack like a mutha'fucka. Everybody's lookin' for work, and the little bit that I had left, I wanted to get off 'fore I came to see you."

Damn, Egypt thought to himself. After all the shit that happened at the funeral, Mello never got around to feedin' the streets. *I gotta get me a new connect. I know mad niggas in the city, and if I link up wit' the right mutha'fucka, I could blow up in no time.*

"Eyg," Chino called his name, "you heard me, dawg?"

"Huh? Naw, my nigga, whatchu say? I was zoned out for a second."

"I said, is it cool for me to pay you $9,000 now, and the other $8,500 tomorrow?"

"Yeah," Egypt nodded his head. "That's cool."

"Bet."

Chino reached in both of his coat pockets and pulled a knot from each one. "Here," he handed Egypt the money, "that's $4,500 a clip."

Egypt counted the money a stack at a time, and then popped his glove compartment. After stuffing the money inside, he locked it and told Chino to reach under the passenger's seat.

Chino reached down and pulled out the brown paper bag. "Aye, this a half a chumpee, right?"

"Ain't that whatchu asked for?"

"Yeah," Chino nodded his head. "I just wanted to make sure." He reached inside of the bag and pulled out a white slab covered in plastic wrap. It was nine inches long, three inches wide, and one inch thick. "Umm mmm mmm." He smiled like a little kid on Christmas morning. "This that buttah right here. I can smell it through the packaging."

Egypt looked at his Cartier, and then returned his focus to Chino. "Yo, gotta bounce, my nigga. And make sure you got my chicken by tomorrow night. I don't wanna have to come lookin' for you," he warned with a deadly expression on his face.

"Nigga, my word straight like Indian hair," Chino quickly shot back. He gave Egypt some dap and then climbed out of the Porsche. As he hopped back in his Bronco and pulled off, Egypt started the ignition, and the sounds of Jim Jones' *Byrd Gang Money* erupted from his customized sound system.

Just cleaned my fancy car/ Picked up my fancy clothes/ And we only in the hot spots, no/ We got the bar/ We got the bar/ This is Byrd Gang Money/This is Byrd Gang Money/ Spendin' that Byrd Gang Money.

As he slowly pulled away from the curb, a black Mercedes G63 pulled up beside him, blocking off the front of his car. Mashing down on the brake pedal, he whipped out his .357 Magnum, and aimed at the Benz through his windshield. Just as he finger-fucked the trigger, the tinted driver's side window rolled down and Daphney was staring at him.

"Turn the music down." He couldn't hear the words, but he read her lips. He cut the music off and threw the transmission in *park*.

"Daph, what the fuck is you doin'?" he snapped at her when he climbed out of the car. "I almost shot ya ass." He showed her the .357, then placed it back on his waist.

"Come take a ride wit' me," she said in a calm voice. "We need to talk."

Askari

Chapter Eleven

"Daph, what's good?" Egypt asked as he settled into the passenger's seat.

"When you and Zaire was standing outside of my house, I heard what you was saying about Sontino," she revealed as she cruised down the block and made a right turn on Columbia Avenue.

"N-N-Naw, it wasn't even like that," he stuttered. I was just sayin', like, like, Zaire, like I was just tellin' Zai, you know, like how Sonny gon' play us like that." His palms were sweaty and his heart was beating like an African drum. He wasn't sure if she had already talked to Sonny, but just in case she didn't, he was doing his best to clean up his words.

"Play y'all?" she asked while whipping the Benz with one hand. Her other hand was wrapped around the compact .380 that was concealed in her jacket pocket. The barrel was aimed at Egypt's stomach and if he said the wrong thing, she was more than ready to leave his guts on the upholstery. "Play y'all how?"

"You know," he shrugged his shoulders and sunk into the seat, "by fuckin' wit' the ol' head Grip."

"And what's so wrong about that?" She questioned his mind state, wondering if she would be able to trust him.

"That nigga killed Mook and Nasty, and his young buls shot me up. And for all we know, he could have killed Easy and made it look like Sheed did it."

"Damn, I never even looked at it from that angle," Daphney said. "Maybe that's the reason he showed up at the funeral and started blazing." Just then, she remembered a book that her father instructed her to read, 48 Laws of Power. "He very well could have set everything up, and then made himself look like a hero, just to get Sonny to trust him."

"And that's the shit that I'm talking 'bout, Daph. After everything we been through, how Sonny gon' turn around and start fuckin' wit' this nigga?"

"So, whatchu wanna do about it?" she asked. Her left index finger was gently placed on the trigger, and if he gave her any inclination that he was still loyal to Sonny, she was ready to let him have it.

After a brief pause, he looked her straight in the eyes and said, "I wanna be my own boss. I wanna do my own thing."

Daphney smiled at him and removed her index finger from the trigger-guard. Still whipping the Benz truck with her right hand, she said, "What if I can make that happen for you?"

"Huh?" Egypt replied, looking at her skeptically.

"I'm not in the habit of repeating myself," she checked him. "You heard what I said."

She pulled the Benz over on the side of the road and threw the transmission in *park*. She then turned her body towards him and rested her arms on the leather console that separated the two front seats. "You know who my daddy is, right?"

"Yeah," Egypt nodded his head. "Alvin Rines, the boss of the YBM,"

"And do you know who my son's father was?"

He searched his brain, but couldn't come up with an answer. "Nizzaw, I don't think you ever told me about your son's father. Who is he?"

"Who was he?" she corrected him.

"A'ight, well who was he?"

"Mook."

Completely brain-fucked, Egypt just sat there with his mouth wide open. "Hey yo Daph, hold up," he paused for a moment, taking the necessary time to get his head together. "A'ight, I might have heard you wrong, but did you say Mook?"

"Yes," she nodded her head in the affirmative. "He's Dayshon's father. He was my first love, my everything."

"Does Sonny know?"

"Nobody knew, just me and Mook."

"Well, if Mook was your baby dad, then how the fuck did you end up wit' Sonny?"

"To make Mook jealous," she revealed her true intentions. "You gotta remember, before my daddy went to prison, Mook was his top lieutenant. He left everything to Mook, his money, his connect, and the responsibility of looking after his family. At the time, I was just a little girl and Mook was like my big brother. But as I got older and grew into a woman, the dynamics of our relationship began to change. I first noticed when I was sixteen. Every time I started fucking with a nigga, Mook would flip out and chase him away. Initially, I thought he was being the overprotective big brother; but obviously that wasn't the case."

She paused for a moment, and then continued, "On my eighteenth birthday, he called my house and told me that he was coming to take me shopping. It wasn't unusual for him to lace me with random shopping sprees, so I really didn't think anything of it; especially since it was my birthday. He picked me up in his Maserati and we drove to New York. I was anticipating a day of shopping and upgrading my wardrobe, but Mook had other plans. Instead of hitting up the diamond and fashion districts, he drove us to Central Park and took me on a romantic carriage ride. It was then that he expressed his true feelings for me, and he told me that he wanted me to be his woman. I was head over heels in love with him, but up until that point I had never said anything. So, when he expressed his true feelings for me, I wasted no time expressing my true feelings for him."

"Our love was a real one, but we still had to sneak around because of my daddy. He knew that daddy would never approve of him dating me, so we did our best to keep it a secret. In the meantime, I got pregnant with Dayshon, and when Mook found out, he panicked. So, to cover his tracks and throw daddy off, he married his side bitch, Saleena." She gave Egypt a second to let it all soak in before she went on.

"As time went on, we continued to sneak around, but eventually I became tired. So, I gave him an ultimatum, either divorce that bitch, Saleena, and be with me and the baby, or I was leaving."

"And he chose to stay with Saleena," Egypt said, already knowing that part of the story.

"Yeah, he stayed with that bitch," she replied with venom dripping from her tongue. "So, I moved on and did me. We remained friends, but nothing more."

"So how did you link up wit' Sonny?"

"One day, Mook called me and asked me to meet with his young bul to show him a house in Cheltenham. I already knew who Sontino was, but he didn't know me. Now, don't get me wrong, Sonny's a fly ass nigga, but I never wanted him. The only nigga I ever wanted was Mook, but Mook was on some bullshit. Anyway, I started fucking with Sonny just to make Mook jealous, but then he got killed and I found out that I was pregnant with Keyonti. And at the end of the day, I really did fall in love with Sontino, but now..." her voice trailed off and she took a deep breath.

"I'm sayin', though," Egypt looked at her with a confused expression. "What does any of this have to do wit' me?"

Daphney looked at him through squinted eyes. "You wanna be your own boss and I can make that happen for you. But first, you gotta do something for me."

"And what's that?" Egypt asked, folding his arms across his chest.

Daphney sat back in her bucket seat and casually placed her left hand back on her pistol. Attentively reading his body language, she said, "You gotta help me kill Sontino."

Egypt went quiet and Daphney continued to watch him like a hawk. All he had to do was utter the wrong words and he was finished. His eyes searched around the front seat, looking for a hidden camera. This shit had to be a set up. "Yo, Daph, stop fuckin' around."

"I'm dead ass serious," she replied without batting an eye.

"How I'm 'posed to know this ain't a set up? For all I know, you coulda told Sonny what I said and he sent you to line me up."

She leaned over the center console and used her tongue to part his lips. He was rigid at first, but after a couple of seconds, he began to kiss her back. She removed her left hand from her jacket pocket and gently caressed his dick through his jeans.

"Do you still think I'm fuckin' around?" she asked in a passionate voice, still stroking his meat through his jeans.

"I don't know," he breathed heavily. "You're gonna have to do a lil' more to convince me."

She squinted her eyes and seductively bit down on her bottom lip. Without saying another word, she unbuckled his jeans and then used her tongue to make his toes curl.

***

A Half an Hour Later

"You wanna run that by me again?" Carmine asked, looking at Fat Petey with a raised eyebrow. He, Fat Petey, and Anthony Marco, his war capo from South Jersey, were sitting in the living room of a small row home in South Philly.

"His name's Egypt, and he's connected to Sontino," Fat Petey repeated his last statement. "He's a major coke dealer from North Philly, and the other guy that we seen in the video, the one that looks just like him, that's his twin brother, Zaire."

Carmine got up from the couch and stood in front of the window. A glass of Bourbon was clutched in his right hand and a Marlboro Menthol was dangling from the right side of his mouth. He took a drag on the Marlboro, removed it from his lips, and exhaled the smoke. *Was this a set up?* He wondered. *Did Grip kidnap and whack Roberto, just to have me take the blame?*

He looked to his right where Anthony was sitting in a rocking chair. He was slowly rocking back and forth, and taking short pulls on the Cohiba that was nestled in between his left thumb and index finger. The slim, gray haired Italian reminded Carmine of George Clooney, but unlike Mr. Clooney, he was a stone-cold killer, and Carmine was glad to have him on his team.

"Alright, Anthony, now tell me again what you know about this kid, Sontino."

"Well, as you already know, I used to get my coke and heroin from Mook, and Sontino was his second in command. There was a couple of times when Mook couldn't bring me my monthly ship-ment, so he sent Sontino instead. From what I could tell, he was a good kid. He never gave me any problems."

"When was the last time you seen him?"

"A couple of years ago. A little after Mook got whacked."

"Did he ever mention Grip?"

Anthony rubbed the stubble on his chin and slowly nodded his head. "You know what, Carmy, he did. Right after Mook got whacked, he drove down to Jersey to pick up the money that I owed Mook for my last shipment. We had a few drinks and ended up rem-iniscing about Mook. He told me that Mook was like a father to him."

"Come on, Anthony, get to Grip," Carmine said, gesturing for Anthony to speed up his story. "What did he say about Grip?"

"He told me he was gonna do to Grip what Grip did to Mook, chop his fuckin' head off."

"And that's the piece that doesn't fit," Carmine added. "If Son-tino hates Grip, and he's lookin' to whack him, why in the hell would he help Grip set me up? We've gotta be missin' somethin'."

Fat Petey knocked down his double-shot of Vodka, and then looked over at Carmine. "You know what I'm thinkin', Carmy, I'm thinkin' Roberto got whacked behind somethin' personal, a broad, maybe."

"Oh, yeah, Petey, and what makes you say that?"

"Because, if they wanted to whack him and make it seem like we did it, they would have whacked him at the club. They wouldn't have kidnapped and tortured him. They would have caught him leavin' the club, slid up behind him, and put two in his friggin' head. Boda Boom. Boda Bing."

Carmine didn't respond, but he realized that Fat Petey was on to something. He whipped out is cell phone and dialed Chatchi's number. The phone rang a couple of times, and then Chatchi's voice eased through the phone.

"Whatever you have to say, mijo, it better be good," he threat-ened.

"Did you receive the video that I uploaded to your phone?"

"Yeah," Chatchi confirmed. "But I need more. I need names and locations."

"The guy who followed Roberto and Chino out of my club, his name's Egypt and he's connected to The Moreno Family," Carmine snitched.

"The Morenos?" Chatchi questioned. "Now is not the time for you to be fucking around, mijo. I know that you and The Morenos are having problems. And aside from that, me and Gervin are tight, so why would he harm my nephew? You must really think I'm stupid, mijo."

"Chatchi, I'm tellin' you the truth. These guys are connected to The Morenos," Carmine insisted.

"So, lemme guess, now I'm supposed to send the devil knocking on your enemy's door, and only because you say so?"

"Listen, you border-hoppin', wet-back motherfucker. I'm sick of this fuckin' shit," Carmine shouted into the phone. He was sick and tired of playing games and was ready to let his nuts hang. "You want a war, motherfucker? I'll take you to fuckin' war."

Chatchi laughed at him. "Your twenty-four hours to live just went down to twenty-four seconds."

Click.

Enraged, Carmine bashed his cell phone against the wall. "Fuck those motherfuckers," he shouted. Fat Petey and Anthony were looking at him like he was crazy, and then looked at one another with terrified expressions.

"Carmy, are you friggin' crazy?" Fat Petey asked with his arms stretched out wide. "You're gonna get us all killed."

"Rally the fuckin' troops," Carmine demanded while pacing back and forth. "I don't give a fuck if we gotta drive down to Texas in a fifty-car caravan. I want those sons-of-bitches dead."

Crash.

A Molotov cocktail crashed through the living room window and exploded just a couple of feet away from Carmine's feet.

Ba-Boom.

Large flames and thick black smoke instantly filled the living room. The left sleeve on Carmine's Versace sweater caught fire and he frantically tried to pat it out. Fat Petey and Anthony hopped out of their seats, but before they had the chance to do anything, rapid gunfire ripped through the living room wall.

Bdddddoc. Bdddddoc. Bdddddoc. Bdddddoc.
Ba-Boom.

Another cocktail was tossed into the house and the flaming kerosene-filled bottle instantly bolstered the raging inferno. The smoke was thick, the flames were scorching, and the bullets were flying indiscriminately.

Bdddddoc. Bdddddoc. Bdddddoc. Bdddddoc.

Carmine was crawling on all fours, heading towards the back door. Anthony was crouched down behind the china cabinet in the dining room. And Fat Petey was shuffling from right to left like a headless chicken.

"Petey, get down," Anthony yelled over the gunfire.

Bdddddoc. Bdddddoc. Bdddddoc.

Bullets danced up Fat Petey's chest, lifting his rotund body off of the floor. After twisting in the air, he landed on top of the dining room table and the oak wood frame toppled over.

The smoke was so thick that Carmine could barely see what lie ahead of him. Still crawling on all fours, a bullet ripped through his left leg, and he fell on the carpet, spread eagle.

"Stay down, Carmy, I've got you covered," Anthony yelled. He let off a couple of shots, and then grabbed his boss by the back of his collar and drug him into the kitchen. The bright-orange flames were spreading throughout the house and Carmine could feel the heat seeping up his right pants leg.

"Anthony, get me outta here," he shouted.

"Just stay down, Carmy. I've got you."

When they finally made it to the back door at the back of the kitchen, they were coughing uncontrollably, desperately in need of fresh air. Anthony turned the door knob and pulled it open.

Boom.

The colossal blast of a riot-pump at point blank range hollowed out his chest and he flew backwards, clean across the kitchen.

Carmine looked up and the last thing he saw was the three-dimensional horns that protruded from Diablo's forehead.

Boom.

Askari

Chapter Twelve
Back At La Casa Moreno

"Damn, bro, that's some gangsta ass shit," Rahmello acknowledged. He was referring to Sonny's narration of Grip's life story,
and the fact that his grandfather came to America as a Cuban immi-
grant and hustled his way to the top was the illest shit in the world
to him.

Sonny smiled at him. "I know, right? And this is the legacy
that's being handed down to us."

The bedroom door opened up wide and Grip stepped through
the threshold. He was comfortably attired in a navy-blue track suit
and a fresh pair of white Nikes. A tall glass of V8 vegetable juice
was clutched in his right hand, and his eyes went from Rahmello to
Sonny, and then back to Rahmello. Approaching the California
king-sized bed, he smiled at his grandsons. "How's everything coming along, fellas? And why is that young lady sleeping outside in
the hallway? There's a total of twenty-five bedrooms throughout
this house. Certainly, she could have used one."

"We good," Sonny assured him. "And as far as Oli, she stepped
outside so me and Rahmello could talk. She must have fell asleep
while she was waiting."

Grip nodded his understanding, and then fixed his gaze on the
young man who was the spitting image of himself. They had the
same light complexion, the same grade of wavy hair, and the same
blue eyes. "And as for you, Rahmello, are you feeling any better?"

Rahmello was speechless. His respect for the old man was so
profound that he was afraid to say something stupid.

Grip laughed at him. "Well damn, boy, say something."

Rahmello stared into his blue eyes and said, "I look just like
you."

"That's for damn sure," Sonny interjected, making his grandfather and little brother laugh.

"Damn, I wish y'all father was here," Grip said. "I missed out
on so much when it comes to y'all that I really don't know what to
say or do to make things right."

"I don't know about Sonny, but I'm good," Rahmello said. "I always knew I had that gangsta shit up in me, and now I know why. I've got the blood of a boss."

Grip nodded his head, and then looked at Sonny. "What about you?"

"I can't even front, it's a part of me that wanted to get at you, but I'm puttin' that shit behind me. We're family, and at the end of the day, that's the only thing that matters."

Grip smiled and extended his hand to give Sonny a pound. "Respect."

"Respect," Sonny repeated and then solidified their truce with a pound.

"So, what we gon' do about the Italians?" Rahmello asked, even though he already knew they had nothing to do with Easy's murder. He figured that somebody had to pay for what happened, and if he kept the focus on the Italians, he could keep Olivia safe.

Grip took a swig of his vegetable juice and wiped his mouth with the back of his left hand. "Little Angolo's a done deal, and if I had to bet my last dollar, I'd say that Carmine won't live to see tomorrow."

"And what makes you say that?" Sonny asked.

"Just trust me," Grip replied. As he knocked down the rest of his vegetable juice, his cell phone vibrated in his pocket. After grabbing the phone and seeing that Chatchi was the caller, he quickly accepted. "Chatchi, what's goin' on, my brother?"

"Gervin, we have a major problem, homes."

"A problem?" Grip asked. "What type of problem? Is it Joaquin?"

"No," Chatchi replied. "It's his son, Roberto. He was kidnapped and murdered a couple of weeks ago while partying in your city. Initially, I suspected Little Angolo and Carmine, the both of them are dead by the way, but before Carmine crossed over, he provided me with information that connects your family to the situation with my nephew, eh."

"Information?" Grip inquired. "What type of information?"

126

"The video of the actual kidnapping, mijo. I have it, and just so you know, Carmine identified two of the culprits as members of your organization." Confused, Grip looked back and forth between Sonny and Rahmello, hoping they weren't the two culprits that Chatchi was talking about. "Send me the video so I can see it for myself. I'm pretty sure this is a misunderstanding, but whatever the case, I fully intend to get to the bottom of it."

"As you should," Chatchi replied with a threatening undertone. "We've come too far to have a misunderstanding of this magnitude, so I sincerely hope that this information was incorrect."

"I totally agree," said Grip. "The alliance between our families is greatly valued by me and my grandsons." He cut his eyes at Sonny and Rahmello who were sitting there looking at him skeptically.

"And me and Joaquin feel the same way, mijo. In any event, we really need to sit down and talk. Aside from this situation with Roberto, we need to go over the final details pertaining to Joaquin's escape."

"Absolutely," Grip concurred. "In fact, my plane for Cuba is taking off in a couple of hours. I'm going to be over there for the next few months, and Joaquin's asylum status is one of the things I'll be working out with the Castros."

"Cuba? In a couple of hours?" Chatchi questioned. "This is unacceptable, mijo. I've called for a mandatory meeting with The Conglomerate, tomorrow at midnight. Everyone is expected to attend, so your trip to Cuba is gonna have to wait."

Grip sighed and gently rubbed the hair on his chin. "What's the location?"

"The Waldorf Astoria," Chatchi answered. "In New York City. And Gervin," he paused for a couple of seconds, "I'll be expecting you to have answers pertaining to my nephew."

Click.

"Yo, what happened?" Sonny asked. "You look madder than a mutha'fucka."

Grip didn't answer. He was too busy uploading the video footage that Chatchi sent to his phone. As the video began to play, he gritted his teeth and slowly shook his head from left to right. "God-damnit," he complained, and then handed the phone to Sonny. "What the hell was this about?"

"What was what about?" Rahmello asked, feeling left out of the loop. He was hanging halfway off of the bed, trying his hardest to see the phone for himself. "Yo, Sonny, what is it?"

"A major goddamned problem," Grip stated with a salty voice.

Sonny was quiet, borderline stuck on stupid. The last thing he was expecting to see was a video of Breeze and the twins kidnapping Mexican Bobby. "Yo, Sonny, lemme see that shit," Rahmello demanded, and then snatched the phone away from Sonny's hand. He watched the video for a couple of seconds, scratched his head, and then looked up at his grandfather. "Who sent this to you?"

"A very good friend of mines," Grip informed him. "And he's claiming that we had something to do with the kidnapping and murder of his nephew. Initially, I didn't understand why. But after watching that fuckin' video, it's pretty goddamned obvious."

"No disrespect to this friend of yours," Rahmello said, "but his nephew was a mutha'fuckin' rat. This nut ass nigga even had the nerve to have the shit tatted on his mutha'fuckin' neck."

"A rat?" Grip looked at him with a creased brow. "Who told you that?"

Rahmello got quiet. He looked at Sonny, and Sonny answered the question for him. "Our connect told us."

Grip folded his arms across his chest. "And who in the hell is your connect?"

"Columbian Poncho and his brother, Juan."

"Poncho and Juan?" Grip repeated with a sour face. "You mean the Nunez Brothers? Them mutha'fuckas from Medellin, Colum-bia?"

"Yeah," Sonny confirmed. "What's the big deal? The Mexican nigga was a rat, and we put him down. He testified against some niggas down in Mexico, and to get even, Poncho and Juan paid a hunnid blocks to rock his stupid ass."

Grip took a deep breath and vigorously massaged the back of his neck. "Do the two of you even realize what you've done?" He looked back and forth between the two brothers, eagerly waiting for an answer.

"Listen, dawg, it is what it is," Sonny said as he got up from the leather recliner. "It's not like we can bring the nigga back, so fuck him. His ass shouldn't have told."

Grip was blown away by the arrogance that rolled of the tip of his tongue. "Sontino," he said his name in a low, but stern voice, "that boy was a somebody."

"Oh, I know," Sonny quickly shot back. "He was a fuckin' rat."

"Stop saying that shit," Grip snapped at him. "He wasn't a rat. His name was Roberto Alverez. He was the son of Joaquin Alverez, the boss of the Sinaloa Cartel, and these mutha'fuckas want answers."

Far from impressed, Sonny shrugged his shoulders. "A'ight, and?"

"Goddamnit," Grip shouted, and then violently threw his empty bottle of V8 against the wall, smashing it to pieces. "Joaquin is one of the most powerful men in North America. Even behind bars that little mutha'fucka's a goddamned giant, and furthermore, he's our strongest ally in The Conglomerate."

"Nigga, who the fuck is you talkin' to?" Sonny matched his intensity, and then got up in his grill. Deep seeded feelings of hatred shot throughout his body and he was seconds away from jellying the old man's biscuit.

Grip took a step backwards and quickly rolled up his sleeves. "Boy, I'ma tell you right now, this ain't the tree you wanna be climbin'. Grandson or not, I ain't got no problems cruisin' over yo' monkey ass."

"Sonny, chill out," Rahmello said as he grabbed the back of his shirt tail. He looked at his grandfather and conveyed the same message. "Hey, yo, cool out, ol' head. Y'all niggas is buggin' right now."

Sonny calmed down and Grip did the same. Muhammad, who was walking down the second story hallway, appeared in the doorway and looked at Grip. He started to say something, but Sonny didn't give him the chance. "Nigga, mind ya fuckin' business," he snarled at the old man. "This a family issue and ya mutha'fuckin' ass ain't family. So, either keep it the fuck pushin', or I swear to God I'ma pop ya fuckin' top."

Muhammad was fuming. He looked at Grip, and Grip signaled for him to keep it moving. As he left the room, Grip cracked his knuckles and returned his gaze to Sonny. In a calm voice, he said, "You're not going to like this, but in order for us to make things right and avoid a full-blown war, we're going to have to give up the twins."

"Give up the twins?" Sonny asked, looking at him like he was outside of his mind. "Nigga, you trippin', I ain't throwin' my young buls under the bus. Fuck them taco-eatin' ass niggas."

"Sontino, you just don't get it," Grip tried to reason with him. "It's either them or us."

"Well, I guess it's gonna have to be them," Sonny declared. "And by them, I'm talking 'bout the Cinnamon Bagel Cartel, or whateva them niggas call they'self. 'Cause I ain't givin' up my young buls. Them Mexicans will have to kill me first."

"And believe you, me," Grip assured him, "they'll have no qualms about adhering to your request."

Sonny couldn't believe his ears. After all of the Black Mafia stories that he heard about his grandfather, he was starting to smell the bitch in his blood. *Yo, this nigga's a fuckin' turkey*, he thought to himself. *My nigga, Mook, woulda told them Mexicans to suck his dick.*

Pacing back and forth, Grip searched his mind for a diplomatic resolution. "Alright, so you're telling me that the Nunez Brothers were the ones who put you up to this shit?"

"Yeah," Sonny replied in a nonchalant manner. As far as he was concerned, the Mexicans bled like he bled and breathed the same air, so bitching up wasn't an option. "It was only business," he continued ever so casually. "They told me that Mexican Bobby snitched on some of their peoples down in Mexico, and they cut me a check to get him outta here."

"Those slimy sons-of-bitches," Grip snarled through clenched teeth. "They fuckin' played you. Roberto wasn't a rat. He wasn't even connected to the cartel. He was a goddamned boxer."

"But what about his neck?" Sonny asked with his arms stretched out. "This nigga had the tattoo of a rat eatin' a piece of cheese, and directly above the rat it said 'La Ratta'."

Grip scowled at him and did everything in his power to refrain from smacking his face off. Attempting to calm himself down, he took a deep breath and exhaled. "La Ratta was his nickname," he explained in a low voice, "The name was given to him for his boxing style. He was known for trapping himself in a corner of the ring and then viciously fighting his way out like a caged rat. He was far from a government witness. He was good fucking kid, and whether you like it or not, somebody's gonna have to pay for what happened to him."

"La Ratta," Rahmello said aloud, thinking about Mexican Bobby's tattoo. He flexed his jaw muscles and cracked his knuckles as images of the little Mexican strapped down to the workshop table flooded his mind. He looked at Sonny and slowly shook his head. "Yo, I think we might've fucked up, bro."

"You're goddamned right y'all fucked up," Grip admonished them. He sat at the foot of Rahmello's bed and rested his face in the palms of his hands.

"Yo, somethin' ain't right," Sonny insisted. A confused look covered his light skinned face and his body temperature was slowly escalating. "If main man wasn't a rat, then why the fuck did Poncho and Juan pay us to kill him?" His question elicited an uneasy silence. And for a brief moment, they just sat there staring at one another.

"They paid y'all to kill him because of me," a feminine voice stated. Completely caught off guard, the three men looked at the bed room door and saw Olivia standing in the threshold.

***

Askari

"So, you still think I'm bullshittin'?" Daphney asked in a husky voice. She was down on all fours, positioned on top of Egypt's bed, and popping her fat ass against his pelvis.

"Ahn ahn," Egypt replied with a lustful undertone, loving the way her ass was twerking against his body one cheek at a time. Her pussy was gobbling up his dick and he was stretching her walls with every stroke.

"Ummmm," Daphney expressed her pleasure. She was so wet that her creamy white nectar was caked up at the base of his dick and slowly dripping down her inner thighs. "Goddamnit, nigga, fuck this pussy," she demanded, and then rocked backwards to meet his oncoming thrust.

Egypt gripped her by the waist and forcefully rammed his eleven inches deep inside of her, causing her body to jolt forward. "Nizzaw, where you going?" He breathed heavily and gripped her waist even tighter. "Don't run. I'm givin' you whatchu asked for." His dick was so big and his stroke was so strong that she was cumming for the third time in fifteen minutes.

"Ahhhhh," she cried out as she continued to pop her ass against his pelvis. "Murder this pussy," she panted. "Nigga, murder this shit. Ahhhnnnnn."

In total compliance, he pounded her box like a jack-hammer and she collapsed on the bed. Her eyes were closed and her mouth was wide open.

He felt so good that she wanted to scream, and scream she did. With her face buried in the pillow and her ass tooted in the air, he squatted over top of her and placed his hands on both of her shoulders.

"Yes, baby, yes," she continued to purr. "Fuck me like a boss. Shit."

Her words drove him crazy and he started going ham. Pinning her down to the bed, he fucked her pussy with fast, long, hard strokes. "Bitch, you like this dick, don't you?"

"Yes," she screamed. "Fuck yes."

Her pussy was so tight and wet that every other stroke he had to pull out to keep his composure. "Damn, Daph, you got that juice

132

box, fa'real. Sheesh." He slipped back inside of her and continued to punish her slippery womb. Her ass was jiggling like Jell-O, and every time he looked at her left butt cheek and saw the tattoo of Sonny's name, he pumped harder and faster. "That nigga don't be fuckin' you like this, do he?"

"No," she cried out "This... This shit is somethin' different, somethin' special. Damn."

His manhood was so long and thick that her walls were stretching like elastic and she could feel herself about to cum for the fourth time

***

It was 11:15 p.m. when Zaire walked through the front door of the trap house that he shared with his twin. After a long hectic day, he was dead tired and the only thing he cared about was getting some much-needed rest. He punched in the code to their Brink's home security system, slipped out of his Timbs, and tossed them aside. As he removed the fur coat that Daphney let him borrow from Sonny's closet, he looked around the living room and noticed that bricks of cocaine were scattered all around. There had to be at least two hundred in total.

"Yo, what the fuck is this nigga thinkin'?" he said to himself, knowing that Egypt stole the work from Sonny's stash house in Cheltenham.

"Hey, yo, Egypt," he shouted from the bottom of the stairs. He knew that his twin was upstairs getting some pussy because he could hear the headboard banging against the wall and the lustful moans of a woman.

Looking at the bricks piled up on the coffee table, Zaire shook his head in contempt. Not only was Egypt out of pocket for stealing the work from Sonny's stash house, his stupid ass had the audacity to have a chick inside of the spot with incriminating evidence laying around in plain view. Enraged, he darted up the stairs and approached Egypt's bedroom door. He started to knock, but instead he gently pushed it open.

Daphney was lying on her back with both of her legs propped up on Egypt's shoulders. Her left hand was gripping the base of his dick like a dildo, and he was slowly dipping his shaft in and out of her honey pot. "Ahhhhnnnnn. Shit. Fuck me slow, daddy. Just like that, like that. Ummmmm!"

His slow strokes became harder and faster, and his shoulder-length dreads began to bounce around wildly. The pressure from her hand gripping the base of his dick was increasing the blood flow to his plum-sized head, making his massive member larger than it already was. Pushing her legs away from his shoulders, he slipped out of her and stood to his feet. "Get on ya knees and eat this dick up," he commanded as beads of sweat dripped down his face and cascaded down his muscular chest.

Kneeling before him, Daphney spat on his dick and stroked him with both hands. She then kissed the tip of his juicy bulb, opened up wide, and brought him to the back of her throat. "Ummm," she moaned with a mouthful of dick and gently caressed him with the base of her tongue.

"You gon' let me cum in ya mouth?" Egypt asked her with a devilish grin.

Stroking him with both hands and making over-exaggerated slurping noises, she looked him in the eyes and nodded her consent. She kissed the tip of his head one last time, then removed her hands and tilted her head back, patiently waiting for his creamy load.

"Ssss. Damn," Egypt groaned as he stroked himself at top speed. His toes began to curl, gripping up the satin bed sheets, and he looked up at the ceiling.

"Hurry up and gimmie that shit," Daphney demanded as she finger popped her pussy. "I earned it, so give it to me. I wanna taste every fuckin' drop." He looked down and the sight of her beautiful face drove him over the edge. His dick began to throb like a beating heart and a thick stream of cum sprang from the depths of his balls and splashed against her forehead. He hunched forward and another gush of creamy jizz shot from his pistol and landed on her left cheek.

"Ummmm," Daphney moaned as she stuck out her tongue, fishing for every single drop.

Zaire was standing in the doorway, stuck on stupid, with his jaw hanging to the floor. His twin brother was balls deep in his big homie's bitch, and he couldn't believe it. He shook his head and wiped his eyes, hoping that his peepers were playing tricks on him, but they weren't. This shit was real. Tears welled up in his eyes and goosebumps covered his dark brown skin. The man in violation was the same man who came into the world two minutes and twenty seconds before he did, and the man being violated was without a doubt one of the men he was willing to die for.

He gently closed the door and wiped away the lone tear that dripped from his left eye. "Damn, Eyg, what the fuck you done got us into, dawg? Damn."

Askari

Chapter Thirteen
Back At La Casa Moreno

"Oli, whatchu talking 'bout?" Rahmello asked, shooting her a funny look. "Whatchu mean they had him killed because of you?"

"Roberto," she spoke in a cracked voice. "He was… He was my boyfriend."

"Your what?" Rahmello snapped. He was looking at her like he wanted to split her wig to the banana meat. "Your boyfriend? Fuck you mean that nigga was your boyfriend? You was steppin' out on me?"

"No," she quickly replied as the tears began to fall from her eyes. "This was before I even met you," she clarified. "Me and Roberto was together for almost two years. I met him back in 2012 when me and my girls went to Cancun for spring break. Roberto was my first love, my everything, but when Papi found out, he demanded that I break it off with him. He also threatened that if Roberto ever came looking for me, he would have him killed."

Feeling what he perceived to be betrayal, and hurt beyond words, Rahmello asked her the million-dollar question, even though the answer was obvious. "So, lemme guess, he came lookin' for you, huh?"

She nodded her head and wiped away the snot that dripped from her nose.

"How long ago?"

She didn't answer.

"How long ago, I said?"

"A couple of months ago," she revealed, and then shamefully lowered her head.

"You fucked that nigga, didn't you?"

When she looked away and refused to answer, Rahmello could feel the core of his heart ripping at the seams. "Is that his baby?"

"I don't know," she sobbed. "I mean, I don't think so. I hope not."

"Oli, you outta pocket, yo, straight up." Not only was he embarrassed, he felt stupid. The love that he had for her was so strong that he was willing to deceive his own brother just to protect her, and now he realized that he couldn't even trust her. "You's a grimy ass bitch, Oli. Straight up, shorty, you grimy as shit."

"Baby, I'm sorry," she pleaded. "I didn't mean to hurt you." She approached the bed and tried to hug him, but he forcefully pushed her away. "But Mello," she sobbed, still trying to wrap her arms around him, "I'm sorry. I swear to God, I wasn't trying to hurt you."

"Oli, don't fuckin' touch me," he snarled at her, then pushed her in the chest and she fell to the floor, just a couple of feet away from Grip. "Get ya thotty ass outta here."

"Young lady," Grip said as he helped her to her feet, "which one of the Nunez Brothers is your father? Juan or Poncho?"

"Poncho," she answered. She was rubbing her baby bump and looking at Rahmello, but he refused to make eye contact.

"Do you know where I can find him?" he continued in a soothing voice. "You know, so we can sit down and straighten everything out."

"I think they went back to Columbia, but I'm not sure."

"Back to Columbia?" Grip asked. "For what reason?"

She folded her arms across her chest and defiantly looked away.

"Young lady, I need you to help me," Grip said in a smooth, condescending voice. "Our safety depends on your cooperation, so please, if you have any information pertaining to your father's whereabouts, I need you to tell me. I only want to talk to him."

Olivia looked him in the eyes and took a deep breath. "After everything that happened at the funeral," she began, then stopped abruptly when Rahmello shot her a look that said, *Bitch, you doin' too much. Shut ya stupid ass up.*

Sonny noticed the look and it instantly raised a red flag. He looked back and forth between her and Rahmello, and then stepped in between their line of eye sight. Folding his arms across his chest, he looked at Olivia with a raised brow. "After everything that happened at the funeral?" he inquired. "You mean my pop's funeral?"

Slowly, she nodded her head in the affirmative and then wiped the tears from her eyes. "When they found out about the cop lady being killed, they panicked, and my Uncle Juan told them to come back to Medellin."

Sonny positioned himself in front of her, and his eyes became dark, thin slits. "Fuck is that supposed to mean? Are you tellin' me that Poncho and Juan had somethin' to do wit' my pops gettin' killed?"

"Umm hmm," she replied, looking at him with doe-like eyes and silently praying that he acknowledged her innocence. Unfortunately, his body language exuded the opposite. His chest was slowly rising up and down, his nostrils were flaring, and he was anxiously biting down on his bottom lip.

"Young lady," Grip interjected, "how do you know all of this?"

Completely terrified, her petite body began to tremble. "I was... I was there when it... When it happened," she managed to say through her sniffles. "They killed him in the back... In the back of the bodega, in my Papi's office."

"They?" Sonny vehemently questioned. "Who the fuck is they?"

"Papi, Chee-Chee, and my brother, Estaban," she snitched them out.

"Chee-Chee?" Sonny screwed up his face. "The lil' scruffy lookin' mutha'fucka who was at the bodega the last time I was over there?"

"Umm hmm, that was him," she confirmed, then instinctively took a step backwards.

"What the fuck did they kill him for?" Sonny tweaked out. "What the fuck did he do?" His words embodied so much anger that Olivia was flinching like a battered housewife.

"Estaban," she sobbed. "I heard him tell Papi dat ju papa was de one who killed our brother, Angelo." She was so afraid that her Columbian accent was seeping into her English.

"Angelo," Sonny repeated. He searched his mind and quickly remembered the name. Poncho had mentioned his son, Angelo, when they were talking outside of the funeral home, just minutes before the shooting started. He also remembered the sarcastic remarks that rolled off of Poncho's lips as they stood beside his father's hearse. *Ju papa was a fine man, Sontino. It's a shame dat he died so violently.*

Sonny was heated. Images of Easy being gunned down and stuffed in the trunk of his Jaguar played inside of his mind like a horror movie, and he completely lost it. Enraged, he whipped out his Glock .40 and snatched Olivia by the back of her head. She attempted to scream, but the sound was cut short when he forcefully shoved the barrel between her lips and separated the teeth from her gums.

"No," Rahmello shouted as he rolled off of the bed and crawled towards them. "Sonny, what the fuck is you doin', bro? She's carrying my seed."

Olivia was shaking like a Parkinson's patient. Her big, wide eyes were glued to the back of the gun, and the warm urine that darkened the front of her Juicy Coutures was beginning to make a small puddle on the carpet below.

"Brozay, I'm beggin' you," Rahmello pleaded. "Don't do me like this."

Sonny scowled at him. "Nigga, you knew about this shit, didn't you? Didn't you?"

Rahmello was at a loss for words. Shaking his head, he said, "Come on, bro, chill."

"Nigga, answer the fuckin' question."

"Yeah," he replied in a soft, depleted voice. "She told me about it back at the hospital. I was gonna…"

"Gonna what?" Sonny interrupted him and gave him the look of death. "You was gonna let them niggas get away wit' killin' pops, and damn near killin' our whole fuckin' family? Just to protect this bitch?" He pushed the Glock so far down Olivia's throat that the knuckle on his trigger finger was pressed against her top lip. Her eyelashes fluttered and she damn near passed out. The blood from her broken teeth was running down the sides of her mouth, and she gagged so hard that a thick clump of snot-laced vomit shot from her nose and landed on the back of Sonny's hand.

"Sonny, please," Rahmello shouted when Sonny's index finger slipped inside of the trigger-guard. "I was gonna hold pops down, I swear it. I was gonna kill them niggas by myself. And the only reason that I didn't tell you what happened is because I didn't want nothin' to happen to Oli."

"Sontino," Grip's voice boomed in his right ear. "Let her go, we're going to need her. She has to tell Chatchi about her and Roberto, and explain why Poncho wanted him dead."

"No," Rahmello protested. "Them Mexicans will kill her."

"Nigga, what the fuck you think I'ma do?" Sonny snapped at him. "Them niggas killed my mutha'fuckin' pops, and now I'ma murder they whole fuckin' family."

"Bro, please," Rahmello cried. He was propped up on his right knee and his hands were pressed together as if he were praying. "If nothin' else, think about my baby, bro. She's carryin' my baby."

Sonny was shaking with rage. Everything inside of him wanted to paint the walls with Olivia's blood, but he couldn't bring himself to take the life of a woman and her unborn child. Frustrated, he pulled the Glock out of her mouth and tossed her on top of Rahmello. She coughed and gagged, and Rahmello wrapped his arms around her, desperately trying to calm her down.

Sonny aimed the barrel at her face and said, "The only reason I'm not gon' kill you is because of that baby. But if it wasn't for that," he slowly shook his head and looked back forth between her and Rahmello, "I woulda popped ya fuckin' top."

Gently, Grip grabbed him by the arm and pulled him into the hallway. Closing the door behind him, he said, "Sontino, you seriously need to learn how to curb your anger."

Sonny didn't respond. His left hand was still wrapped around the Glock and the only thing he think about was killing Poncho. *Sleep well, my friend.* Those were the words he remembered Poncho saying as he walked past Easy's hearse and climbed into the white Benz.

"Tomorrow night we have to drive to New York City to meet with The Conglomerate," Grip continued in a calm voice. "The meeting was called by Chatchi, and he specifically told me that he's expecting answers pertaining to the situation with Roberto."

Sonny was looking at him like he was crazy. "Nigga, we just found out that the Columbians killed my pops, killed your son, and the only thing you're worried about is the next nigga's son? Is you fuckin' crazy, dawg?"

Grip sighed and began to pace back and forth. "Listen, Sontino, and listen closely. These Mexicans are not to be fucked with. I know you're probably thinking that I'm afraid, but I'm not. I'm just being cautious. These Mexicans are cut from a different cloth. They're a different breed. They're the type of mutha'fuckas that you just don't go against."

"Oh, yeah, and why is that?" Sonny asked him.

"You just don't," Grip responded, incapable of coming up with a better answer. "For example, in the snap of a finger, they basically dismantled the entire Gervino Crime Family. Little Angolo, dead. Carmine, dead. And if we don't hand over those goddamned twins, we're going to be next."

"Yo, how many times I gotta fuckin' tell you?" Sonny bellowed. "Under no circumstances are you or anybody else touchin' my fuckin' young buls."

"Well, what do you suggest?" Grip retorted. "Because I'm tellin' you right now, we only have about twenty-four hours to figure this shit out."

Sonny gritted his teeth and scowled at him. He started to call him out for being a bitch, but decided that it wouldn't make any difference. The Mexicans had already taken his heart. After wiping away the tears of rage that trickled down the sides of his face, he stuffed the Glock .40 in the small of his back, and took off down the hallway.

"Sontino," Grip called out behind him. "Where are you going? We need to figure this shit out."

Sonny didn't reply. He just continued walking and ice-grilled Muhammad, who was coming up the hallway in the opposite direction.

"Muhammad, where the hell is Gangsta?" Grip asked the lanky old man as he slowly approached him.

"I was just about to ask you the same thing," Muhammad said. "He stormed out of the house about a half an hour ago."

"Goddamnit," Grip sighed, knowing that Gangsta went looking for Detective Sullivan.

"What's the problem?" Muhammad asked him. He'd been working for Grip for over thirty years, so it wasn't hard to tell when his boss was upset.

"The trip to Cuba," Grip said. "We have to reschedule."

"Reschedule?" Muhammad looked at him skeptically. "Why?"

"Because tomorrow night we have to drive to New York City to meet with The Conglomerate."

"The Conglomerate? But your next meeting isn't until July. Did something happen?"

Grip sighed. He knew that The Nunez Brothers were long gone, and that Sonny would rather wage war than sacrifice his twins. "It's Sontino," he said, and then gave a look that could only mean one thing. "Unfortunately, for the sake of business, that's what has to happen."

"Should I have him stopped at the front gate?" Muhammad asked with a sense of urgency. He absolutely hated Sonny, and for the past two years he'd been patiently waiting for Grip to give him the green light. "We can take care of this situation right now."

"Not at all," Grip said. "That would defeat the purpose. It has to be done in front of The Conglomerate. The sacrifice of my own flesh and blood for the sake of one of its chairmen is something that will undoubtedly be appreciated."

"I see," Muhammad expressed his acquiescence. "But what about the other one," he gestured towards the bed room door, "Rahmello?"

Grip smiled at him and slowly rubbed his hands together. "We're still going to need a figure head for the family, right? Well, who better than the grandson who looks just like me?" he said with a slight chuckle. "It'll be like the sixties all over again."

Muhammad smiled back and saluted him with a light bow. "Long live The Moreno Family."

***

Back At the Twins' Trap House

Zaire was laying on his bed smoking a Vanilla Dutch when he heard Egypt and Daphney walking down the hallway and descending the stairs. He sat up and listened closely. A couple of seconds later, he heard the front door open and close, so he got up from his bed, and approached his bed room window. After pulling back the curtains and ascending the blinds, he peered down and shook his head in disappointment. Egypt was escorting Daphney to the black Benz truck that was parked across the street from their house. His right arm was draped across her shoulders, and she was holding him around the waist, and strutting with a slight limp. "Damn," Zaire said aloud, referring to the way she was walking. "Ya triflin' ass got the Ghost Dick." That's what he and Egypt called it whenever they fucked some new pussy. And just like any other chick who ever had a dose of the twins, he knew that the only reason Daphney was walking funny is because she was still feeling the heaviness of Egypt's dick pressed against her spine, and would feel it for at least another hour.

"Yo, this shit is crazy," he said to himself as she wrapped her arms around Egypt's neck and kissed him passionately. Their chemistry was so intense that he began to wonder how long the two of them had been creeping behind Sonny's back. After releasing their embrace, she climbed into the Benz, closed the door, and started the ignition. As the truck came to life and the halogenic lights illuminated the block, the tinted driver's side window rolled down, and she was saying something that Zaire was incapable of hearing. Egypt nodded his head a couple of times, and then leaned inside of the SUV to kiss her once more.

Moving away from the window, Zaire took another pull on his Dutch Master and inhaled deeply. His heart was beating rapidly and a plethora of goose-bumps popped up on his arms. He sat on top of his bed and released the Haze smoke. "Eyg, what the fuck is you doin, dawg?" He couldn't believe that his twin was stupid enough to put them in such a predicament. He was dead wrong, and Zaire knew it would only be a matter of time before his reckless actions got the best of him.

The front door opened and closed, and he could hear Egypt coming up the stairs. A few seconds later, the light from the hallway illuminated the dark room as Egypt opened his bed room door and stepped inside. A look of determination was written across his face and he was cracking his knuckles one at a time.

"How long you been home?" Egypt asked him.

"About thirty minutes," Zaire responded, giving him a look that insinuated he knew exactly what Egypt was up to.

"A'ight, so you seen the work that's downstairs in the livin' room?"

Zaire nodded his head.

"Do you know who I had in my room?"

Again, Zaire nodded his head.

"A'ight, so I'm assuming that you know what's goin' on?"

"Yeah, I know what's goin' on," Zaire responded. "But why? Why would you do this to Sonny? Why would you do this to us?"

Egypt was happy to hear the word "us". This assured him that come hell or high water, his twin was rocking out with him. He sat down beside Zaire and took the Dutch from his hand. After taking a nice long pull, he said, "Listen, bro, there's a time and a place for everything. Our time is now, and our destination is the top. Sonny ain't the same, Zai. The money done went to his head, and now he's turnin' his back on everything that made him. He turned his back on Mook, and without Mook, niggas would be broke and stuck in the hood right about now. You're my twin brother, we came from the same womb, and we both believe in loyalty. I just need you to be loyal to the right mutha'fucka, and that's Mook."

"But what about Sonny?" Zaire asked. "He was the one who groomed us and put us in position. Don't get me wrong, I got crazy love for Mook, but at the end of the day, he wasn't the nigga who fed us when we was starvin', Sonny was."

Egypt released the Haze smoke that was festering in his lungs, and then took another pull on the Dutch Master. "Naw, Zai, Mook was the one who made sure we ate. By feedin' Sonny, he was feedin' us, and that's the realest shit I ever spoke. And now that Mook's gone, and he left Sonny the whole empire, this nigga got the nerve to make moves wit' the nigga who killed him. Naw, bro, it ain't goin' down like that," he shook his head from side to side. "I ain't lettin' that shit ride."

"So, whatchu sayin', Eyg? You gon' kill Sonny?"

Egypt shrugged his shoulders. "It's the only way, but for now we gotta chill. It's just like I said, there's a time and a place for everything."

Zaire took a deep breath and sighed. He knew that siding with Egypt and going against Sonny was a bad move, but at the same time, Egypt was his twin brother and he couldn't see himself turning his back on him. "A'ight," he continued after collecting his thoughts, "what's the situation wit' Daphney? How does she fit into the equation?"

"She is the equation," Egypt explained. "She's the one callin' the shots. She has a connect on standby, just waitin' to flood us wit' work. And the second she gives us the green light, we gotta make that shit count."

Zaire reached out for the Dutch Master, and then placed it to his lips. After taking a deep pull, he said, "So, what we gon' do about the work that's downstairs? You know he's gonna flip the fuck out when he finds out that somebody hit the stash house."

"That's simple," Egypt replied. "Me and Daph already got that figured out. We're gonna blame it on Sheed. Who's to say he didn't hit the stash house before he shot up the funeral?"

"I feel you, bro, but how we gon' move it?" Zaire asked and then exhaled a cloud of smoke. "If we pop up outta nowhere and start movin' birds like crazy, Sonny's gonna know it was us. At the very least, we gotta get somebody else to move it, somebody that he'd never expect."

"Chino," Egypt smiled at him. "I'ma have him and his team movin' the work for us. Trust me, bro, Sonny will never figure this shit out. All we gotta do is stay on point, continue to play the flunky role, and as soon as Daph gives us the go ahead, we gon' cock back, squeeze, and send his ass to the fuckin' moon."

Zaire hit the Dutch Master one last time and then stubbed it out in the ashtray. Looking at Egypt, he extended his right hand and said, "Whatever the situation, I gotcha back, bro."

Egypt smiled at him and accepted his right hand. "I already know, Zai. I already know." As he got up from the bed and began walking towards the door, Zaire called out to him.

"Hey, Eyg."

"What's poppin', bro?"

"I don't trust, Daphney."

"I don't trust that bitch, either," Egypt concurred. "And as soon as we kill Sonny, we killin' that bitch, too."

"More or less."

Askari

Chapter Fourteen
Delaware County, Pennsylvania

Detective Sullivan was sitting at the computer in his home office. A hot cup of cappuccino was resting on the wooden coaster to the left of his keyboard, a chocolate bear Claw was nestled in between his left thumb and index finger, and his right hand was casually placed on top of his mouse. He clicked on the Google website and curiously surfed the internet looking for any and everything he could find on Agent Long. There had to be a connection between him and The Moreno Crime Family, and Sullivan was determined to find it. His wife, Rebecca, and their six-year-old daughter, Chelsey, were sound asleep, but he vowed to stay awake the entire night if he had to. Nothing or no one would stop him from breaking this case.

"Gervin," he said aloud as he typed in the characters, "Moreno. Search." In a matter of seconds, his 19-inch monitor was flooded with images of Grip and a slew of Philadelphia gangsters, past and present. He saw pictures of the legendary Sam Christian, Nudi Mims, Aaron Jones, King Tut, and Lil' Man to name a few. But the only picture that piqued his interest was a 1955 mug shot of an adolescent Grip. The young hoodlum appeared to be no older than fifteen. He was holding a police identification card, and his icy blue eyes were distant, yet determined at the same time. A stitched up two-inch gash was prominently displayed above his right eye, and his pink lips were fixed into a slight smirk. It was the look of a young gangster thirsty for recognition.

"You little bastard," Sullivan spoke to the picture. "They should have locked your little ass up and threw away the goddamned key."

He moved the mouse and clicked on the *News* option. Almost immediately, a surplus of news articles dating back to the early 60's popped up on the screen. For the past year and a half, he'd been studying the boxes of police reports that were connected to Grip and his organization, but to actually see the news articles that the citizens of Philadelphia had to witness firsthand was a different experience. One after another, for forty minutes straight, he meticulously went through the articles and crime scene photos that vividly depicted the crimes and atrocities committed at the behest of The Moreno Crime Family. Looking at these items, he developed a better understanding of the dreadful mystique that hovered above Grip and his organization like a black cloud. There were stories of entire families being slaughtered in cold blood, with the children being drowned in bath tubs, stories of witnesses being burned alive in the middle of the street in broad daylight, and horrific narrations where the spouses of their enemies would wake up in the morning only to find the decapitated heads of their husbands laying on the pillows beside them. True savages, The Moreno Crime Family were every bit of the Boogey Man stories that spread throughout the streets of Philadelphia like urban legends.

As he continued scrolling down the screen, a particular news article from February 18th, 1975, piqued his interest.

Gervin 'Grip' Moreno, Acquitted in the Murders of His Sister and Her Fiancée. The Couple's Infant Child is Still Missing, Presumed to be Dead.

"What the hell was this about?" Detective Sullivan said aloud as he clicked on the article and began to read.

Yesterday, a Philadelphia jury consisting of five women and seven men acquitted Gervin Moreno on two counts of first-degree murder and kidnapping. The charges stemmed from the murders of his sister, Angela Moreno, and her fiancé, Russell Fitzgerald.

On the morning of January 10th, 1974, residents on the 2200 block of Carpenter Street called the police reporting the sounds of loud gunfire erupting from the Fitzgerald residence. Upon their arrival, the police discovered the dead bodies of Angela Moreno and Russell Fitzgerald. Ms. Moreno's body was discovered in the living room. Her hands were tied behind her back and a T-shirt that was used as a blindfold was wrapped around her face. Mr. Fitzgerald's body was discovered on the second floor, in the couple's bedroom. He was also blindfolded and held captive with his hands tied behind his back. Both were murdered execution style with a single bullet to the back of the head. It was also determined that the couple's one month old child, Terrance Moreno, was missing from the South Philadelphia row home. His whereabouts are currently unknown.

According to eyewitness accounts, Gervin Moreno was seen walking into the house moments before the shooting erupted, and was seen leaving the house immediately after with the crying infant cradled in his arms. The murder weapon, a .357 Magnum, was discovered at the scene and, according to the authorities, Mr. Moreno's fingerprints were successfully lifted from the gun. His bloody fingerprints were also discovered on the clothes line that was used to tie up the victims.

Despite this incriminating evidence, after a two-month long trial, the jury acquitted Mr. Moreno on all charges, and aside from the fact that the witness was murdered prior to trial, the district attorney is claiming that Mr. Moreno tampered with the jury and that the verdict was fixed.

Detective Sullivan was ecstatic. "You son-of-a-bitch," he exclaimed. "The missing kid, he's Agent Long. DEA Agent Terrance Long is Terrance Moreno. He's Grip's nephew."

He Googled the name Terrance Moreno, but nothing came up. "Come on, you motherfucker, I know you have to be in here somewhere." He knew that in order for people to believe him, he would need unequivocal proof. Otherwise, his assertion would only amount to conjecture. Determined to bolster his position, he clicked on a website that specialized in background checks, and punched in the two names.

As he sat there waiting for the information to process, the unexpected happened. And for the first time, he wished that he'd taken Rebecca's advice when it came to decorating his office.

"Didn't anybody ever tell you not to sit with your back to the door?"

The warmth of the intruder's voice caressed the peach fuzz on his left earlobe. The phonemic of the voice was husky and deep, and the smell of menthol rolled off the tip of his tongue. Detective Sullivan slowly removed his hand from the mouse and stoically looked at the monitor, careful not to make any moves that would get the noodles knocked out of his noggin. The feeling of cold steel against the right side of his neck was enough to let him know that shit was real.

"What are you doing in my house, Terry?" He had no doubts whatsoever pertaining to the intruder's identity.

Gangsta cocked a bullet into the chamber and pressed the tip of the silencer to the back of his wig.

"Sshhh." He continued to whisper in Sullivan's ear. "We wouldn't want to wake up the wife and kid, now would we?"

At the mention of Rebecca and Chelsey, Sullivan became defensive, immediately fearing for the safety of his family. Realizing he had to do something to protect them, his eyes scoured the top of his desk looking for something that he could possibly use as a weapon. To the left of his 19-inch monitor, he spotted the 10X12 picture of him, Rebecca, and Chelsey. It was the same exact picture they used to grace the front of their holiday greeting cards. Dressed in red and green sweaters and standing in front of a decorated Christmas tree, the young family looked as though they didn't have a care in the world. The light from the hallway shimmered off of the picture frame and Sullivan caught a glimpse of Gangsta. A black handgun that was equipped with a two-inch silencer was clutched in his right hand, and he was standing directly behind him.

"You really don't have to do this, Terry." He was talking through clinched teeth and doing his best to bide some time, hoping that Gangsta would slip up and give him the opportunity he needed to protect his family.

"Sure, I do," Gangsta replied, still whispering in his left ear. "You know too much, so for me to even consider letting you live, I'd be trading my life for yours, and obviously that's not an option."

"Aren't you tired of this shit, Terry?"

"Tired of what?" Gangsta asked with a raised brow.

"How does it feel, Terry?" Sullivan raised his voice a few octaves, attempting to play with Gangsta's psyche.

"What the fuck are you talking about, Sully?" Gangsta shot back and tightened his grip on the P89. He knew that he was doing way too much talking, but before he killed his mark he needed to know the extent of Sullivan's information and the names of the people that he shared it with.

"How does it feel, Terry? I want you tell me."

"Pussy, what the fuck are you talking about?"

"The feeling of knowing that the same motherfucker who turned you into a monster was the same motherfucker who murdered your parents back in '74."

Gangsta was stunned. He was expecting to hear some off the wall bullshit, but the allegation that Grip was the one who murdered his parents was so left field that he honestly didn't know how to respond. "Yo, what the fuck are you talking about, Sully?"

"I'm talking about Grip. That rotten motherfucker murdered your parents and now he's manipulating you into doing his dirty work," Detective Sullivan quickly replied. He wasn't sure how long his psychological game would last, but he had to make the best of it.

"That's bullshit," Gangsta vehemently stated. "Uncle G didn't kill my folks, the Italians did."

Detective Sullivan laughed at him. "The Italians? Is that what he told you? Was that the battery that he placed in your back? That black-hearted motherfucker killed your parents and I can prove it."

"Prove it?" Gangsta questioned with a screwed-up face. "How the fuck can you prove something that never happened?"

"All you have to do is tap the mouse," Sullivan insisted. The screen saver of him, Rebecca, and Chelsey was bouncing across the screen, but with the click of the mouse Gangsta was in for a rude awakening. "I've got the news article from February 8th, 1975, the day after Grip was acquitted for the murders of your parents. He was arrested and tried for the crimes, but somehow he managed to pay off the jury and they let him walk."

The look on Gangsta's face was nothing short of incredulous. He fixed his eyes on the screen saver, and said, "Mutha'fucka you better not be lying."

"I'm telling you the God honest truth," Sullivan propounded.

Gangsta started to reach for the mouse with his left hand, but he pulled it back. "Nah, mutha'fucka, you click on the mouse, and I swear to God, if you're lying to me I'ma fuck ya wife in the ass and make you watch."

Detective Sullivan took a deep breath and released a long sigh. Slowly, carefully, he reached for the mouse and clicked the button. The results of his background check popped up on the screen, so he clicked the backwards arrow in the top right corner and the news article appeared on the screen. "There's your proof."

With the lips of the silencer still pressed against Sullivan's neck, Gangsta leaned forward and meticulously read the article. He couldn't believe his eyes. Everything that Sullivan was saying was right before him in black and white. Not only was Grip charged in the murders of his parents, the evidence against him appeared to be overwhelming.

Detective Sullivan breathed deeply, realizing that this was the moment he'd been waiting for. Gangsta was so caught up in reading the article that he wasn't paying him any mind. But, just as he was about to make his move, he noticed something in the bottom left corner of the picture frame. It was Chelsey. She was standing in the doorway, dressed in her Sponge Bob pajamas set, and wiping the sleep out of her eyes. Her favorite teddy bear, Mr. Fluffy, was dangling from her right hand and Sullivan could tell that she had the slightest idea that an intruder was in the midst of their home.

"Daddy, can I have a glass of warm milk? I can't sleep."

Her squeaky little voice caught Gangsta by surprise. "What the fuck?" He turned to look in her direction and Sullivan made his move. He hopped to his feet and punched Gangsta in the stomach with a short, left hook.

"Chelsey, run."

The little girl released a piercing scream as Gangsta nearly dropped to his knees. He desperately tried to recover from the unexpected blow, but Sullivan was already digging in his ass. His left hand was raining blows on the right side of Gangsta's face and his right hand was struggling to rip the P89 from his grasp.

"Aaaagggghhhhh," Chelsey continued screaming. "Daddy, stop."

Still struggling for the possession of the gun, Sullivan looked at his baby girl and aggressively shouted. "Chesley, get the hell out of here. Go."

"Pussy, get up off me," Gangsta snarled at him, returning a couple of blows in the process, warming up the detective's rib cage. They tumbled around the small office, knocking over every single item that they came in contact with. Gangsta was forty something pounds heavier, but it didn't show. Detective Sullivan was a man on a mission and, with the safety of his family hanging in the balance, he fought with the intensity of a Roman gladiator. His right hand nearly had the gun ripped away from Gangsta's hand, but a solid hook to the bridge of his nose knocked him backwards. The velocity of his tumbling body pulled the P89 loose and the pistol fell on top of a stack of papers. Hungrily, they both dove for the gun, savagely fighting for its possession. Gangsta had his hands wrapped around the silencer and Sullivan had his left hand wrapped around the wood grain handle.

"Daddy, stop fighting," Chelsey continued to scream. "Aaaagggghhhhh."

In a twist of fate, Sullivan managed to slip his index finger inside of the trigger guard. Still struggling for possession, he aimed the barrel to the best of his ability, and let off a shot.

Pfft.

The bullet sliced through Gangsta's right arm like a hot knife to a block of government cheese. He stumbled backwards and fell to the floor, clutching his wound.

Chelsey stopped screaming. Confused, she looked at the red circle that embellished the front of her shirt, and then looked up, and gazed into her father's brown eyes. In a soft, innocent voice, she said, "Daddy, it's burning."

Sullivan shrieked like a wounded bear. He dropped the Godforsaken piece of metal, and ran towards her, catching her body in the crook of his arms just before she hit the carpet. "Chelsey," he shouted. "Oh, my God. Chelsey, no."

As he frantically ripped the front of her Sponge Bob shirt and examined the gunshot wound to her solar plexus, Rebecca emerged from their bed room and stepped into the hallway. "Ronald," she pronounced his name with a whiny undertone. "What the hell is going on out here? Why is she making so much noise?"

She wiped the sleep out of her eyes and looked closely. Her daughter was covered in blood, and her husband was begging the little girl to wake up. "Chelsey?" She mumbled before screaming, "Chelsey." She placed her right hand over her heart, and then ran down the hallway at top speed. She snatched the girl away from her father and held her like a newborn baby. "Chelsey," she whispered in her ear. "Wake up, baby, please."

When Chelsey failed to respond and her head lolled to the side, Rebecca went into a frenzy. Violently, she shook her daughter like a rag doll, attempting to bring her back to life, but it wasn't working. Her beautiful, sweet, innocent Chelsey was dead at the tender age of six and there was nothing she could do to change it.

Sullivan was devastated. He was so caught up in grieving for his little girl that he forgot about Gangsta. His wife was screaming bloody murder, asking God "why," and the both of them were covered in the warm blood of their only child.

"Damnit," Gangsta groaned as he slowly got up from the floor. Clutching his arm, he looked at the grieving family, and then spotted the P89 lying on the carpet. When he reached down to pick it up, a stream of blood dripped down his arm, trickled off the tips of his fingers, and dotted the beige carpet. "Fuckin' bitch," he complained, instantly realizing that his DNA was all over the office.

"Ronald," Rebecca sobbed, "what the hell happened to her?"

Her words snapped him out of his trance, and he remembered that Gangsta was lying on the floor behind him. He spun around and reached for the P89, but it was too late.

Pfft. Pfft. Pfft.

The bullets collapsed the back of his melon like a deflated football, burst out the side of his forehead, and left Rebecca with a face full of blood. It happened so fast that initially she couldn't understand why the weight of his dead body had her pinned to the hallway floor. Completely stunned, she used the back of her right hand to wipe the blood out of her eyes, and then looked up to see Gangsta standing there with the smoking gun clutched in his right hand.

"No," she cried out. "Jesus, please."

Pfft. Pfft.

The bullets ripped through her eyeballs, replacing them with bloody red marbles. Her body convulsed, and then slowly, peacefully, abruptly came to a stop.

"Damn," Gangsta sighed. He was shaking his head and regretfully looking down at the human sandwich. Rebecca was on the bottom, Chelsey was wedged in the middle, and Sullivan was lying on top. "Damn," he repeated. The last thing he ever wanted to do was kill an innocent woman and child, but in the same vein, he understood that sometimes you can't avoid the unexpected. Looking at the blood that was dripping from his right hand, he continued shaking his head from left to right. "Fuck, man. Now, I gotta burn these mutha'fuckas up. Damn."

Askari

Chapter Fifteen

A black 2014 Chevy Impala was parked up the block from Sonny's Upper Dublin estate, and Arnold Troutman, the lead investigator for Savino and Associates, was sitting behind the steering wheel. His Apple iPad was downloading the video footage from his dash-cam, and he was looking at Daphney through a pair of night-vision goggles. "Mmm mmm mmm," the skinny white man said to himself, and then took a bite of his roast beef and provolone on rye. "Talk about making a bad situation worse." Unbeknownst to Daphney, the top-notch investigator had been watching and recording her every move for the past three hours.

His assignment began earlier that evening when he received a text message from Sonny stating that he needed an extra pair of eyes to watch over his family. Troutman was fully aware of the ambush at Easy's funeral, and he quickly offered his assistance. He'd been working for Sonny for the past year and a half, and just a couple of weeks ago, Sonny paid him $10,000 for tracking down Mexican Bobby, so obviously he was eager to make a fast buck. After strapping on his bullet-proof vest and loading up his 9mm, he packed a couple of sandwiches, filled up his coffee thermos, and headed out the door.

Upon his arrival, he noticed that Sonny was driving up the block in his Porsche Spyder, so he activated his dome light, flashed his high beams, and rolled down his window. The gray car pulled up beside his Impala, and the tinted driver's side window retracted into the bullet-proof door.

"Sontino, I'm locked and loaded," Troutman said, and then held up the black 9mm that was lying on his lap.

Sonny nodded his approval, then reached inside of his glove compartment and grabbed the white envelope that was lying beside a pack of Backwood. He handed the envelope to Troutman, and the skinny white man stuffed it inside of his jacket pocket.

"It's $15,000 inside of the envelope," Sonny told him. "I paid you an extra $5,000 for taking the job on such a short notice."

Troutman smiled at him. "Thanks, Sontino."

"Don't even mention it," Sonny said as he waved him off. "But, listen, I gotta make a few runs, so all I need you to do is stay on point. And if anybody, Trout, I mean anybody, comes to my house other than me or the twins, they're an enemy."

"I'm ready to rock and roll, Sontino, trust me. But just so I know, exactly who am I watching out for?" Troutman asked.

"My wife and kids," Sonny informed him. "My mom and grandmom were supposed to have been here too, but they left a little while ago."

"So noted," Troutman confirmed as he gently caressed the top of his pistol. "Now, as far as your wife, does she know that I'm here?"

"Naw." Sonny shook his head. "That shouldn't even matter because her and the kids are done for the night, and they ain't got no business leavin' the house. All I need you to do is keep your eyes open, and remember what I said about a mutha'fucka comin' to my house. If it ain't me or the twins, they're an enemy, and I'm expectin' you to handle that shit accordingly."

"Absolutely," Troutman assured him. He stuck his right hand out of the window and embraced Sonny with a firm handshake. "Don't you worry about a thing, Sontino. I've got it covered."

"More or less," Sonny replied, and then reached under the passenger's seat and pulled out a black FNH .45 and two extended clips. "Here." He handed the pistol and the two ladders to Troutman. "Just in case shit get real, you can hold it down accordingly. Because that punk ass nine you packin' ain't gon' do nothin' but make a mutha'fucka mad."

Troutman chuckled. "All right, Sontino, whatever you say."

"More or less," Sonny replied, wrapping up the conversation. The only thing on his mind was getting back to the hospital to check on Rahmello. He nodded at Troutman, giving him a look that conveyed a clear-cut warning, and then pulled off slowly.

As Troutman sat there examining the massive handgun, the bright lights on the front of Daphney's Benz illuminated the block as the SUV emerged from behind the stone wall and drove towards him. He started to flag her down, but decided to remain incognito as he thought about Sonny's words. *Her and the kids are done for the night, and they ain't got no business leavin' the house.* Hoping that Daphney wouldn't see him as she drove by, he crouched down in the driver's seat and waited for the SUV to cruise past him. When it reached the corner and made a right turn, he brought the Impala back to life and followed the Benz truck from a safe distance.

That was three hours ago, and during that time, he collected enough video footage to prove that a double cross was in full effect. After dropping the kids off at a house in Uptown Philly, she drove to the Bad Landz and linked up with Egypt. They drove around aimlessly, then pulled over on a dark block, and made the SUV rock back and forth, clearly indicating that they were engaging in sexual activity. After that, they drove to Sonny's stash house and loaded the back of the SUV with large quantities of cocaine, and then traveled to Egypt's trap house where they unloaded the work, and spent a total of forty minutes inside of the house doing only God knows what.

Troutman had it all on video, and the last thing he recorded was Daphney and Egypt sharing a juicy kiss in the middle of the street before she hopped back in the Benz and returned to the estate. Now, she was climbing out of the SUV and strutting across the driveway with a slight limp.

Taking a deep breath, Troutman grabbed his iPad from the passenger's seat and prepared an email that was addressed to Sonny. After pressing *Send*, he shook his head from left to right, and settled back in the driver's seat. "Sontino's gonna be fuckin' pissed."

***

Ring. Ring. Ring.

"Leave it," Egypt's voice came through the speakers, replacing his automated answering service.

Beep.

"Eyg, where the fuck is y'all niggas at?" Sonny questioned. He was using the Bluetooth in his Porsche Spyder and cruising up City Line Avenue. "I've been callin' you and Zaire for damn near an hour. It's a lot of shit goin' on, and the three of us need to get together as soon as possible. So, hit me back the second you get this message. And Eyg, wherever you at, watch ya body, bro."

After disconnecting the call, he reclined back in his butter leather seat and continued cruising. The heat was bumping, the windows were cracked, and the Kush smoke was heavy and thick. He thought about calling Daphney to tell her he was sorry, but he didn't. The streets were hectic enough and they demanded his undivided attention. Stopping at a red light, he looked to his left and saw the TGI Fridays where he and Mook had a meeting with Grip two years prior, right before Mook was murdered. When the traffic light turned green, he whipped into the empty parking lot, and stopped in the same exact spot where he and Mook were sitting in Mook's Bentley. He threw the transmission in *park*, and then took a long pull on his Backwood. As he exhaled the smoke, he reflected back on the conversation they had just minutes before Mook made his proposal to Grip.

***

Two Years Earlier

"Yo, you know I believe in you, right?" Mook took a pull on his Backwood, and then looked over at Sonny, who was reclined in the passenger's seat, gazing off into the distance.

"You believe in me?" Sonny looked at him skeptically. "Whatchu talking 'bout, bro?"

"I'm talking 'bout you and ya potential," Mook said as he exhaled a cloud of Haze smoke. "Outta all my young buls, I just want you to know that I'm expectin' the most outta you."

"Outta me?" Sonny raised his voice a couple of octaves. "Me, Sheed, and Tommy be doin' the same exact shit, so why are you expectin' the most outta me? What makes me so different?" He leaned across the center console, reaching out for the Backwood, and Mook passed it to him.

"Don't get it twisted, I fucks wit' Tommy and Sheed, but you...You're cut from a different cloth," Mook tried to explain.

"Them niggas grew up and made a choice to embrace the streets, but niggas like you and me, we was made for the streets. The same shit that niggas like Tommy and Sheed need to think about, is the same shit that's second nature for niggas like you and me. We're not the same. Some niggas was born to lead, and others were born to follow."

"But what if you're givin' me too much credit?" Sonny asked, and then took a pull on the Backwood. "Who's to say that I'm not a follower, as opposed to bein' a leader? I mean, shit," he shrugged his shoulders, "I follow you."

Mook smiled, appreciating the confidence that his young nigga had in him.

He grabbed the Backwood from Sonny and took a deep pull. Exhaling the smoke, he said, "In order for a nigga to be a great leader, he has to learn how to be a great follower first. I wasn't always the leader that you see today, I used to follow behind my ol' head, Alvin. I watched him closely and studied his mannerisms. I studied the way he talked, the way he walked, the way he treated his family, the way he treated his team, and the way he dealt wit' these mutha'fuckas in the streets. He was a true to life boss, and he showed me the blueprint. He taught me how to win, and over the past few years, I've been teachin' you everything that he taught me."

He hit the Backwood once more and then tossed it out the window. Returning his gaze to Sonny, he said, "Now, as far as ya'self, ya pop was a boss nigga, and the best of that nigga was passed down to you. I'm tellin' you, Sonny, the streets are yours for the takin', but first you gotta learn how to watch these niggas. They fear what they don't understand, and they hate what they can't conquer. But most of all, and you can mark my words, everybody has an agenda, niggas and bitches. So, you really gotta watch these mutha'fuckas, especially, when it comes to makin' and maintainin' this money."

"Bro, where is this shit comin' from?" Sonny asked, still looking at him skeptically. In a weird way, he had the feeling that Mook

knew that something bad was about to happen to him on some Tu-pac type of shit, and that he was dropping these jewels while he still had the chance. The feeling was so intense that warm tears were welling at the rims of his eyes and his trigger finger was beginning to itch.

"Yo, calm down," Mook said as he reached across the center console and wiped away the single tear that fell from Sonny's left eye. "I love you like a son, and I'm only tellin' you the same shit that Alvin told me. This is the blueprint, and if you take it and run wit' it, you can't go wrong. I mean, look at me and the moves that I made over the years. That little three-bedroom project down Rich-ard Allen done turned into a muthatfuckin' mansion, and that lil' cherry-red Lex I was pushin' done turned into a fleet of nothin' but foreigns. And this is the crazy part, my crib's so secluded that I ain't even gotta take the keys outta the ignitions. I just hop in one of them mutha'fuckas and be out. This is the life, my nigga. And if you play the game the way it's 'posed to be played, you can make it ya des-tiny."

Sonny looked at him and nodded his understanding. "I feel you, bro. But on some real shit, I already know what it takes to win. I just need you to tell me what it takes to lose, so that way I can do everything in my power to avoid it."

Instead of responding, Mook shot him a look that said, Fuck outta here wit' the bullshit. You know damn well what it takes to lose.

Sonny smiled at him mischievously. "A'ight, man, damn. But if there was one thing that trumped everything else, what would it be?"

"The tongue," Mook replied without an ounce of hesitation. "Sayin' the wrong thing to the wrong mutha'fucka can put a nigga down faster than anything else."

"Damn," Sonny said, looking at him with a shocked expression. "The tongue, though? Out of everything that can bring a nigga down, you chose to put the tongue at the top of the list?"

"Absolutely," Mook confirmed. "I mean, look at it like this, if every fish in the sea kept his mouth shut, they'd never get caught."

Sonny shook his head and smiled. "More or less."

***

Back to the Present

After reminiscing about one of the last conversations that he had with Mook, Sonny realized that he couldn't afford to make a slip, especially with Grip lurking in the background. He wanted to trust the old man, but he couldn't, his handshake wasn't matching his smile. The older Moreno was quick to stress the importance of family, but when they found out the Columbians killed Easy, he didn't even care. He was only concerned about Mexican Bobby and the Sinaloas. And most importantly, why was he so willing to hand over his empire? There had to be a reason and Sonny was determined to find out.

Everybody has an agenda, Mook's voice resonated in the back of his mind. *So, you really gotta watch these mutha'fuckas, especially when it comes to makin' and maintain' this money.*

The nostalgic thoughts of his big homie brought tears to his eyes. No matter how hard he tried, he couldn't come to terms with the fact that his grandfather was responsible for killing his best friend and father figure. There was simply no way he could let the old man get away with what he had done. Retribution would come eventually, but first he needed to know more about this organization that Grip referred to as "The Conglomerate."

Vrrrrrm. Vrrrrrm. Vrrrrrm.

He reached in his coat pocket and pulled out his cell phone. "An email?" Sonny said aloud, looking at the screen with a screwed-up face. "Why the fuck is Troutman sendin' me an email? He could have just called." He pressed the *Gmail* symbol at the top of the screen and meticulously read the message.

Sontino, you need to see this! It's a video of your wife!

"A video of Daph?" He scratched his head. "Yo, what the fuck is this nigga talkin' about?"

After downloading the attachment, he went to his video App and pressed *play*. Looking at the video, it didn't take long for him to realize what was going on. His young bul was fucking his wife, and together, they were plotting to take him under.

Hate.

Anger.

Punishment.

Revenge.

Those were the four words that bounced around Sonny's mind as he sat there looking at the video. "These rotten, ungrateful mutha'fuckas," Sonny said to himself as he shook his head in contempt. He was watching the portion of the video where Egypt and Daphney were parked on Lawrence Street, making the Benz rock back and forth. "After all the shit I did for you mutha'fuckas, y'all really gone do me like this? Me, though?"

A couple of minutes later, the video was showing the Benz truck pulling into the driveway of his stash house, and Sonny damn near jumped out of the car. "Yo, what the fuck is y'all doin'?" For twenty minutes straight, duffle bag after duffle bag, he watched his wife and one of his closest friends stab him in the back. Infuriated, he called Egypt's cell phone. But once again, he didn't answer.

"Call Nipsy," Sonny spoke into his Bluetooth.

The phone rang a couple of times, and then Nipsy's voice came through the speakers. "Big homie, what's poppin'?"

"Aye, yo, Nipsy, call Egypt on the three-way for me, and if he answers don't tell him I'm on the phone,"

"A'ight, but whatchu want me to say?" Nipsy asked. He could sense that something was wrong, but he knew better than to question Sonny's motive.

"Just tell him that you need some work for the block, and that you're comin' through to pick it up," Sonny instructed. He fired up a Newport and sat there waiting to see if Egypt would answer.

"Hol' up, bro. I'm callin' this nigga right now."

Ring. Ring. Ring.

"Nipsy, what's poppin'?" Sonny could here Egypt's voice come across the airwaves. He started to snap out, but he remembered the conversation that he had with Mook. Sayin' the wrong thing to the wrong mutha'fucka can put a nigga down faster than anything else.

"Aye, yo, Nipsy, what's up dawg?" Egypt was beginning to lose patience with the silence on the other end of the phone.

"Ain't shit, bro. I'm just try'na get right wit' one of them white bitches you be fuckin' wit'."

"Oh yeah," Egypt paused for a second. "A'ight, well talk to me. I talk back. You need a skinny bitch, or a fat one?"

"I only need a skinny," Nipsy said, indicating that he was looking for a half of a brick, opposed to a whole one.

"A'ight, just get at me in the mornin' and I gotchu."

"A'ight," Nipsy agreed. "That's a good look. But, when and where do you want me to meet you?"

"I'm at the spot on M&M. Just come through around eight o'clock."

"A'ight, bro, I'll see you, then."

Click.

After making sure that Egypt was no longer on the line, Nipsy spoke to Sonny. "Bro, you heard him?"

"Yeah, I heard that pussy ass nigga," Sonny replied.

"So, whatchu want me to do?" Nipsy asked.

"Meet me at Club Infamous in about an hour," Sonny told him. "And come by ya'self."

Click.

After disconnecting the call, Sonny threw the transmission in gear and slowly pulled out of the parking lot. His destination was Southwest Philly, and the man he was going to see was known for knocking the noodles out of a mutha'fucka's biscuit. He activated his Bluetooth and said, "Call The Reaper."

***

Back at ADX Florence

U.S. Marshal, Wayne Mitchell, was working a double shift at the behest of Big Angolo, and although he would have much rather been lying in bed beside his beautiful wife, because he was needed at the prison, he was there. The young Marshal knew exactly who

Big Angolo was, and he respected that in which the old man represented, power.

There wasn't a soul on the compound who didn't respect Big Angolo. The Italian mafia was hands down the most successful criminal enterprise that the world had ever seen, and with the help of Hollywood classics such as *The Godfather*, *Casino*, and *Goodfellas*, the mob became America's taboo infatuation. And for the people who occupied the super-max prison, it was somewhat of an honor to be in the presence of a true to life mafia don, a man who was groomed and molded by the legendary "Boss of All Bosses," Mr. Lucky Luciano, himself.

"Mr. Gervino," Mitchell whispered into his cell. "Here." He opened the tray slot and handed Big Angolo the manila envelope. "I'll be making my rounds at the top of every hour, so when you're finished taking care of business, just flag me down to get my attention."

"Alright, Mitchie, thanks." He removed the phone from the manila envelope and stood in front of the window. Taking a deep breath, he punched in the password, called Carmine, and placed the phone against his ear.

Ring. Ring. Ring.

"I'm friggin' busy," he heard Carmine's voice. "Call back."

Beep.

"Goddamnit," Big Angolo expressed his frustration. He hated the fact that his grandson was so rude, and he wished that it was 1964 instead of 2014, so that way he could have rolled up his sleeves and taught the young punk a lesson or two. "Call me as soon as you get this message."

He laid the phone on the window sill, and then looked down at the snow-covered compound. For as far as he could see, there were barb-wire fences, concrete slabs, pull up and dip bars, basketball courts, and a fifteen-foot-high concrete wall that the prisoners used to play handball. "Me and my crazy life," the old man said aloud as he slowly shook his head from side to side. His life on the inside was rough, but had he really wanted to, he could have escaped ADX Florence years ago, but he couldn't. His being there was the only way that the federal government would allow The Conglomerate to maintain its existence.

The Conglomerate was officially founded in 1952 by Lucky Luciano, but its connection to the federal government, namely the C.I.A., began ten years earlier, in 1942. It was during the second world war, and the United States military was so focused on sending their troops to eastern Europe that they quickly became short staffed on the home front. Fearing a sabotage on the eastern seaboard, the U.S. military in conjunction with the C.I.A., sought to beef up security on the New York harbor, specifically the docks along the west side of Manhattan. At the time, the docks were controlled by the local unions, and the unions were controlled by Lucky Luciano, who was serving a fifty-year sentence in upstate New York. Seeking to curry favor with the United States government, Mr. Luciano agreed to have his soldiers secure the harbor, and he promised the C.I.A. that nothing would leave or come through the docks without his approval. This was the first of many deals between the C.I.A. and the mafia.

The second deal was in 1948, immediately after the war. Attempting to break up the labor strikes that were put in place by the Facist regime, the C.I.A. once again called upon Mr. Luciano. During the war, the Facist regime, headed by Hitler and Mussolini, had essentially wiped out the mafia in Italy. But as the American liberating forces moved throughout Sicily, Southern Italy, and France, with the help of Mr. Luciano, they reconstructed the mafia as a tool to break up the labor strikes. In turn, the mafia was given the green light to resurrect the European heroin trade that was reduced to nothing under the Facist regime. Historically, this became the origin of the heroin network known throughout the world as 'The French Connection'.

In the end, Mr. Luciano was tremendously rewarded. He was granted a pardon and "deported" back to Italy, where the C.I.A. placed him at the helm of the world's heroin trade. Being the master-mind that he was, Mr. Luciano formed a partnership with the biggest cocaine and heroin suppliers from South America to Asia, and together they became The Conglomerate. In 1952, with the support of the C.I.A., they submitted a petition to the United Nations, requesting the authority to operate as a worldwide entity, with a clear understanding that they would take care of the U.N's dirty work whenever they were called upon to do so. The petition was granted, and they were given free rein to conduct business on a worldwide scale.

Indecorously, in 1989, Manuel Noriega, one of the largest cocaine suppliers in the world and a chairman of The Conglomerate, was getting too big for his britches. Aside from being mixed up in the infamous Oliver North/Iran Contra scandal, he was financially supporting the Contadora Treaty, a grassroots movement that was calling for peace in Central America. The upper echelon of the C.I.A. was furious because the conflicts in Central America had been propagated by them as a means of justifying the United States' invasion of Nicaragua and Panama, where cocaine was being confiscated and shipped back to the states to be distributed throughout the inner cities. Enraged, the C.I.A. wanted Noriega to pay with his life. They reached out to Big Angolo, the sole inheritor of Mr. Luciano's seat in the wake of his death, and told him that they wanted The Conglomerate to dispose of Noriega in the same manner that they had done to Patrice Lumumba and Che Guevare. Unfortunately, this presented a major problem. Unlike Lumumba and Guevara, Noriega was one of their own and they flat out refused to assassinate him, and as a result, the C.I.A. made The Conglomerate its number one target in America's so-called "War on Drugs".

After handing over tons and tons of cocaine and heroin, and forfeiting billions in U.S. currency, The Conglomerate was forced to cut a deal. But because Noriega was already in prison, the Panamanian drug lord was no longer an option. Playing hard-ball, the C.I.A. made it crystal clear that in order for The Conglomerate maintain its existence, they had to sacrifice two of its chairmen, specifically, Big Angolo and Pablo Escobar, the cocaine cowboy of Medellin, Columbia. The deal was etched in stone, and twenty-five years later, Pablo was dead and gone, and Big Angolo was a God-father buried alive.

Vrrrrrm. Vrrrrrm. Vrrrrrm.

Big Angolo picked up his cell phone and glanced at the screen. The incoming call was a number that he didn't recognize. He started to send the caller straight to voice mail, but his instincts told him otherwise. Reluctantly, he accepted the call and placed the phone against his right ear.

"Big Angolo?" the caller questioned.

"Who the fuck is this?"

"It's Terrance, your grandson. Your daughter, Angela, was my mother."

Askari

Chapter Sixteen

"Terrance," Big Angolo spoke into the phone. "You're the federal agent, Gervin's muscle. I know who you are. What the hell are you callin' me for?"

"I'm callin' because I need to know what happened to my parents," Gangsta explained. He was tearing up I-76, heading back to Philly. The revelation that Grip had something to do with the murders of his mother and father was eating him alive, and he needed answers.

Big Angolo sighed. "What are you askin' me, kid?"

"I'm askin' you if Uncle G was the one who killed my folks, and if he did, why?"

Big Angolo thought back to the day that he learned about the murder of his daughter and warm tears began to trickle down his wrinkled face. He'd made many mistakes in life, and for the most part he learned to live with regrets, but the murder of Angela and Russell was something that he would never come to terms with.

"Big Angolo?" Gangsta questioned the silence on the other end of the phone. "Are you still there?"

The old man wiped the tears from his face and nodded his head slowly. "Yeah, Terrance, I'm still here."

"I need you to tell me what happened," Gangsta insisted.

"Your mother," Big Angolo spoke in a low voice, "was my beautiful angel, my first daughter, and the apple of my eye. I loved her dearly, but things were complicated back then. In the late thirties, my boss, Mr. Lucky Luciano, sent me and my crew to Havana, Cuba to open up casinos and hotel resorts. I had a nightclub on Zanja Street, and it was there that I met and fell in love with your grandmother, Gabriella. She was drop dead gorgeous, and she stole my heart from the moment I laid eyes on her. I was struck by a thunderbolt, madly in love with this beautiful black woman.

"Over the next ten years, your grandmother became my everything. We had two beautiful children, Gervin and Angela. Now, your grandmother didn't know it, but back in the states I had a young Italian wife named Carmen, and we had a son," he paused

173

for a second and thought about the recent demise of his namesake, "your uncle, Little Angolo."

"I understand all of that," Gangsta interrupted him. "But why did Uncle G kill my folks?"

"I'm gettin' to it," Big Angolo checked him. "Just let me explain the entire story, so that way you'll have a clear understanding. Alright, now where the hell was I before you interrupted me?"

"You were tellin' me about your two families," Gangsta reminded him, slightly annoyed by the old man's procrastinating.

"That's right," Big Angolo agreed. "Now, like I was sayin', I was basically livin' a double life, dividin' my time between Cuba and the states, tendin' to the needs of both families. But like I said, things were different back then, especially when it came to interracial relationships. It was considered taboo for a guy like me, a white man, to have a serious union with a black woman, but I didn't care. I loved Gabriella and I loved those kids. My only problem was my boss, Mr. Luciano. I was married to his niece, and he didn't appreciate the fact that I had another family, especially one with a black woman. Cuban or not, Gabriella Moreno was darker than chocolate, and took pride in the fact she was a daughter of West Africa. It was rocky at first, but eventually me and Mr. Luciano came to an understanding. Because Gabriella was living in Cuba and Carmen was back in the states, the two of them would never know about one another, and therefore Carmen wouldn't have to live with the shame of knowing that her husband had another family with a black woman.

"Everything was working out nicely and I was able to keep both of my families happy. But in 1953, my entire world was flipped upside down. That son-of-a-bitch, Fidel Castro, made a power play to take over Cuba. We did everything we could to stick him in the fuckin' ground, but that slippery, bushy beard havin' motherfucker was relentless. He was heavily guarded at all times, and his banditos were ruthless beyond words. And before I knew it, the guys in my crew were dropping like flies. Murder contracts were placed on the heads of my family, and the only option I had was to get 'em outta Cuba and bring 'em to the states. Obviously, this presented a major

174

rift between me and Mr. Luciano. He understood that Gabriella and the kids were my family, but at the same time he made it clear that if I had any dealings wit' em when I brought 'em to America, he would have me whacked. So, unfortunately, when I brought 'em to the states, I was forced to turn my back on 'em. It hurt like hell and I swear to Christ that I didn't wanna do it, but at the time I didn't have a choice.

"For years, I was forced to watch 'em from a safe distance, and every month I would send money through my underboss, Mikey. In 1955, Gervin went to jail for a murder, and when he came home in the early sixties, he quickly made a name for himself. By then, Mr. Luciano was dead and gone, and because I didn't have to worry about any backlash, I reached out to Gervin."

"I already know this," Gangsta interrupted him once again. "Uncle G wanted to be a made man, but y'all wouldn't allow it because he wasn't a hundred percent Italian. So, to earn his respect he started the black mafia and took y'all to war. I already know the history. All I'm askin' is that you tell me what happened to my mom and dad. Why the fuck did Uncle G kill 'em?"

"It was because of me and the alliance that I formed with your mother," Big Angolo revealed.

"The alliance that you formed with my mom?" Gangsta questioned. "Are you tellin' me that my mom was caught up in the streets?"

"Absolutely," Big Angolo confirmed. "And by the time she was killed, she was arguably the biggest heroin supplier in Philadelphia. Gervin didn't know it, but in 1971, on your mother's twenty-first birthday, she came to see me. I couldn't believe it, I finally had the chance to sit down and talk to my beautiful baby girl, and I was so happy. I couldn't stop smiling. I'll never forget this day, we were sitting in my restaurant on Oregon Avenue enjoying a nice meal and everything was great. Initially, I assumed that Angela was just a daughter yearning for the love and affection of her father, but your mother, my daughter, fugget about it." The old man chuckled. "She had balls the size of watermelons."

"Whatchu mean by that?" Gangsta asked him.

"She was a wolf in sheep's clothing, a chip off the ol' block, I promise you. And it didn't take long for me to figure out that she couldn't have cared less about my love and affection. I mean, can you imagine? we're sitting at my private table and I'm talking to my little girl for the first time, and the only thing she cared about was a heroin connection. I was stuck, completely speechless, and taken aback. I'm tellin' you, kid, this daughter of mines was drop dead gorgeous, and I remember this shit like it was yesterday. She was draped in pearls, wrapped in a full-length mink, and staring at me with the same blue eyes that her mother used to rob me outta my heart."

"So, what did you do?"

"I gave her what she asked me for, and before I knew it, she was buying fifty keys a month. Apparently, her and your father were branching away from Gervin. He was too loud, spending his time in the spotlight, and basking in the glory of being a ghetto celebrity. One day he's riding around the slums of South Philly in a Rolls-Royce with the heavyweight champion sitting in the passenger's seat, and then the next day he's on the Channel 9 News acting as a bodyguard for Elijah Muhammad. Now, your father on the other hand, he was a man's man, a gangster's gangster. He was the quiet type. He walked lightly and carried a big stick, so naturally him and Gervin would often bump heads.

"In 1973, about a year before your parents were killed, they broke away from The Moreno Family and started their own thing. Your mother was the brain and your father was the brawn. Gervin was livid, especially when he found out that Angela and Russell were getting their heroin from me. Rumor had it that he placed a murder contract on your mother, but because she was pregnant at the time, he told his goons to wait until she gave birth. Then after she had you, they killed her."

"Who?" Gangsta asked. "Who killed her?" By now, he was breathing heavy and warm tears were running down the sides of his face. "It was Grip and who else?"

"It wasn't Gervin," Big Angolo said. "It was that skinny moth-erfucker, Muhammad, and that school boy. I forgot his name, but I heard he's a judge in the federal court."

"Gregory Johnson," Gangsta blurted out. "Judge Gregory John-son."

"Exactly," Big Angolo confirmed. "That's his name, Gregory Johnson. Supposedly, he killed your mother and father to solidify his position in The Moreno Family."

"But, what about the newspaper article?" Gangsta pried. "It said that Grip was the one who killed my folks. The district attorney had a witness who saw him leave the house immediately after the shootin', and they said that he was holdin' me in his arms."

"That's news to me," Big Angolo claimed. "As far as I knew, he had Gregory and Muhammad make the hit. Anything outside of that was never brought to my attention."

An eerie silence invaded the airwaves as both men sorted through his thoughts. Big Angolo was thinking about Angela's beautiful face, and Gangsta was thinking about the man who raised him, the same man who robbed him of his mother and father.

"Hey, Terrance," Big Angolo broke the silence. His voice was calm and steady. "What the hell is goin' on out there? I told Gervin and Little Angolo to put their differences aside and come together for the sake of our family's legacy. What the fuck happened?"

"Power," Gangsta insisted. "Those arrogant mutha'fuckas couldn't stand the thought of being on the same level, so to settle the score once and for all, they chose to wage war on one another, with Sontino and Carmine doin' all the dirty work."

"Sontino?" Big Angolo questioned. "Who the fuck is that?"

"He's Grip's grandson, and the new boss of The Moreno Crime Family."

"Gervin has a grandson?"

"He has two of them, Sontino and Rahmello. And the crazy part about it, Sontino wasn't even fuckin' wit' him. Actually, Sontino was try'na kill him, but being the slimy mutha'fucka that he is, Grip found a way to manipulate Sontino into trustin' him."

"So basically," Big Angolo interjected, "Little Angolo and Gervin were puttin' my great-grandsons on a collision course, just so one of 'em could out do the other, and solely inherit my empire?"

"Yep, that's exactly what happened," Gangsta told him.

"Alright, so what about the Mexicans? How in the hell did they get mixed up in it?"

"The Mexicans?" Gangsta asked. "What Mexicans?"

"You know, the Sinaloa Cartel, them crazy sons-of-bitches down in Texas. Did Gervin use them to go after Little Angolo and Carmine?"

"The Sinaloa Cartel?" Gangsta questioned. "Big Angolo, you lost me."

"Goddamnit, the fuckin' Mexicans!" The old man overstated. "They're the ones who whacked Little Angolo, and now they're comin' for Carmine. And speakin' of Carmine, I just called him a few minutes ago and he didn't answer. I'm thinkin' they might've whacked him, too."

"I don't know," Gangsta spoke the truth. "Grip never told me nothin' about the Mexicans, but at the same time, I wouldn't put it past him. Ever since he returned to the states, he's been killing any and everything that could possibly stand in the way of him takin' over The Conglomerate. He even killed Joey."

"Joey?" Big Angolo raised his voice. "Gervin whacked Joey? Why?"

"Because Joey knew too much. He knew about The Conglomerate, and once Little Angolo was outta the way, Grip knew that Joey would come for his spot."

"Goddamnit," Big Angolo snapped. He was shaking with rage and doing everything in his power not to break the phone in half. "What the fuck is Gervin thinkin'?" he continued to shout. "Is he losin' his fuckin' mind?"

"I don't know, fam, but calm down," Gangsta told him. "You shoutin' all in my mutha'fuckin' ear. Just take a minute to calm down."

Big Angolo took a deep breath and exhaled slowly. He started to say something, but stopped when he heard a voice at the door. It was Mitchell. He was patrolling the tier when he heard the old man shouting. "Mr. Gervino," he spoke in a low voice, just above a whisper. "Keep it down, you're gonna get us pinched."

Big Angolo ice-grilled him, then quickly pulled off his left shoe and threw it at the door. "Get the fuck away from my goddamned cell."

"I was only try'na tell you that you're too loud," Mitchell explained. "If somebody hears you, we'll both be in trouble."

"Goddamnit," the old man bellowed. He tossed his other shoe and it crashed into the door with a loud bang. "If I gotta say it one more fuckin' time, I'm gonna rip your head off and shove it down your fuckin' neck. Now get:"

As Mitchell walked away from the door, Big Angolo returned his attention to Gangsta. "Listen, kid, I know a way that we can fix this shit, but I'm gonna need your help."

"I'm all ears," Gangsta replied. "Whatever I gotta do to take down Grip, I'm ready to make it happen. That slippery mutha'fucka killed my folks, and I can't rest until I get him outta here."

"That judge of his, I need you to pay him a visit," Big Angolo spoke in a clear voice. "And before you whack him, you have to get him to sign an arrest warrant and extradition papers for Joaquin Alverez."

"It's funny you mentioned this bitch ass nigga," Gangsta said as he parked his Ford Excursion a block away from the Judge's estate. "He's at the top of my shit list." He ejected the spent magazine in his P89 and replaced it with a fresh one.

"Whatever you do, Terrance, just make sure that you get him to sign the papers."

"Trust me," Gangsta replied in a chilly voice. "He's gonna do a whole lot more than sign some mutha'fuckin' papers. This is the beginning of the reckoning." He cocked a bullet into the chamber, and then disconnected the call.

***

Hidalgo County, Texas

"Mijo, where are you?" Chatchi spoke into his cell phone. He was sitting behind his desk at The Honey Comb Gentleman's Club. A mountain of cocaine was sprawled out on top of the desk, and he was so high that he couldn't feel his face.

"We're at the Marriot Hotel in Center City, Philadelphia," Jorge informed him. "We're waitin' for the next move, so whatever you want done, just let us know and we'll carry it out to the tee."

Chatchi leaned forward and pressed his face against the glistening white mountain. After inhaling the white powder, he coughed a couple of times and then sat back in his chair and wiped the residue away from his face with the back of his right hand. He was sweating like a glass of cold water in the middle of a desert, and he couldn't stop his jaw muscles from flexing.

"Before I cut Chico's heart out and fed it to my German Shepherds, he mentioned the name Olivia Nunez," Chatchi told him. "I want you to talk to Diablo, him and Roberto were close. Ask him if he knows anything about this chica named Olivia."

"Gimmie a second," Jorge spoke into the phone. "I gotta go wake him up, he's out in the living room sound asleep on the couch." As he spun around to leave the room, he jumped backwards and dropped the phone on the floor. The tatted-up assassin was standing right behind him.

"Who's next?" Diablo asked.

"Don't be sneakin' up on me like that, eh," Jorge shouted at him. He was clutching his chest with his left hand and his eyes were bigger than golf balls. "You almost gave me a heart attack, homes. Don't be doin' that shit."

"Who's next?" Diablo repeated his question. He couldn't have cared less about Jorge's complaining. He had one mission, one mission only, and that was to slaughter the mutha'fuckas who kidnapped and murdered Roberto.

"Olivia Nunez," Jorge said after calming himself down. "Are you familiar with the name?"

Diablo squinted his eyes. Olivia Nunez was a name that he was all too familiar with, and he cursed himself for not thinking of it sooner. "She was Roberto's girlfriend," he stated in a cold, heartless voice. "The bitch broke it off a lil' while back, but Roberto was still in love wit' her." He looked at Jorge with a sinister glare. "That bitch had somethin' to do wit' this, didn't she?"

"I'm not sure," Jorge said as he held up his index finger, gesturing for him to wait a second. He reached down to pick up his cell phone, and then placed it against his ear. "Chatchi, you still there?" He listened closely, but the only thing he heard was a loud snort.

"Ay yi yi," Chatchi blurted out, and then coughed for a couple of seconds. After wiping the coke from his nose, he said, "Talk to me, mijo. Does he know her?"

"Yeah, he said that the chica was Roberto's ex-girlfriend," Jorge informed him. "Is she connected to what happened?"

"I don't know, mijo, that's for you to find out. Chico told me that Roberto and this chica, Olivia, had a major falling out, and then after that her father called Roberto and threatened to kill him. And guess what else, her father is Poncho Nunez,"

"Columbian Poncho?" Jorge questioned. "He's a chairman of The Conglomerate, him and his brother Juan. Why would they make a move against us? If it wasn't for us and our tunnels, they wouldn't have a pipeline to smuggle their yahyo into the states. So, why would they kill Roberto and jeopardize our business relationship? It doesn't make any sense."

"Maybe you're right," Chatchi acknowledged. "But I've been calling him and Juan for the last ten minutes, and neither one of them has yet to accept my calls. I need you to find them."

Click.

Jorge looked up to tell Diablo what was going on, but the young Mexican was already gone. He looked on the table where he left his car keys, and they were missing as well. The devil was headed for the Nunez residence and the only thing that was strong enough to stop his wrath was the power of God.

Askari

Chapter Seventeen
A Half an Hour Later in Southwest Philadelphia

On the corner of 54th and Kingsessing, the hawk was out and Jack Frost was showing his icy ass. The wind was blowing, making a cold night even colder, and the snowflakes that cascaded from the starless sky were clinging to everything they touched, quickly accumulating by the inch. The large intersection was essentially deserted. But for the sake of chasing money, a crew of young hustlers dressed in all black was posted beneath a dimly lit street light, selling everything from Percocet 30s to dimes of heroin.

"Yo, where the fuck is the doe at?" Murda Mont complained as his hungry eyes scoured the area looking for any signs of a customer. He was frustrated to say the least, and because he was used to taking money instead of making money, the fact that he'd been standing in the cold for the last two hours just to make a hundred dollars had him mad as shit.

"Oh, so now y'all ain't got nothin' to say?" He was looking back and forth between his homies, Doo Dirty and Killah Kye. Doo Dirty was sipping on the Cup of Noodles that he just got from his baby mother's house, and Killah Kye was puffing on a Dutch Master. He snatched the Dutch from Killah Kye and took a deep pull. "I know one thing," he said through a cloud of smoke, "I'm 'bout to say fuck trappin', I was makin' more money when I was runnin' around the city robbin' niggas."

"You and me both," Killah Kye conceded. Like Murda Mont, he was a stick-up kid by nature, and ever since they bailed out of jail a couple of weeks ago, he'd been following behind Doo Dirty, attempting to be a drug dealer.

Murda Mont exhaled a cloud of smoke and then fixed his gaze on Doo Dirty. "Yo, how the fuck is you talkin' all this money shit and ya so-called block only doin' a couple hunnid a night? Now, when me and Kye was doin' our thing before we got knocked, we was touchin' about six hunnid a night. And we wasn't standin' outside in the cold." He looked at Killah Kye and gave him some dap. "We was robbin' the niggas that was standin' outside in the cold."

Doo Dirty wolfed down the rest of his chicken flavored noodles, and then tossed the container in the trash can that was chained to the light post. "A'ight, but what if y'all tried to rob a nigga like me?" he asked, and then reached behind his back and whipped out a .45 semi-automatic. "He woulda put a Tootsie Roll in ya dumb ass."

Murda Mont looked at Killah Kye and they burst out laughing. "Nigga, ya pretty-boy ass ain't doin' nothin'." They took turns grinding him up, but deep inside, they both knew he was worthy of the name 'Doo Dirty.'

"Yeah, a'ight," Doo Dirty replied as he placed the .45 on his right hip. "Let a nigga try me."

As they went back and forth, arguing about who caught the most wreck, a smoke-gray Porsche with tinted windows and chromed-out rims cruised by at a slow pace.

"Yo, who the fuck was that?" Murda Mont asked. He was looking at the red tail lights, and reaching for the .357 that was tucked in his belt. Being a stick-up kid, he was always paranoid, knowing that a mark from his past could be seeking revenge at any given time. "Who the fuck was drivin' that Porsche?" he reiterated. "I couldn't see through the tint."

Doo Dirty shrugged his shoulders and pulled the draw string on his hood, attempting to shield his face from the blistering wind. "I don't know, but that Porsche was chunkier than a mutha'fucka. I think it was a 918," he continued, and then sparked up the Newport that was dangling from his lips. "That's a limited edition. They don't even make 'em like that. It probably set a nigga back a couple hunnid thousand."

Killah Kye looked at Murda Mont and shook his head slowly. "Yo, that's some nut ass shit," he lamented, regretting the fact that they missed out on a golden opportunity. "We shoulda robbed that nigga."

Murda Mont hit the Dutch Master one last time and then tossed it to the ground. He would have never told his two homies, but he was super concerned about the driver of the Porsche. "Yo, I'm done for the night, dawg. I'm takin' it down." After giving his niggas some dap, he started to walk away, but stopped in his tracks. "Yo, there he go again," he overstated. "Look." He pointed up 54th Street, directing their attention to the halogenic lights that illuminated the top of the block. Removing his Sig Sauer, he looked back and forth between Killah Kye and Doo Dirty. "This nigga's up to somethin', dawg. I'm tellin' you."

"It don't even matter," Killah Kye replied. He reached under his Sean John coat and whipped out a nickel-plated 9mm. "I'm ready to jam this nigga."

"Hol' up," Doo Dirty waved him off. "Chill out for a minute. I think he's lookin' for my baby mom's house. That's probably why he's drivin' so slow." Murda Mont looked at him skeptically. "Ya baby mom's house?"

"Yeah," Doo Dirty nodded his head. "He's probably lookin' for her sister, Keyshia. You know she be fuckin' wit' one of them niggas that play for the Sixers."

"Umm mmm mmm," Killah Kye sighed. "Ol' freaky ass Keyshia. Every time I turn around she got a ballin' ass nigga comin' to see her. She need to stop playin', and bust that thing open for a real nigga."

Murda Mont shot him a look that said, *Nigga, shut the fuck up.* He then returned his attention to Doo Dirty. "Naw, bro, look," he pointed at the coupe, "he can't be lookin' for Keyshia. He just drove past the house for the second time. I'm tellin' you, bro, this nigga on some other shit."

Killah Kye shrugged his shoulders and cocked back the top of his burner. "Well, fuck it then, if he try'na get froggy, I got a clip full of hollows that'll make his ass leap."

"You and me, both," Doo Dirty said. He snatched the hammer from his waist and cocked a bullet into the chamber.

As they stood erect, guns cocked, and ready for action, the Porsche Spyder cruised down the block and stopped on the opposite corner. The base line of Tupac's, *My Ambitions Az A Ryda*, was thumping from the trunk, and the halogenic headlights were so bright they had to look away until their eyes made the proper adjustments.

Slowly, the smoke-gray coupe coasted through the intersection and pulled up beside them. The tinted driver's side window retracted into the bullet-proof door and a calm silence replaced the music. The car's interior was too dark for them to see Sonny's face, and the only thing they saw was the bling of his earrings. The VS stones were shining bright, similar to the eyes of a black cat in the middle of a dark alley on the darkest night.

Licking his chops, Murda Mont took a step closer. "Damn, homie, whatchu lost?" His .357 was clutched in his right hand and discreetly tucked behind his right leg.

Sonny remained calm and took a pull on his Backwood. As he exhaled the smoke, it seeped from the car and mingled with the cascading snowflakes. "Whatchu deaf, nigga?" Murda Mont fired off another question.

"This nigga's gotta be deaf," Killah Kye backed him up. "Either that, or he's the dumbest mutha'fucka walkin' on two legs."

The dome light cut on and Sonny was sitting behind the steering wheel, puffing his Backwood. They assumed he was staring at them, but actually he was looking at the man creeping up behind them.

"Yo, y'all know this nigga?" Murda Mont asked.

"Naw, we don't know this nigga," Doo Dirty and Killah Kye answered in unison.

"But I'ma tell you what I do know," Killah Kye continued. He took a step closer and aimed his ratchet at Sonny's face. "I know them some big ass diamonds."

"Yeah, them jawns blingin' like a mutha'fucka," Doo Dirty interjected. "And if I was main man, I'd be takin' them shits off 'fore this pound get to barkin'."

"And if I was you," a voice spoke up from behind them, "I'd be steppin' the fuck off 'fore this pump action knock a limb off ya mutha'fuckin' ass."

They spun around just in time to see Rayon The Reaper cocking the lever on his sawed-off shotgun.

Click. Clack.

Shaking like a room full of fat bitches twerking for a pork chop, they lowered their weapons, and looked at him with pleading eyes. Not only was Rayon a Southwest legend, he was hands down the craziest mutha'fucka to ever walk the streets of Philly, and they wanted no parts of him.

"D-D-Double R," Murda Mont stuttered. "H-H-He witchu?"

The Reaper wasn't in the business of explaining himself, so he didn't. Instead, he moved the shotgun from face to face, and gritted his teeth. "Get y'all lil' asses outta here," he demanded. "Now."

The three men quickly backed away from the corner. Doo Dirty cut his eye at Murda Mont, and shook his head slowly. "Yo, how the fuck is this nigga on the streets? Ain't he 'posed to be on death row?"

The Reaper heard what he said, but he paid him no mind. He had bigger fish to fry. After climbing in the passenger's side of the Porsche, he laid the shotty on the floor and looked at Sonny. The loyalty that he had for the young hustler was iron clad. Not only did Sonny give him the $50,000 for killing Tommy in the county jail, he looked out for his mother, and hired Savino to represent him at trial. The Reaper was fighting a triple homicide, and the district attorney was seeking the death penalty. But because Sonny got him Savino, he beat the case. Now, he was back on the streets, guns cocked, and ready to commit murder for the sake of a dollar.

"Yo, why is you just now callin'?" The Reaper asked. "I seen you on the news, and I heard about the situation witcha pop."

Sonny flexed his jaw muscles and pulled off slowly. In many ways, he was embarrassed to tell The Reaper why he contacted him. But at the same time, his thirst for blood was stronger than his pride. He grabbed his iPhone and pulled up the video of Daphney and Egypt, and then passed it to The Reaper.

Completely shocked, the dark-skinned black man looked at Sonny, and then returned his attention to the video. Initially, when Sonny first called, he assumed that the target was either Grip or Carmine, but now he realized that the situation was much deeper.

"For a nice check, I'll chop a mutha'fucka up and feed him to his kids," The Reaper promised. "But for you, my nigga, I'll gut a

Askari

mutha'fucka from his neck to his balls, and then bend him over and rip his lungs out his ass."

"I already know," Sonny replied as he veered right and hopped on the expressway. "But it ain't just him. That stankin' ass bitch gotta get it, too."

The Reaper gave him a quizzical look, uncertain as to whether or not he heard him correctly. "Hold up, fam, just so we on the same page, is you sayin' that you want me to body ya wife?"

"Not at all," Sonny clarified, and then looked at him with a sinister glare. "I don't want you to kill her." He returned his eyes to the road and mashed down on the gas pedal. "I'ma kill that bitch myself."

***

Back at La Casa Moreno

Rahmello was lying in bed staring at the ceiling. Olivia was down the hall in another guest room, being attended to by Heldga, and Grip was in his office calling all around looking for Gangsta. Muhammad was sitting in his living quarters, fantasizing about choking the life out of Sonny, and Ahmed and Mustafa were outside patrolling the property.

"These bitches ain't shit," Rahmello said to himself as he lay there thinking about Olivia and Mexican Bobby. "I gave this bitch my heart and she threw it back in my face. And now, all because I was try'na protect her stupid ass, Sonny's gonna cut me off. I know it."

The bedroom door creaked open and Grip peeked inside. "Rahmello," he addressed his grandson. "You okay?"

Rahmello looked at him, and then returned his gaze to the ceiling. "Yeah, I'm a'ight."

"Do you mind if I come inside and talk to you for a minute?"

"Nah," he sighed, "you good." His fingers were interlocked between his head and the pillow, and the gunshot wound to his leg was beginning to itch.

Grip closed the door behind him and took a seat beside the bed. He could see that Rahmello was hurting and he knew why. "It's that girl, isn't it?"

Rahmello gritted his teeth and cleared his throat. "Man, fuck that bitch." He spoke a good game, but internally his ego was bruised and his heart was aching.

"Well, you know the saying," Grip smiled at him, "show me a man that's down and out, and I'll show you a sucker for love,"

Irritated, Rahmello ice-grilled him and sat up to position his back against the padded headboard. "Ah," he winced from the pain that shot up his left leg. "Goddamn."

"Whoa now, take it easy," Grip said as he reached out to help him scoot back. He propped the pillow against the headboard, then settled back in his seat as Rahmello reclined on the silk fabric.

"What's up wit' Sonny?" Rahmello asked. "Is he mad at me?"

Grip chose his words carefully, knowing that this was the perfect time to test the waters and see if he could get Rahmello to turn against his brother. "Of course, he's mad at you, would you expect anything less? You know how hot-headed and stubborn your brother can be."

"I know," Rahmello acknowledged as he lowered his head. "I shoulda told him about the Columbians, but I didn't want him to hurt Oli. Now, he's probably gonna kill us both."

"It's possible," Grip conceded. "But what if he only kills your woman, and then leaves you alive to deal with the heartache? You know, just to teach you a lesson?"

Rahmello's light skinned face became beet-red. A lone tear trickled from his left eye and he anxiously bit down on his bottom lip. "If he kills Oli, then he better kill me too. Because if anybody," he looked at Grip with a menacing stare, "and I mean anybody, touches my girl, I'm goin' dead at 'em."

"As you should," Grip replied with a sarcastic undertone, realizing that Rahmello's threat was directed towards him as well. "But Sontino's your blood. Isn't blood thicker than water?"

"That's only in certain cases," Rahmello propounded. "Your blood is your blood, but you still need water to live, and Olivia's my life. Yeah, she did a nigga dirty, but that's still my baby."

"So, what do you plan to do when Sontino extracts revenge?"

Rahmello didn't answer. There was nothing else to say. Digressing, he brought up the situation with the twins. "How do we address this situation wit' the Mexicans? You know how Sonny is. He'd rather die than turn his back on one of the homies."

Grip took a deep breath and gently caressed the hair on his chin. "You know, I'm glad that you mentioned it. The Sinaloas are gonna come down hard if we don't come up with a reasonable explanation. They already have the video of those dirty ass twins kidnaping Roberto, and if we don't turn them over, they'll wage war on our entire family."

"But what about Oli?" Rahmello perked up. "Is there any way that we can keep her out of this?"

"I'm not sure," Grip said. "I mean, we're still going to have to explain why the twins did what they did."

"I think we should blame the Italians," Rahmello suggested. "We can say that they paid the twins to kill him, just to have the blame fall on our family. Plus, from what Sonny told me before we fell out, one of the shooters from my pops funeral was connected to Carmine. So, all we gotta do is play our cards right, and everything should go smooth."

Intrigued by his grandson's wit, Grip smiled at him. "You know, Rahmello, that's not a bad idea. But in order for this to happen, we need to track down and kill the twins, because without them, we won't stand a chance."

"I know," Rahmello acknowledged. "But, Sonny, I know my brother, he's not gonna bend. Like I said before, he'd rather die than turn his back on the twins."

"Alright, but what if get Sontino out of the way?"

Rahmello looked at him with a raised eyebrow. "Whatchu mean get him out of the way?"

"No, not like that," the old man quickly replied. He cracked his knuckles and slowly shook his head, realizing that Rahmello would never go along with killing Sonny. "I was talking about the twins," he lied. "If you tell me where I can find them, we can get Sonny out of the way, and handle the situation ourselves."

Rahmello took a deep breath and sighed. "I don't know," he expressed his uncertainty. "I already went behind his back with the Poncho and Juan situation, and if I cross him again, I know it's gon' be a problem."

"Alright, well if that's the position you wanna take," Grip said as he stood to his feet. "I guess we'll just have to give up your girl-friend." As he headed for the door, Rahmello stopped him.

"Hey, yo, Grip, hol' up."

The old man smiled, knowing that he pressed the right button to play with Rahmello's emotions. He removed the smile on his face and turned around slowly. "What is it?"

"Marshal Street."

"Come again."

"The twins," Rahmello said. "That's where you can find them."

"Marshal and what?"

"Marshal and Montgomery Avenue," he replied in a low voice. "It's the second house from the corner, on the left side of the street."

"And this is where they live?"

"Nah," Rahmello shook his head. "That's the house they sell weight from. They live out of town, but on the weekends, they stay in the hood to be close to the money."

Rubbing his hands together, Grip smiled at him and said, "Trust me, Rahmello, you did the right thing."

"I'm saying, though, whatever you do, don't tell my brother that I was the one who gave up the twins. Because if he finds out, he gon' fuck around and kill me. It's either that, or I'ma have to defend myself and kill him first."

"Don't worry about it," Grip assured him. "It'll never make it that far."

Askari

Chapter Eighteen
Poncho's New Jersey Estate

The Xanaxs that Marisol ingested prior to taking a shower were beginning to take toll as she emerged from the bathroom and plopped down at the foot of her bed. Her curly, salt-and-pepper hair was wrapped up in a white towel, and her damp body was snuggled under a soft-pink, terry cloth bathrobe. She took a deep breath, enjoying the aroma of her kiwi scented shampoo, and then released a long sigh of frustration. For the life of her, she couldn't understand how Olivia could turn her back on their family, and throw Poncho and Estaban under the bus. She loved her daughter dearly, but disloyalty was a crime that she would never condone.

As she lay there thinking about Olivia, her cell phone vibrated on the nightstand. Sluggishly, she rolled over to grab it, and seeing that the caller was Poncho, she quickly accepted. "Papi," she addressed him, her voice full of excitement. "How are ju callin' me right now? Ju and Estaban are flyin' back to Columbia, no?"

"No, mami, we didn't leave," Poncho told her. "De situation from earlier today wasn't as bad as we first thought. De people on de news are blamin' everything on de Italians, so we have no worries."

"So, where are ju?" she pried. "Why didn't ju come back home?"

"We're not too far away. We're at de Red Roof Inn, right off of Route 1," Poncho informed her. "I got a call from Juan as we were drivin' to de airport, and he tol' us to lay low for a couple of days. You know, just in case." He paused for a moment, and then asked about his daughter. "How's Oli? Tell her I'm sorry for what I did and said to her."

Marisol snapped, "Do not speak dat name to me ever again."

Poncho was blown away by what she told him. She and Olivia were the best of friends, and up until now, she was Olivia's number one supporter. "Mamacita, what happened? What did she do?"

"Dat ungrateful bitch is no longer a part of dis familia. She is dead to us all."

"But, what did she do?"

"She betrayed us," Marisol quickly replied. "She turned against ju and Estaban, and as far as I'm concerned, she too is an enemy."

"I no understand," Poncho said. "She betray us, how?"

"After ju and Estaban left for de airport, she beg me to take her to de hospital to see Rahmello. I tell her no, but den she threatened to drive herself. She was crying and very upset, and I did not want her to be driving in dat condition, so I take her myself."

"Did she tell Rahmello about what happened to his poppa?"

"She did exactly dat."

"And what happened after dat?"

"Me and her have a huge fight, and dat's when she cursed ju, papi. Can ju believe it? After everything dat we do for her, she look into my eyes, and curse her own papi."

Upon hearing this, Poncho was hurt, but he didn't let it show. Instead, he focused on the information that Olivia revealed to Rahmello. "Listen mami, I need to know exactly what she say to Rahmello."

"She tol' him dat ju and Estaban kill his poppa at de bodega. I tried to stop her, but she wouldn't listen."

"What did he say when Olivia tol' him dat?"

"He didn't say anything," she said in a low voice, feeling the effects of the two Xanax pills. "He was knocked out cold, and layin' on his hospital bed. But at de same time, he had bodyguards standin' outside in de hallway, and she might've tol' de story to dem. Either way, she betrayed us, and she must never be forgiven."

"Damn it," Poncho sighed. He never anticipated that things would go this far. Not only did he miss his opportunity to kill Sonny and Rahmello, he was now receiving incoming calls and text messages from Chatchi and Joaquin every fifteen minutes. The heat was turning up and he was beginning to feel it.

"Marisol, I want ju to listen to me closely. Stay in de house for de next couple of days, and don't make a peep until I return. No phone calls, no text messages, no Facebook, and no Instagram, ju got dat? Just stay put until I get home, and don't accept any phone calls unless dey come from me or Estaban."

"I gotchu, papi." She could tell from the sound of his voice that something was wrong, so she didn't put up a fuss.

"What about Emilia?" Poncho asked, referring to their housekeeper. "Is she dere witchu?"

"Si, papi. She's downstairs makin' me a pot of tea. Should I tell her de same?"

"Si, mami. Tell her dat we will pay her extra, but until I return, she is not to leave de house."

She was just about to say something, but noticed that her battery was dying. "Papi, I have to go downstairs to get my charger. My phone is about to die." No sooner than she said it, the screen went black and the call was disconnected. "Goddamnit," she complained as she got up from the bed and tightened the belt around her bathrobe.

Stepping into the hallway, she noticed the entire second floor was pitch-black. All of the lights were turned off and she couldn't understand why. The last she remembered, the lights in the hallway were left on. So why did Emilia turn them off? She reached out for the light panel on the wall in the hallway, but when she flipped the switch, nothing happened. The hallway was so dark and the house was so quiet she began to feel frightened. A plethora of goosebumps covered her skin and she could hear the sound of her thumping heart.

Ba-Bump. Ba-Bump. Ba-Bump. Ba-Bump.

Cautiously, she walked the length of the hallway and approached the spiral staircase. Her hands were tightly balled into fists, and her head was on a swivel, slowly moving from left to right looking for any signs of an intruder. Leaning over the balcony and looking down at the ground floor, she noticed that the kitchen was the only room in the house that still had lights.

"Emilia," she called out, hoping to get a response. Unfortunately, the only thing she heard was the tune of her own heartbeat.

Ba-Bump. Ba-Bump. Ba-Bump.

"Why isn't she answering me?" She said to herself as she slowly descended the stairs. Her brown eyes were adjusting to the darkness and she could make out the silhouettes of the furniture that decorated the living room and the main hallway below. As she reached the bottom of the stairs, the piercing sound of a glass hitting the kitchen floor caused her to jump back and clutch her chest with both hands.

Ba-Bump. Ba-Bump. Ba-Bump. Ba-Bump.

Taking a deep breath, she reached for the crucifix that hung from her neck and silently recited *The Lord's Prayer*. The kitchen at the end of the hallway reminded her of a dark tunnel with a bright light gracefully waiting at the end, and strangely, amidst the darkness, within the light, she found a strong sense of hope.

Suddenly, she stopped walking. A huge smile spread across her brown skinned face and she kissed the front of her crucifix. Up ahead, she spotted Emilia moving back and forth from one side of the kitchen to the other. Her Beats by Dre headphones were draped across the top of her head and when she moved past the threshold, Marisol noticed the steaming teapot that was clutched in her left hand.

Moving with confidence and no longer afraid, Marisol approached the kitchen and stared at the young Columbian woman. She was standing in front with her back to the doorway. Her silky black hair flowed down the back of her forest-green bathrobe, and she was nodding her head to the music that thumped from her headphones. Marisol smiled at her, and then took a seat at the marble island in the middle of the kitchen. She started to speak, but a burgundy liquid seeping from the pantry caught her attention.

"Emilia, what's dat?" she asked while looking at the back of her head and pointing down at the substance on the floor. When Emilia didn't respond, Marisol got up from the island and cautiously approached the pantry. What lay before her was so horrendous that she couldn't even scream. The housekeeper's naked body was stretched out in a pool of her own blood. Her arms and legs were grotesquely snapped backwards, fixed into the shape of a swastika, and her once beautiful face was battered beyond recognition. The top of her bone-white skull protruded from the rim of her forehead, resembling the crowning of an infant that was seconds away from birth, and her puffy, zombie-like eyes were fixed on Marisol.

"Help me," the young woman whispered. "Help me, please."

Marisol yelped and hastily spun around, realizing they were not alone. If Emilia was stretched out in the pantry, then who in the hell was standing by the stove?

"Ay dios mio," she cried out and grasped her crucifix with both hands. Her brain was telling her to run, but her trembling legs refused to accept the message. Completely terrified, she stood in front of the pantry looking at the person in the forest-green bathrobe.

Diablo chuckled. Emilia's bathrobe fit him just right. After turning around to face his next victim, he snatched off the blood-soaked terry cloth and stood before Marisol completely naked. His chiseled frame was covered in tattoos, and from the waist up, his golden-brown skin was sprinkled with the coagulated specks of Emilia's blood. His eyes locked on Marisol and he smiled at her, showing off the razor sharp, one-inch incisors that hung from his bloody-red gums.

"Ay dios mio," Marisol repeated. She was clutching her crucifix with both hands and slowly shaking her head from side to side.

Ba-Bump. Ba-Bump. Ba-Bump. Ba-Bump.

Diablo closed his mouth and inhaled deeply, taking in the sweet smell of fear. He then reached up and casually snatched off the hair-covered scalp that clung to the top of his bald head.

Marisol couldn't believe her eyes. The thing walking towards her appeared to be more monster than man. The devil horns that decorated the ends of his forehead were something out of a horror movie, and she was so afraid that she began to feel dizzy.

Ba-Bump. Ba-Bump. Ba-Bump. Ba-Bump.

Diablo smiled once again. He was seconds away from claiming another soul.

Ba-Bump. Ba-Bump. Ba-Bump. Ba-Bump.

"No," Marisol cried. He was a few steps away, looking at her with a twisted expression. "Don't hurt me, please."

She attempted to run and Diablo released a gut-wrenching wail. He then slammed into the front of her face, fangs first.

***

Back at La Casa Moreno

"Alright, gentlemen, there's been a change of plans," Grip said to his men as he entered the dining room and took a seat at the head of the table. Muhammad was seated across from him at the other end of the table, Ahmed and Mustafa were seated to his left, and Shabazz and Aziz were seated to his right. A burning Cohiba was wedged in between his left thumb and index finger, and a serious expression donned his face.

"I had to postpone my trip to Cuba," Grip continued as he looked around the table. He took a pull on his cigar and the cherry shined bright. "Apparently, my grandsons put us in a situation that needs to be rectified immediately."

He released a cloud of smoke and then took another pull. "A couple of weeks ago, the Nunez Brothers, Poncho and Juan, paid them to do a hit on a young Mexican kid who just so happened to be the son on of Joaquin Alverez, the boss of The Sinaloa Cartel. The young man's name was Roberto Alverez, and he was kidnapped in the parking lot of Carmine's strip joint on Delaware Avenue. Initially, the Sinaloas assumed that Carmine and Little Angolo were behind the hit, but now the cartel is focusing on us."

He exhaled a cloud of smoke and blew the foggy mist at the tip of his Cohiba, causing the cherry to flicker and smolder. "And just so you know, earlier this evening, Little Angolo and Carmine were both murdered by the cartel. But before they got to Carmine, his little punk ass sent them a video of the actual kidnapping. I spoke to Chatchi Alverez and he sent me a copy of the video. From what I could see, Sontino and Rahmello weren't present during the incident, but we still have a problem."

"A problem like what?" Brother Shabazz asked him. "If Sontino and Rahmello didn't appear on the video, why are the Sinaloas suspecting us?"

"Those goddamned twins," Grip sighed. "They're the ones who Sontino sent to make the hit. Their faces were all over the video, and I'm assuming that Carmine told the Sinaloas they were connected to the family."

Shabazz looked at Aziz, and then returned his attention to Grip. "So, what did Sontino have to say about this?"

"That grandson of mines," Grip shook his head slowly, "he's proving to be more trouble than I'd ever anticipated. I tried to tell him that the only way to fix this situation was to hand over the twins, but he wouldn't budge. He'd rather go to war and jeopardize my empire than sacrifice those those dirty ass twin brothers. Obviously, this is unacceptable."

"All right, Mr. Moreno, so whatchu want us to do?" Mustafa asked. He was slouched back in his seat with his thick arms folded across his chest.

Grip looked at Muhammad and gave him a head nod. He then got up from the dining room table and left the room without saying another word.

Muhammad cleared his throat and looked the gunman square in the eyes. "The first thing we need to do is get rid of those twins. Sontino wouldn't hand them over. But for the sake of the family, Rahmello did. And as of right now, they're holed up in a house on Marshal Street. So, tomorrow morning at six o'clock sharp, I want the four of you to go around there and take care of business. Do I make myself clear?"

The four men nodded their understanding and looked at the old man attentively. Satisfied with their response, Muhammad continued dishing out instructions. "You'll have to make it clean, in and out, no mistakes. And to prove that the situation was handled, I want their heads, literally. Now, has any of you heard from Gangsta in the last hour?"

"No," they replied in unison.

"All right, well y'all have about seven hours until it's time to get busy, so I strongly suggest that somebody get a hold of him. Also, when you go to make the hit," he looked at Mustafa and Ahmed, "be sure to have your credentials. So, that way if the city cops arrive on the scene, you can flash your FBI badges and tell them mutherfuckers to keep it moving."

Aziz looked around the table, and then settled his eyes on Muhammad. "Where's Sontino? He's the new boss of the family, shouldn't he be here?"

"Sontino's running out of time," Muhammad replied with a devilish grin. "And just so you know, the position that was designated for him is now being handed down to Rahmello."

Confused, Aziz and Shabazz looked at one another. They worked directly under Gangsta, and for the past two years they'd been helping him keep tabs on Sonny. Everything about the young gangster was boss and they didn't understand why Grip was turning his back on him.

"Is there a problem with something I said?" Muhammad challenged, looking back and forth between the two men.

"No, Muhammad, there's not a problem," Aziz replied.

"Good, now somebody get Gangsta on the phone and let him know what's going on."

Out in the hallway, Grip was pacing back forth, talking to Judge Johnson on his cell phone. His right hand was holding the phone against his ear and his left hand was stuffed down in his pants pocket.

"G.J.," Grip spoke into the phone, "you were right about Sontino. We're gonna have to put him down. I wanted so bad to make him the heir to my empire, but he's too much of a loose cannon. I can't control him."

"Alright," Judge Johnson quickly replied.

Grip could sense the vexation in the judge's voice, and it left him with a raised brow. It was uncharacteristic for his old friend to respond with one- or two-word answers, especially when the topic of discussion had a serious nature. "G.J., is everything okay? You sound a little funny."

"Everything's fine," the judge hastily responded, furthering Grip's suspicions.

Grip started to pry, but he didn't. "Alright, well like I was saying, the trip to Cuba has to be rescheduled. Chatchi Alverez is calling an emergency meeting with The Conglomerate. It's tomorrow at midnight, in New York City. There's a lot of shit going on be-tween us and the Sinaloas and I need to fix it before it goes any further."

When Judge Johnson didn't reply, Grip pulled the phone away from his ear and looked at it strangely. Something was wrong, he could feel it. "G.J., are you sure you're okay?"

"I'm fine," Judge Johnson claimed. "But listen, I'm sort of in the middle of something. Let me call you back in a few."

"Alright, my brother, you take it easy."

Click.

Without wasting another second, Grip returned to the dining room and looked at Aziz. "You and Brother Shabazz," he pointed at the two of them, "go check on G.J., and see if he's all right. Matter of fact," he pointed at Ahmed and Mustafa, "the two of you ride along with 'em. Something's not right and I need y'all to see what it is."

Obediently, the four gunmen got up from the table and headed for the door. As they left the dining room, Muhammad stepped to Grip with a look of concern. "What's the matter with G.J.? Is it the Sinaloas?"

Grip took a deep breath and sighed. "I'm not exactly sure, but something's wrong. I can feel it."

"And you're saying this because..."

"I know G.J., and when I told him the news about Sontino, he was distant, almost to the point it seemed as though he didn't even care. That's not like him at all."

"So, how do you suggest we move?" Muhammad asked as he stuffed his hands down in his pockets.

"We're gonna play it by ear," Grip said as he dug in his sweat pants pocket and pulled out a cigar. After removing the stogie from its case, he gestured for Muhammad to give him a light. The skinny man lit the tip of the Cohiba, and Grip took a long pull. "Where the hell is Gangsta?"

"I don't know." Muhammad shrugged his shoulders. "I asked the men and nobody's seen or heard from him in the last hour."

"Goddamnit," Grip sighed, assuming the Sinaloas were already declaring war. He lifted up his cell phone and scrolled through his rolodex. Stopping on Joaquin's number, he pressed the *call* button and placed the phone against his right ear.

Chapter Nineteen
Judge Johnson's Upper Darby Estate

"Pussy, what he say?" Gangsta snarled as he snatched the phone from G.J.'s trembling right hand. The chubby black man was sitting on the concrete floor of his basement. His left hand was cuffed to the furnace on the back wall, and his wife, Alicia, was sprawled out on the floor beside him.

"Oh, so now ya punk ass ain't got nothin' to say," Gangsta antagonized him. "You right." He stuffed the iPhone in his back pocket and then reached down to scoop up the wooden baseball bat that was lying on the floor beside Alicia's bashed in head. Clutching the baseball bat with both hands, he raised it over his head, and then looked down at G.J. with a face full of hate. "Y'all mutha'fuckas killed my peoples and now y'all gon' join 'em."

Crack.

The tip of the bat crashed into the left side of Alicia's head and her warm blood splattered in G.J.'s face.

"Come on, Terrance, she's not even breathing," the judge cried out, regretting the day he didn't kill that crying ass baby when he and Muhammad killed Angela and Russell. "There's no reason to keep hitting her. Can't you see that she's fucking dead?"

"Shut ya faggot ass up," Gangsta commanded. The blood-covered bat was cocked above his head and he was ready to take another swing. "Y'all mutha'fuckas didn't have any compassion when y'all killed my folks, so why the fuck should I have compassion now?"

Crack.

Judge Johnson cried like a newborn baby. The sight of his wife's bloodied corpse was like a dagger to the heart and the pain was immense. "She's already gone, Terrance. For the love of God, just leave her alone."

Stevie Wonder, Ray Charles, and a thousand other blind mutha'fuckas could see that Alicia was no longer among the living, but Gangsta didn't give a fuck. The sound of the wooden baseball bat slamming against her lifeless body was like music to his ears. And besides, he took pleasure in watching G.J. cringe with every devastating blow.

"I'll tell you what," Gangsta said as he lowered the bat and reached down to wipe the blood out of G.J.'s eyes. "If you sign an arrest warrant and extradition papers for Joaquin Alverez, I'll spare you the image of me choppin' this bitch up and tossin' her stankin' ass in the furnace a limb at a time."

G.J. looked at him like he was crazy. "Why would I help you?" he shouted. "You're going to kill me anyway, so fuck you." He conjured up a thick wad of snot and hocked a loogie in Gangsta's face.

Tfft.

The yellowish saliva landed on Gangsta's nose and dripped down to his top lip. Looking at Judge Johnson, he stuck out his tongue and slurped up every drop. "Wrong fuckin' answer." He raised the baseball bat above his head and swung down with a brute force.

Crack.

Crack.

Crack.

"Goddamnit, Terrance, stop."

"Stop what?" Gangsta shouted. His chest was heaving up and down and his face was dotted with Alicia's crimson-red blood. He pointed the baseball bat at the front of her swollen face and shouted, "Nigga, you see this bitch? You see her?"

Judge Johnson took a peek and then quickly looked away. The left side of Alicia's face was completely crushed. Her right eyeball was dangling from the socket, partially attached to a pink piece of flesh that resembled a stretched out Laffy Taffy, and her contorted mouth was wide open.

"Now, stop fuckin' around and put them documents together," Gangsta demanded.

"No," the judge shouted. "I'm not doing a goddamned thing. Fuck you."

Gangsta scowled at him and tossed the bat across the basement floor. "A'ight, so I see I'ma have to turn up the heat in this mutha'fucka." He pulled down the lever on the right side of the furnace and the small iron door opened up wide. An intensifying heat spread throughout the basement, and the burning embers inside of the furnace illuminated his face with a bright red glow.

"Pussy, you gon' put them documents together." He whipped out his P89 and aimed the barrel at G.J.'s groin. "One way or the other."

***

Cartagena, Columbia

Standing on the balcony outside of his master bed room, Juan Nunez was completely at peace. A silk bathrobe from The House of Versace was wrapped around his skinny frame, and his neatly pedicured toes were spilling out the front of his Hermes slippers. A six-inch corn-pipe was nestled in the right side of his mouth and the sweet fragrance of the finest marijuana hung in the air, elegantly blending with the cool breeze that rolled in off of the Atlantic Ocean. His large estate was settled on the northern coast of Columbia, and for as far as he could see, there was nothing but miles upon miles of pitch-black water. The bright, full moon illuminated the calm waves below. Off in the distance, he spotted the silhouette of a large dolphin leaping in the air and submerging back in the water with a silky-smooth splash.

He and his younger brother, Poncho, had come a long way from growing up on a coffee plantation in the mountains of Medellin. And now, after thirty plus years of trafficking cocaine, he was hours away from solely inheriting Pablo Escobar's seat as a chairman of The Conglomerate. The position was once divided between him and Poncho, but this was no longer the case. A half an hour ago, he received a phone call from Chatchi Alverez, and the Mexican kingpin informed him that he had information linking Poncho to the kidnapping and murder of his nephew, Roberto. Not only did Chatchi threaten to take him and Poncho to war, he promised that if Juan didn't do something to rectify the situation, the cartel would shut down the pipelines they used to smuggle their cocaine into the states. Certainly, both scenarios were unacceptable.

As he stood there smoking his pipe and watching the tide roll in, the glass door that separated the balcony from his master bedroom opened up wide and a beautiful Columbian woman dressed in a skin-tight nightgown appeared in the threshold. She had a honey-brown complexion and the face of a young Pam Grier. Her large breasts were firm and round, and the cool air that rolled off the shore made her gum-drop nipples pop like turkey-testers. The thickness of her thighs and hips were reminiscent of Mother Africa, and the curly black hair that flowed down the length of her back carried the aroma of coconuts.

Juan knew the young woman was standing behind him, but his brown eyes never left the ocean. Slowly, she approached him and kissed the left side of his neck.

"Papi," she addressed him in a husky voice, "ju have a phone call." She reached her arms around his waist and handed him the iPhone.

He passed the corn-pipe to his beautiful companion, and then spoke into the cell phone. "Speak."

"Juan, we have major trouble," Poncho blurted out.

"Is dat so," Juan replied nonchalantly. "Trouble of what type?"

"It's de Mexicanos," Poncho vehemently stated. "I think dey know what we done to Roberto."

"Ju make such a claim, why?"

"Not only Chatchi, but Jorge too has been callin' me back-to-back for de last half an hour. I'm tellin' you, dey know what we done. And above all else, I think dat somethin' is wrong wit' Marisol. I talk her a few minutes ago, and den all of a sudden de phone went dead. I tried to call her back, but she no answer."

Juan turned his head to look at the woman and gestured for her to give him some privacy. When the balcony door closed behind her, he continued talking. "Did ju send somebody to check on her?"

"Si," Poncho quickly confirmed. "I sent Estaban and tol' him to bring Marisol and Emilia back to de hotel."

"Where's Chee-Chee?" Juan asked. "Is he close by?"

"He's right here, sittin' at de table by de window. We're in de same hotel room at de Red Roof Inn. Why?"

"Put him on de phone."

The phone went silent and a few seconds later, Chee-Chee's voice came across the airwaves. "Hola, papa."

"It's time, Chee-Chee. Kill him."

"Si, papa."

The line went silent and Juan listened closely. He never imagined the day would come that he had to kill his own brother, but Poncho left him no choice. When he spoke to Juan a couple of weeks ago telling him that he wanted to kill Roberto, Juan told him not to do it, but Poncho was persistent. Eventually, Juan deferred to his brother's desires, but only under one condition, they had to use someone else to make the hit, and that's when they made their proposal to Sonny. The plan was to have Sonny kill Roberto, and then they would kill him to cover their tracks. Unfortunately, Poncho failed to make the hit at Easy's funeral, and now the Sinaloas were seconds away from hopping on that ass.

Juan took a deep breath and wiped away the tears that dripped from his brown eyes. The iPhone was still pressed against his ear and he could hear the popping of Chee-Chee's pistol as the bullets snatched the life out of his only brother. This was hands down the toughest decision that he ever had to make, but Poncho made his bed and now he had to lay in it.

"Jeffe," Chee-Chee spoke into the phone with the calmness of a trained killer. "It is done."

"Good. Now, leave de hotel and drive to de airport. My private jet is waiting for ju."

"Si, papa."

Click.

After disconnecting the call, Juan dialed Chatchi's phone number, and then returned the phone to his ear.

Ring. Ring. Ring.

"Mijo, tell me what I want to hear," Chatchi demanded when he accepted the incoming call.

"We are even," Juan spoke in a low voice. "De situation has been rectified."

"That's only for now, mijo, only for now. My brother, Joaquin, will make the final determination. So, until then, if I was you, mijo, I'd play it real cool. Comprende?"

"Comprende."

"And don't forget," Chatchi reminded him. "We meet tomorrow night at The Waldorf in New York City."

Click.

***

Back in North Philly

When Sonny and The Reaper pulled up in front of Club Infamous, they noticed that Nipsy was already there. He was standing on the corner of Broad and Erie, dressed in all black, and shuffling from side to side, attempting to keep warm. His frost-covered, fur-lined hood was pulled down low, blocking most of his face, but Sonny could still see it was him.

"Yo, who the fuck is main man?" The Reaper asked. He was pointing at Nipsy and looking at Sonny with a raised brow. "And why the fuck is he just standin' there?"

"That's my young bul," Sonny said as he turned off the car and removed the key from the ignition. The Reaper shot him a funny look, and when he reached for the door handle, The Reaper leaned over the center console and pushed him back against the driver's seat.

"Double R, what the fuck is you doin'?" Sonny snapped, looking at The Reaper's right hand pressed against his chest. "Is you fuckin' crazy?"

"Somethin' like that," The Reaper replied as he slowly pulled away his hand. "But more than anything, I'm the nigga that Mook would have wanted to watch ya back and keep you safe."

"Watch my back?" Sonny looked at him like he was stupid. "Keep me safe? Yo, I don't know if Mook ever told you or not, but I'm a fuckin' monster."

"Oh, yeah," The Reaper challenged. "So, why the fuck you call on me?"

208

"Because two monsters is better than one."

"Absolutely," The Reaper agreed. He picked up his shotgun and casually wrapped his left hand around the pistol-grip. Looking at Nipsy, he said, "So, that's ya young bul, huh?"

"Ain't that what the fuck I just said?" Sonny retorted.

"Yeah, and I'm pretty sure that was the same thing you used to say about the little niggas who crossed you. So, who's to say this mutha'fuckas any different? For all we know, he could have a gang of shooters in the tuck just waitin' to hop out and start blastin' at any given second." The Reaper was from the old school, and with twenty-three bodies under his belt, he was a firm believer that death was always around the corner.

"This is a different situation," Sonny assured him. "Just follow my lead." As he climbed out of the Porsche, Mook's voice resonated in the back of his mind. *Everybody has an agenda, so you really gotta watch these mutha'fuckas.*

The freezing cold weather smacked him in the face, but he didn't care, he was on a mission. Looking up and down Broad Street, it appeared to be a typical Friday night. The Checkers restaurant on Germantown Avenue was serving up Champ burgers and apple nuggets. Broad Street Eddie's was serving up watered down drinks. And the BBQ truck that occupied the corner of Germantown and Erie had the three-way intersection smelling like a Kansas City rib shack.

After gesturing for The Reaper to get out of the car, he flagged down Nipsy and pointed at the black Suburban that was parked in the middle of the block.

***

"Yo, Daph, I'm lookin' at this stupid mutha'fucka right now," Egypt spoke into his iPhone. He and Zaire were sitting in the Checkers' parking lot, discreetly tucked behind the tinted windows on the Ford Bronco that they borrowed from Chino about an hour earlier. Egypt received a phone call from Nipsy saying that he needed some work, but it didn't take long for Egypt to realize that the call was a set-up. After talking to Nipsy, he heard the phone click and a second later he heard Sonny's voice come across the air waves. Apparently, Sonny was secretly listening on the three-way. But when Nipsy attempted to end the call, he somehow left Egypt on the line.

"Daph, did you hear what I said?"

"Yeah, I heard you," she replied in a distant voice. She was looking through the blinds on her living room window, staring at the black Chevy Impala that was parked across the street from her house. "Don't you know that mutherfucker had somebody following me?"

"He had somebody following you?" Egypt asked. "Who?"

"I'm not exactly sure, but he's an older white man. I noticed him a little after I left your house. At first, I didn't think anything of it, but when I turned off of Cheltenham Avenue and hopped on Route 309, the motherfucker was still behind me. He followed me all the way back to the house."

"Damn," Egypt said as he kept his eyes on Sonny. He was standing in front of his Porsche and talking to a medium-built, dark skinned man that he'd never seen before. "I'm sayin', though, how can you be so sure it wasn't the feds?"

"Trust me, it's definitely not the feds," Daphney spoke with conviction.

"And what makes you say that?"

"Well, first of all, if the dude was a fed, he would have hopped out back at the stash house and caught us red-handed. And secondly, this is the only way Sontino could have known what we were up to. I'm telling you, this mutherfucker has to be working for him."

She moved away from the window and plopped down on the sofa. "Listen, whatever you do, you have to kill him before he leaves the club. Because if you don't, I'm pretty sure you can figure out what's gonna happen next."

"Don't worry about it, Daph. I got him."

Daphney barked at him. "Nigga, don't tell me you got him, go get him."

Click.

Zaire was sitting in the passenger's seat shaking his head. He was looking at Sonny and nervously biting down on his bottom lip.

"Zai, you ready?" Egypt asked as he reached into the back seat and scooped up his Mack 90. He was so focused on killing Sonny and taking over the Block Boys that he didn't even realize Zaire was sitting beside him crying his eyes out.

"Yeah, I'm ready," Zaire sniffled, and then reached for the .357 that was nestled in his shoulder holster. "I just wish that I wasn't."

"Whatchu mean by that?" Egypt asked as he settled back in his seat. He looked over and the first thing he noticed was the tears dripping down his brother's face. He then noticed the Sig Sauer that was clutched in his hand. The large barrel was aimed at his torso and Zaire was finger-fucking the trigger. "Yo, Zai, what the fuck is you doin'?" His Mack 90 was gripped in both hands, but not once did he attempt to aim the barrel at his twin. "Dawg, I know you ain't sidin' wit' this nigga over me? I'm ya fuckin' brother."

Zaire took a deep breath and used is free hand to wipe away his tears. After Egypt told him about the conversation that he had with Nipsy, and he realized they no longer held the element of surprise, he bitched up and called Sonny the second Egypt left the room. He told Sonny everything he knew, and to prove his loyalty, he offered to kill his own brother.

"You know, it's funny," Zaire said in a cracked voice. "Here we are, sittin' in this old ass truck talking 'bout Sonny. It's almost like the first time we met him, you remember that? Mommy was locked up for shoplifting and granny had just passed away. We was eleven years old, homeless and hungry, afraid to go back to granny's house because the welfare people was try'na put us in a foster home. You remember that? You remember we was livin' on the streets, rippin' and runnin' all day, and when the sun went down we had to break into cars just to have somewhere to sleep?"

'Yeah, I remember," Egypt quickly replied. "But you trippin' right now, Zai. How the fuck you gon' take sides wit' Sonny and ride against me?"

"Because we owe him. If it wasn't for the night that we broke into his mom's car and he found us the next morning, where the fuck would we be?" Zaire shouted. "Him and Miss Annie took us in. They fed us and gave us somewhere to sleep. This nigga damn near raised us, and now you want me to help you kill him? Nigga, fuck that."

Zaire gently applied pressure to the trigger, but before he had the chance to squeeze, he saw The Reaper sliding up on the driver's side door. A 12-gauge shotty was clutched in his hands and the sawed-off barrel was aimed at the back of Egypt's head.

"What the..."

Boom.

The driver's side window exploded with force, and before they knew it, the smell of fresh blood and gunpowder permeated the SUV. Sonny snatched open the passenger's side door and the twin brother's fell to the icy cold ground. Sonny's fur-lined hood was pulled down over his face, and he was looking around the parking lot checking to see if anyone heard the loud blast of the shotgun. Surprisingly, nobody seemed to be paying attention. But in the corner of his left eye he noticed the two teenaged girls who were working inside of the Checkers. Their faces were pressed against the glass front window and their hungry eyes were fixed on the Bronco.

"Double R," he looked at his hit man, "make them nosey ass bitches mind they fuckin' business."

The Reaper spun around and aimed the shotty at the large window, and almost immediately the two girls ran towards the back of the restaurant screaming bloody murder.

Satisfied that the two witnesses wouldn't be able to identify the black Suburban that was parked down the block, Sonny raised his hand in the air, signaling for Nipsy to bring the SUV up to the parking lot. He then looked down and scowled at the blood covered twins. "Fuck is you lookin' all surprised for?"

"N-N-Naw," the twin stuttered. He was trapped between his dead brother and the concrete, and his eardrums were ringing from the loud blast of the shotgun. "I was about... I was about to smoke Egypt, but I never... I never got the chance." He shook away the lingering dizziness and squinted his eyes to adjust his sight. "The shotty," he continued, "it hit him up 'fore I had the chance to do it myself. I was rockin' witchu, bro, you gotta believe me. I was gonna smoke him, I swear."

Sonny looked at him and gritted his teeth. All of the love and devotion that he once had for the twin brothers he found sleeping in the back seat of his mother's car was long gone, and the only thing that could rectify their disloyalty was death.

The Suburban pulled up beside him and he snatched open the back passenger's side door. Looking at Nipsy, he said, "Help me put these mutha'fuckas in the back seat. And hurry the fuck up. We gotta get in the wind 'fore the boys come."

"A'ight," Nipsy replied as he hopped out of the truck and quickly got to work. After pulling Egypt's mutilated corpse off of Zaire, he grabbed him under the arms and lifted his dead weight into the truck. "And Double R," Sonny looked at The Reaper, "check inside of the Bronco and find this nigga's cell phone. I need to see if he saved any text messages between him and that bitch, so that way I can tell how long these mutha'fuckas been plottin' on me."

As The Reaper ransacked the SUV, Sonny pulled out a pair of zip-ties and knelt down beside Zaire.

"Brozay, you gotta believe me," Zaire pleaded as Sonny tightened the zip-ties around his wrist. He wanted to put up a fight and struggle to get free, but he didn't want to make things worse. His best option was to keep cool and talk his way out of it. "I'm tellin' you, Sonny, I ain't have nothin' to do wit' this shit, bro."

"Pussy, stop lyin'," Sonny snapped at him as he snatched him off of the ground and tossed him in the back of the Suburban.

"I swear on my flag," Zaire shouted. He was lying on the floor of the Suburban face first, right beside his dead brother. "Sonny, you gotta believe me, I didn't cross you."

"Nigga, I saw the fuckin' video," Sonny shouted back. "When you pulled up and went inside of the house, Daphney was already there. So, if you wasn't try'na cross me, why the fuck did it take so long for you to call me?"

"I didn't know it was Daphney," Zaire lied. "The only thing I knew was that Egypt had a bitch in his room, and I could hear 'em fuckin'. I never went inside of the room, so how the fuck was I 'posed to know it was Daph?"

Sonny scowled at him, and then forcefully slammed the back door. Looking at The Reaper, he said, "Double R, did you find it?"

"Yeah," The Reaper nodded his head and held up the iPhone. "I got it right here." He tossed him the cell phone, then hopped back in the Bronco and started the engine. "Yo, we gotta get up outta here," he said while reaching over to close the passenger's side door. "I can hear the sirens. They're only a couple of blocks away."

"I know," Sonny said. "I can hear them mutha'fuckas, too." He climbed in the passenger side of the Suburban and Nipsy pulled out of the parking lot with the old Bronco close behind.

"So, where we takin' these niggas?" Nipsy asked.

"We takin' they asses to The Swamp," Sonny spoke in a cold voice. "I already talked to The Butcher and told him to have everything ready."

"The Swamp," Zaire shouted like a bitch, knowing all too well what happened to the mutha'fuckas who were taken to the rural pig farm in Bucks County. "Come on, bro, please. I'm tellin' you the truth and I can prove it."

"You can prove it?" Sonny looked at him skeptically. "Prove it, how?"

"All you gotta do is call Daphney from Egypt's cell phone and let me talk to her. Me and Egypt sound just alike, so she won't know the difference."

"And what the fuck is that gonna prove?"

"Hold up, bro, you ain't let me finish. Whatever she had goin' on wit' Egypt was just between them, so when I mention me, I can guarantee that she ain't gon' have nothin' to say. And that's because I never had nothin' to do wit' this shit."

Sonny thought about it for a second, then shrugged his shoulders. "A'ight, but I'ma tell you right now, if this stankin' ass bitch says anything about you knowin' what was goin' on, I'ma chop ya ass up myself."

Chapter Twenty
Back at Judge Johnson's Estate

"Who the hell is that?" Ahmed asked as he pulled into the driveway and parked his Escalade behind G.J.'s Lexus.

"Who the hell is who?" Mustafa asked. He was sitting in the passenger's seat gently caressing his M-16.

"The mutha'fucka right there," Ahmed overstated. He was pointing towards the west wing of the house where a dark shadowy figure was crouched down and creeping in the opposite direction. "Come on, let's get his ass." He threw the transmission in *park*, snatched up his M-16, and hopped out of the truck.

Mustafa was right behind him. His M-16 was cradled in both hands, and by the time Aziz and Shabazz were out of the truck, he and Ahmed were halfway across the driveway.

Shabazz looked at Aziz and nodded his head. Aziz returned the gesture, and simultaneously they reached behind their backs and pulled out their .41 calibers.

Gangsta was headed back to his truck when the dark colored SUV pulled into the driveway. The federal warrant and extradition papers for Joaquin were safely tucked away in his back pocket, and his P89 was tightly gripped in his right hand. The gunshot wound to his arm was itching and burning, but yet and still he was ready for action.

"F.B.I.," Ahmed shouted. He was aiming his assault rifle at the man dressed in all black, and quickly rushing towards him. "Get on the fuckin' ground."

Gangsta took off running, zig-zagging his way to the back yard. His hoody was pulled down low and he was hoping that the four men didn't see his face.

"Goddamnit!" Ahmed complained. He was running as fast as he could, and aiming his M-16, looking for the best shot possible.

Gangsta was in the zone. He tripped over a snow-covered lawn chair, fell on his ass, hopped back up, and slipped inside of the house through the back door. He was sweating profusely and desperately trying to catch his breath. As he leaned against the kitchen counter, his iPhone vibrated in his hoody pocket, and he quickly grabbed it. Looking at the screen, he saw that the caller was Big Angolo.

"About time," he said to himself as he took a seat at the kitchen table. "Sheesh!"

When the four gunmen reached the back corner of the house, they stopped running and crouched down against the back wall. There was simple no telling what lay around the corner of the house and they didn't want to walk into an ambush.

"Gimmie your coat," Ahmed demanded. He was looking at Mustafa and gesturing for him to hurry up.

As Mustafa peeled out of his coat, Ahmed looked at Aziz and Shabazz. "I'm gonna use the coat as a decoy. Instead of us moving too fast and stumbling into something crazy, I'm gonna toss the coat into the back yard. If the son-of-a-bitch starts shooting, I want the two of you to run around to the other side of the house. So, that way we can block him in from both sides."

"All right," Shabazz said. "But, what if he doesn't take the bait?"

"If he doesn't," Ahmed shrugged his shoulders, "fuck it, we'll just storm the back yard, two at a time, and take his ass down."

The two men nodded their heads, and then looked at Mustafa, who was handing over his winter coat. "So, let's go over this one more time," Shabazz said. "If the mutha'fucka doesn't shoot at the coat, we're gonna storm the back yard?"

"Precisely," Ahmed told him. "Me and Mustafa are gonna take the lead, so just fall back and cover us from behind." He looked at Mustafa. "You ready to do this?"

"Absolutely."

"Alright," Ahmed nodded his head. "In three... two... one." He tossed the coat into the back yard, expecting to hear gunfire, but the only thing he heard was silence. "I guess we'll have to rock out with Plan B." He tightened his grasp on the assault rifle and looked at Mustafa. "I'm gonna go low, so cover me from up top." He did a dive role around the corner and popped up on his right knee, crouched down and ready to fire. Mustafa was right behind him, but they quickly realized the back yard was empty.

"Look," Mustafa whispered. He was pointing at the foot prints in the snow. "He went inside of the house."

Ahmed looked down at the fresh foot prints, and then looked up at the back door. It was slightly ajar and the welcome mat on the back patio was crooked and disheveled. "Come on, we can't let him get away."

As they approached the back door and stepped inside of the house, the first thing they noticed was Gangsta. He was dressed in all black and sitting at the kitchen table talking on his iPhone.

"Gangsta?" Ahmed asked, wondering what the hell was going on. "That was you? Why did you take off running and not say anything? We could have killed you." He lowered is M-16, and Mustafa did the same.

Gangsta looked at the two agents and held up his index finger, signaling for them to wait a second. "Everything's in order," he spoke into his cell phone. "I did my part. The rest is up to you."

"What the fuck is going on?" Mustafa asked, looking at Gangsta with a raised brow. "Where's G.J.?"

"He's waitin' for y'all," Gangsta replied as he disconnected the call and stuffed the iPhone back in his hoody pocket.

"He's waiting for us?" Ahmed asked, giving Gangsta a skeptical look. "He's waiting for us, where?"

"In the depths of hell," Gangsta said with a devilish grin.

Shabazz and Aziz, who were standing behind the two agents, took a step closer and pressed the barrels of their guns to the back of their domes. They knew all along that the man dressed in all black was Gangsta. Prior to pulling up to the house, they were sitting in the back of the Escalade secretly communicating with him through text messages. They told him how Grip and Muhammad were planning to kill Sonny, and gave him the run down on the potential beef with the Sinaloas. In turn, Gangsta told them about the latest information pertaining to the murders of his parents. He also made it clear that he needed Ahmed and Mustafa to come inside of the house. So, that way, they wouldn't have to worry about any potential witnesses.

Ahmed was completely stunned, and the feeling of cold steel pressed against the back of his wig made his eyes pop like golf balls. "You're not gonna get away with this."

"I already did," Gangsta confirmed as he took a couple of steps backwards. "Aziz and Shabazz," he looked at his two hitters. "Do 'em."

Boc.

Boc.

Two clouds of a bloody red mist erupted from their front of their foreheads and the two agents crumbled to the floor.

"So, what's the next move?" Aziz asked.

"Whatchu think?" Gangsta said as he stepped over the two agents and headed out the back door. "We gotta find Sonny and let him know what's goin' on."

***

Jal Laredo Prison Camp, Laredo Mexico

The Catholic chapel on the ground floor of the Level-2 prison was desolate and quiet. The aroma of burning incense and scented candles permeated the sanctuary, giving the room an instant feeling of comfort, and for the first time in his adult life, Joaquin Alverez was ready to make amends for his painful and destructive past. Standing in the threshold of the double oak wood doors, he was draped in a gray jump-suit and wearing a pair of shower shoes. His normally clean shaved face had a five o'clock shadow and his long, Indian hair was slicked back to the nape of his neck.

When he stepped inside of the chapel, the first thing that grabbed his attention was the large crucifix that hung on the wall directly behind the pulpit. With bright, wide eyes he turned his head from left to right, taking in the pastel paintings of the most renowned Catholic Saints, and then settled his gaze on the confessional booth in the back left corner. The large structure was eight feet in length, six feet in width, and was pieced together from the stained wood of an English sycamore. A shiny, brass column divided the booth into two separate chambers, and each chamber was tucked behind a velvet curtain.

The Sinaloa boss walked down the aisle and slowly approached the confessional. His violent ways and corrupt lifestyle couldn't have been further from the Catholic religion, but if the Biblical teachings he learned as a child had the slightest semblance of the truth, he knew that he needed to make atonement for his sins. Not for the sake of himself, but for the sake of his son, Roberto.

After stepping inside of the confessional, he closed the curtain and took a seat on the wooden bench. The small chamber was no bigger than a telephone booth. A 10 X 12-inch window was built into the wall on his left-hand side, and a black screen was fixed into the frame. On the other side of the screen, the institutional chaplain, Father Diaz, was gently caressing his rosary beads and quietly reciting a prayer for world peace. A burning candle was positioned on the wooden shelf beside him, and the flickering wick illuminated the booth with a dismal glow. After saying "Amen" and kissing the front his rosary, he marked his body with the symbol of the Holy Cross, and turned his face towards the window. "Yes, my son."

"Forgive me, Father, for I have sinned," Joaquin requested in a low voice. The palms of his hands were clammy and moist, and he was too embarrassed to the look the priest in his face. "I have committed great atrocities for the better part of my life, and I'm afraid that my son is going to be punished for my evil ways. He was recently murdered and I was hoping that you could pray for his soul."

Father Diaz took a deep breath and exhaled slowly, recognizing the face of the man who was sitting in the next booth. Not only was he the most dangerous man in all of Mexico, he was the hand that pulled the strings on "Diablo," and the middle finger that was aimed at the sky telling God to "Fuck off."

"Father," Joaquin continued, "is there any atonement for the soul of my son?"

Carefully choosing his words, Father Diaz looked straight ahead and told the little man what he wanted to hear. "The Bible teaches us that a son shall inherit the sins of his father, but nonetheless, our God is a God who loves. He's a God of understanding, a God who forgives."

"So, my son will be forgiven?"

"Ah, yes, he'll definitely be forgiven. Just ah, say three Hail Mary's, and give a donation to the church in whatever way you see fit." He blew out the prayer candle and quickly departed from the booth. "God bless you, my son."

When Joaquin returned to his cell, he lay on top of his bed and fished out the cell phone that was buried inside of his pillow. After pressing the POWER button, he punched in his security code, and noticed that he'd missed two calls. One of the missed calls came from Chatchi, and the other one came from Grip. Completely bypassing the latter, he dialed the numbers to Chatchi's cell phone and placed the phone against his ear.

Ring. Ring. Ring.

"Hola," Chatchi answered in a loud voice. He was still at the gentleman's club, coked up, and anxiously pacing back and forth throughout his office.

"Mijo, now is not the time for you to be treating your nose," Joaquin scolded him. "You need to be focused on the issue at hand."

"I am," Chatchi propounded. "And just so you know, I got to the bottom of what happened to Roberto."

"It was the Italians, wasn't it?"

"Unfortunately," Chatchi replied, "that's not the case. The Gervinos had no involvement whatsoever, but I know who does."

"Who?" Joaquin demanded. "Tell it to me now." He was so mad that his English was beginning to break down.

"It was The Moreno Crime Family," Chatchi revealed. "They were actin' on the orders of Poncho Nunez."

"Gervin?" Joaquin questioned. "Acting on the orders of Poncho Nunez? That doesn't make any sense. Gervin is superior to Poncho, so why would he take orders from him?"

"It wasn't Gervin," Chatchi explained. "It was his grandson, Sontino. Poncho paid him to take out Roberto, and the guys that

Sontino used to make the hit, we know who they are, we have them on video."

"And how do you know all of this?"

"Aside from the information that we got from Carmine, I spoke to Juan Nunez and he explained everything in detail."

Joaquin paused for a moment, giving his brain the opportunity to digest the new information. "Alright, now for what reason did Poncho want Roberto dead?"

"His daughter," Chatchi told him. "Her name is Olivia and she was Roberto's girlfriend. Poncho didn't approve of their relationship, and him and Roberto had a heated argument. After that, Poncho reached out to Gervin's grandson, and he paid him to make the hit."

"Where is Poncho now?"

"Poncho's a done deal. Juan had him clipped as a sign of good faith. He's claiming that he had nothing to do with the situation, and that he wanted to show his loyalty."

"And what about this kid, Sontino?" Joaquin asked him. "Is he dead yet?"

"Not yet, but we're in the process of trackin' him down."

"Does Gervin know about this? Does he know that his grandson murdered my Roberto?"

"I'm not exactly sure, but I'll know sooner rather than later. I called a mandatory meeting with The Conglomerate. It's tomorrow at midnight. And trust me, mijo, by the end of that meeting we'll know everything that we need to know. Any and all debts will be paid in full."

Joaquin looked at his phone and saw that he had an incoming call. It was Big Angolo calling him from ADX Florence. "Alright, homes, now back to the Gervinos. Are you absolutely sure that Little Angolo and Carmine had nothing to do with my son?"

"A hundred percent, mijo, a hundred percent."

"But they paid the price anyway?"

"I mean, it was a mistake, a casualty of war," Chatchi explained, attempting to make light of the situation. "And at the end of the day, it doesn't really matter. Gervin and Sontino are both connected to the Gervino Family."

"Technically your right, but at the same time we both know that the Morenos and Gervinos operate as two separate entities. This could turn out to be a major problem."

"A problem?" Chatchi laughed it off. "We have Diablo for such problems."

Joaquin took a deep breath and flexed his jaw muscles. Chatchi didn't understand the severity of the situation, but he did. "Listen, mijo, I have an incoming call. I'll be calling you back within the next couple of hours, so stay by the phone. And mijo, put away the yahyo and get some rest. Midnight is right around the corner and you need to be clicking on all cylinders. We can't afford to make a bad situation worse."

After disconnecting the call, he accepted the incoming call from Big Angolo. "Mr. Gervino," he addressed the mafia don with the utmost respect, "I'm glad that you called. We need to talk."

***

Back at Poncho's New Jersey Estate

When Estaban pulled up in front of his parent's mansion, an eerie feeling shot throughout his body. He'd been calling Marisol back-to-back for the last fifteen minutes, but every time he called, the phone went to voicemail. "What de fuck is goin' on?" he asked himself while climbing out of his Benz.

The large house was completely quiet, and from the looks of things, it appeared as though nobody was home. As he approached the front door, he immediately recognized that something was wrong. The front door was slightly cracked open and all of the lights were turned off. Confused, he looked around the front yard and calmly removed the .380 handgun that was tucked down in his waist band. Cocking a live round up into the chamber, he pushed the door open with the tip of his boot and cautiously slipped inside of the house.

"Mama," he called out, slowly moving forward with the .380 leading the way. "Emilia."

He listened closely and the only thing he heard was the tick-tocking of the grandfather clock that was positioned on the wall to his left.

Tick. Tock.

Tick. Tock.

Tick. Tock.

Stepping into the main hallway, he noticed that the only light in the house came from the kitchen. As he began walking in that direction, an unfamiliar fragrance smacked him dead in the face. It was strong and rancid, similar to the smell of raw chitterlings but a little more gamey. "Yuck." He used his free hand to cover his nose and mouth and shook his head disdainfully. "What de fuck is Emilia cookin'?"

When he reached the end of the hallway and stepped into the kitchen, the first thing he spotted was the large pot that was sitting on top of the stove. Hot steam was seeping through the cracked lid and the odor was so strong that he couldn't help but to cough and gag. "Mama," he continued to call out. "Emilia."

Aiming the .380 from left to right, he approached the stove and turned down the dial. The bubbling pot came to a halt and the blistering steam was reduced to a simmer. "What de fuck is goin' on around here?" He looked around the kitchen and everything seemed to be in place, but there were no signs of Marisol and Emilia. "Where de fuck did dey go? Dey shoulda been here waitin' for me."

After looking around, he lifted up the pot lid and damn near had a heart attack. Emilia's swollen, decapitated head was staring at him from inside of the pot. The skin on her face was stretched out and leathery, and directly underneath, he caught a glimpse of the well-done flesh that was dangling from her cheek bones. "Yo, what de fuck is dis?" He dropped the pot lid and backed away from the stove. "Is dis a fuckin' joke?"

"Esta... Estaban," he heard a voice calling his name.

"Who de fuck is dat?" He was waving the .380 from side to side, ready to blow a mutha'fucka's head off.

"In—in here," Marisol continued to whisper. "In—in de pantry."

"Mama?" Estaban questioned the voice. When he approached the pantry, he dropped his pistol and covered his mouth with both hands. He was completely stunned and didn't know what to do. His mother's naked body was connected to Emilia's headless corpse, and the two bodies were stitched together in the 69 position. Marisol was lying on top and her swollen head was nestled in between Emilia's thighs.

"Mama," he cried out. "What happened? Who done ju like dis?" He knelt down beside her and scoured her body from head to toe. She was a bloody mess, and Estaban couldn't believe what he was seeing. The skin on her back was ripped away and he could vividly see the whites of her rib cage. He wanted to help her, but when he tried to move her body, she released a gut-wrenching scream.

"Mama," he continued to cry. "Who de fuck done dis? Tell me now."

Marisol turned her head to the left and her entire body began to tremble. "Esta... Estaban... run."

"Mama, I can't hear ju." He leaned forward and placed his ear beside her mouth. "Say it to me again, I couldn't hear ju."

"He... He's coming."

He looked at her skeptically, unable to hear what she was saying. "Mama, I gotta get ju some help," he cried like a baby. "Ju need help."

"Di... Diablo."

"Diablo?" He gave her a funny look. "Huh?"

"Be... Behind ju."

"Mama, I can't hear ju," he sobbed. "Say it to me again."

He waited for an answer, but it never came. She took her last breath and her body went limp. "Mama," he shouted and shrugged her shoulder with brute force. "Don't go, mama. Come back to me, please." He reached out to hold her, but stopped moving when a cold hand gently caressed the back of his neck. He stumbled forward and quickly spun around. Looking up, the first thing he noticed was the devil horns that protruded from Diablo's forehead. The small Mexican was covered in blood and a large Butcher's knife was clutched in his right hand. Estaban was frozen with fear. He wanted to strike out and avenge the murder of his mother, but he couldn't move.

"I am Diablo," the little Mexican spoke in a demented voice. *"Fear me."*

Askari

Chapter Twenty-One
Sonny's Old Trap House on Fairhill Street

Vrrrrm. Vrrrrrm. Vrrrrrm.

Sonny looked at his iPhone, and then returned his attention to Zaire, who was strapped down to the chair at the other end of the dining room table. The Reaper was standing behind Zaire and his sawed-off shotty was pressed to the back of his noggin. Nipsy was in the living room sitting on the couch, and Sonny's pit bull was watching him closely.

"Nipsy, come over here and take the duct tape off his mouth," Sonny demanded.

"A'ight, but first you gotta get ya dog," Nipsy told him. "This nigga lookin' like he 'bout to eat a mutha'fucka."

"Damu," Sonny said in a deep, dominant voice. "Get ya ass up-stairs."

The large pit bull looked at him and then looked back at Nipsy. His cropped ears were standing at attention and a deep growl was festering in the back of his throat. Urrrrr.

"Now," Sonny commanded.

The muscular dog trotted up the stairs and Nipsy got up from the couch. Obediently, he stood next to Zaire and snatched off the gray tape, causing the twin to grimace in pain.

"Damn," Zaire complained, looking at Nipsy like he wanted to punch his face off. "Fuck you do it all hard for?"

"Nigga, shut the fuck up and listen," Sonny barked at him. He leaned across the table and pointed his finger in Zaire's face. "You got one chance to prove that you ain't have nothin' to do wit' this shit." He grabbed Egypt's cell phone off of the table and put it on speaker. After dialing Daphney's number, he slid it across the table, and then sat back and folded his arms across his chest.

Ring. Ring. Ring.

"About fuckin' time," Daphney said when she answered the phone. "Is it done? Did you kill him?"

Her words hit Sonny straight to the heart. It was one thing to see her and Egypt on video, but to actually hear his own wife plotting his murder was a completely different thing. Enraged, he continued listening to the conversation.

"Egypt," Daphney's voice boomed from the phone. "Did you hear me?"

"Yeah," Zaire responded, pretending to be Egypt. "We got him, two to the chest and one to the head."

"We?" Daphney questioned. "Who the fuck is we?"

"Me and Zaire," he replied. "I know he wasn't a part of the plan, but I was thinkin' that if I brought him wit' me, shit would go a lot smoother."

"A'ight," she said. "But from here on out, I don't need you to do any thinking, that's my job. I do the thinking and all you gotta do is follow my lead. Oh yeah, and as far as your brother, I didn't make a deal with him. I made a deal with you. So, whenever we need to take care of business, you can just leave his ass out of it."

Zaire looked at Sonny and gave him a look that said, *I told you so.* He returned his attention back to the phone call. "So, whatchu want me to do wit' him? You want me to leave his ass at the club and just wait for somebody to find him?"

"Hell no," she quickly shot back. "That's my mutherfuckin' establishment. Why the fuck would I want a dead body poppin' up at my place of business?"

"A'ight, so then whatchu want me to do wit' him?"

"I'm sayin', like, don't y'all have a place to take the mutherfuckers that y'all want to turn up missing?"

"Yeah," Zaire confirmed. "We got a spot in Bucks County. It's a pig farm right off of Route 611."

"Good, well then take his ass there."

Click.

Zaire looked up at Sonny and nodded his head. "You see, bro, I told you. I told you I ain't have nothin' to do wit' this shit. It was all Egypt."

"You's a funny mutha'fucka," Sonny said as he got up from the table and walked over to Zaire. "You think I'm stupid, don't you?"

"Bro, what is you talking 'bout?" Zaire asked, looking at him with pleading eyes. "You heard it for ya'self, I wasn't involved."

"Nigga, you made me kill my fuckin' young bul," Sonny snarled at him. "He was innocent and he lost his life because of you."

"Yo, you're trippin', bro. Straight up."

"Not at all," Sonny confirmed. He reached down and lifted up Zaire's left pant leg, revealing the scar tissue from a gunshot wound. "Just like I thought, *Egypt*."

Egypt lowered his head and accepted his fate. He tried to pull a fast one but it didn't work. When The Reaper aimed the shotgun at the back of his head, he saw him out the corner of his eye and ducked down just in time. The bullet whizzed by his left ear and struck Zaire on the right side of his forehead, knocking the gravy out the back of his biscuit. When Sonny snatched open the passenger's side door and they fell out the Bronco, he pretended to be his twin brother, thinking he could prove his innocence and possibly live to see another day.

"Damn," he sighed. "How the fuck did you know it was me?"

Sonny gritted his teeth and looked at him like he wanted to break his fucking neck. "I caught a glimpse of that scar when I was puttin' ya stupid ass in the back of the truck," he spoke through clenched teeth. "And I knew that Zaire wasn't the one who got shot that day, it was you. That's how the fuck I knew who you was."

The Reaper and Nipsy were completely dumbfounded. They would have never figured out that Zaire was actually Egypt, The Reaper in particular. He could have sworn that he shot Egypt in the back of his melon.

Vrrrrrm. Vrrrrrm. Vrrrrrm.

Sonny looked at his vibrating cell phone, but ignored the incoming call. "Nipsy," he spoke in a calm voice. "Go in the kitchen and grab the sharpest knife you can find. I got a little bit of work to do."

***

The Philadelphia International Airport

"Come on, Sonny, answer ya fuckin' phone," Gangsta said as he handed his bags to the TSA agent. He'd been calling Sonny back-to-back for the last hour, trying to put him onto game, but he couldn't get through.

"Don't you think me and Aziz should stay back?" Shabazz asked him. "So, that way, we can tell him what's goin' on."

"Nah," Gangsta shook his head. "Big Angolo told me to bring y'all wit' me. Credentials or not, it wouldn't make sense for just one agent to be transporting a federal prisoner by himself, especially, from one country to another. So, I've gotta take y'all wit' me, it's the only way we can pull this off."

Aziz sighed, "But I'm saying, if we don't get in touch wit' Sonny, he's gonna walk right into an ambush. We can't let him go out like that."

"I know," Gangsta agreed. "But at this point, there's nothing else we can do. Big Angolo made it clear that he wants us in Mexico by the morning. We have to pick up Joaquin and have him in New York by midnight."

"New York?" Aziz gave him a questioning look. "I thought we had to put him on the first thing smokin' to Cuba?"

"Initially, that was the plan, but things got switched around at the last minute," Gangsta explained. "According to Big Angolo, we gotta have him at the Waldorf Astoria by midnight. It's the only way we can straighten out the differences between our families."

"All right," Shabazz nodded his head. "But at the very least, I think you should call him one last time."

Gangsta did as he suggested, and once again, the phone went straight to voicemail. It was against his better judgement to leave a message of such magnitude but he did it anyway. "Sonny, it's Gangsta. Whatever you do, you can't trust Grip. Him and Muhammad are plannin' to kill you. I've been try'na call you for the last half an hour, but you're not answering. Hopefully, you'll get this message before it's too late."

Frustrated, he disconnected the call and switched his phone over to plane mode. Looking at Shabazz and Aziz, he said, "Come on, y'all, we got a flight to catch." He headed towards the runway and the two men followed behind him.

***

An Hour Later Back At La Casa Moreno

Grip was a nervous wreck. He was sitting behind the desk in his office, chain smoking and nervously watching his security monitors. His top soldiers were missing in action, and worst of all, Joaquin wasn't accepting his phone calls. "Ain't this a bitch," he said aloud. "I've been chasing behind this mutha'fucka for two years now, going out of my way to put him in position, and this is the goddamned thanks I get? I should have listened to G.J. and Muhammad, and killed his ass when I had the chance."

"Killed who?" Rahmello asked as he limped into the office. His anxiety was getting the best of him, and he was tired of lying in bed looking up at the ceiling.

Grip started to speak, but his vibrating cell phone demanded his attention. Hoping that the caller was Joaquin, he snatched it up and looked at the screen.

"Who's that?" Rahmello asked.

"It's your bother," Grip said as he accepted the call and placed the phone against his ear. "What?"

"Nigga, don't be whattin' me," Sonny snapped back, daring the old man to say something crazy.

Grip took a deep breath and gently caressed his beard. In a calmer voice, he said, "Pardon me, Sontino, I'm just a little frustrated."

"Oh, yeah, well I'm just callin' to let you know that I took care of that situation."

"What situation?"

"The twins, Egypt and Zaire," Sonny clarified. "I took care of business."

"Is that right?" Grip perked up and damn near hopped out of his chair. "Are you shittin' me right now, or did you really take care of business?"

"Ain't that what the fuck I just said?"

"That's good," Grip smiled at Rahmello. "Real good. We're gonna need 'em for the meeting tomorrow, and you know what I mean when I say that, right?"

"Absolutely, I'm two steps ahead of you," Sonny said, placing emphasis on the word "ahead."

"That's good," Grip confirmed. "Now, about tomorrow night, we're leaving La Casa Moreno at nine o'clock, sharp. It's about a two-hour drive, so I need you to be on time."

"That's a no go," Sonny declined. "I've got a lot of shit to take care between now and then. So, it'll be better for me to just meet you there."

Grip was reluctant to agree, but he realized that he didn't have a choice. "All right, but just for a little insurance, would you mind if I came to pick up the twins? You know, just in case."

"I don't see that being a problem," Sonny said in a calm voice. "I'm at the club on Broad Street, so just come through and holla at me."

"All right," Grip replied. "I'm on my way."

Click.

"Yo, why are you smilin' so hard?" Rahmello asked him as he disconnected the call.

"Because your brother," Grip continued smiling, "he finally came to his senses and did the right thing."

"What did he do?"

"He took care of those goddamned twins. That's what he did. And believe me when I tell you, that was the best decision he ever made."

"So, what about Oli?" Rahmello asked him. "Now that we have the twins, we can keep her out of this, right?"

"We won't even mention her name."

***

At Club Infamous

Sonny was all alone in the Block Boy Room. A burning Dutch Master was nestled between his left thumb and index finger, and he was standing in front of the picturesque glass front window, looking down at the empty dance floor. Nipsy and The Reaper were at The Swamp getting ready for what he had planned for Daphney, and the headless bodies of the twins were downstairs in the basement wrapped up in old blankets.

"Talk about the worse day ever," he said to himself, and then took a pull on his Dutch Master. As he exhaled the smoke, his cell phone vibrated in his pants pocket. He pulled it out and saw that it was a text message from Troutman.

How much longer do you want me to watch the house? The bedroom lights were just turned off, so I'm assuming that she's done for the night.

After reading the text message, Sonny hit him right back.

I already got the information I needed, so you can go. I can handle the rest.

Troutman replied a couple of seconds later.

All right, buddy, you take it easy.

After looking over the last message, Sonny noticed he had a missed call from Gangsta. He clicked on his voicemail App and pressed *play*.

"Sonny, it's Gangsta. Whatever you do, you can't trust Grip. Him and Muhammad are plannin' to kill you. I've been try'na call you for the last half an hour, but you're not answering. Hopefully, you'll get this message before it's too late."

Sonny couldn't believe what he was hearing. He looked down at the diamond ring that his grandfather gave him and anxiously bit down on his bottom lip. "This grimy ass nigga," he snarled through clenched teeth. "He was settin' me up the whole time." He started to walk away from the window, but a slight movement in the corner of his eye stopped him dead in his tracks. Looking down at the front of the club, he saw three mutha'fuckas creeping towards the back staircase. They were dressed in all black and strapped with M-16s.

"Yo, this nigga's really try'na park me." He tossed the Dutch Master and ran over to the bar. Reaching under the bottom shelf, he pulled out a Thompson M-1 that was equipped with a 150-round drum. After cocking a bullet into the chamber, he ran back to the window and aimed down at the three assassins. "Hey, yo, dick heads, look up here."

Three gunmen looked up and before they had a chance to react, a loud burst of gunfire shattered the window.

***

Back at La Casa Moreno

Muhammad was sitting at the dining room table eating a plate of spaghetti when Grip stepped into the room and approached him. "I've got some good news," Grip said as he took a pull on his Cohiba. "Sontino took out the twins."

Muhammad dropped his fork and used a napkin to wipe the corners of his mouth. "Come again."

Grip smiled at him. "Sontino, he did the right thing. He took out the twins, and now we gotta go pick 'em up. We're gonna need 'em for the meeting tomorrow night."

"But as far as Sontino, we're still gonna kill him, right?"

"Not at all," Grip replied. "I'm proud of him. He did what he had to do for the sake of his family. Now, don't get me wrong, he's still a little rough around the edges. But in due time, I'll smooth him out."

Muhammad's face turned to stone and he shook his head slowly. Taking a deep breath, he said, "I think I might have fucked up."

Grip looked at him skeptically. "You think you might have fucked up? What the fuck is that supposed to mean?"

"After everybody went missing, I took it upon myself to reach out to Chatchi."

"You reached out to Chatchi?" Grip raised his voice a few octaves. "And told him what?"

"I told him the truth about Roberto," Muhammad revealed. "I told him that Sontino was the one who ordered the hit, and I gave him the address to the house in Upper Dublin and told him about the club on Broad Street."

"You did what?" Grip shouted at him.

"I did it for the sake of the family," Muhammad tried to explain. "I did it for us. They already got to G.J. and Gangsta, and I knew that they were coming for us next. Plus, you told me that you wanted Sontino dead. I thought that I was doing the right thing."

Without saying another word, Grip reached behind his back and whipped out his .10 millimeter. He cocked the hammer back and aimed the barrel at Muhammad's face.

"Come on, Grip, please. I only did it for us."

"And I'm doing this for my grandson."

Boom.

Muhammad's brains burst out of the back of his dome and splashed against the wall behind him.

His mouth was wide open and he was looking at Grip with a shocked expression.

Boom. Boom. Boom.

The next three rounds flipped him out of the chair and left him twisted against the back wall.

"Yo, what the fuck is goin' on?" Rahmello asked as he limped into the dining room. He was looking at Grip, and then looked down and saw the lanky old man twisted up in the corner.

"Come on," Grip said as he breezed right by him and headed for the front door. "We've gotta get to Club Infamous. The Mexicans are coming to kill your brother."

***

Back at Sonny's Upper Dublin Estate

"I knew this mutherfucker wasn't dead," Daphney snapped out. She was sitting in the back seat of Troutman's Impala. His blood-covered cell phone was clutched in her right hand, and his dead body was stinking in the front seat. "I knew that pussy ass Egypt wasn't man enough to handle his fuckin' business. Now, I've gotta kill this mutherfucker myself."

Looking at Troutman, she realized that it wasn't a good idea to leave a dead body in front of her house. "Fuck it, I guess I'ma have to push his ass over to the passenger's side, and then drive him up to the garage. I'll figure the rest of this shit out later."

As she reached for the door handle, the door was snatched open, and a pair of hands snatched her out of the car. Initially, she thought it was Sonny, but when she looked up and saw the tatted-up face, the three-dimensional devil horns, and the razor-sharp teeth, she screamed at the top of her lungs. "Nigga, who the fuck is you?"

"Me?" the Mexican smiled at her, showing off his one-inch fangs. "I am Diablo, the one who God sent to punish the world."

To Be Continued...
Available NOW!
Blood of a Boss 4: Rahmello's Betrayal

About the Author

My pen name is *ASKARI*, but I'm known throughout the city of Philadelphia and surrounding counties as S-Class. Prior to writing books, I was one of the hottest up and coming rappers in the city. This was in the early 2000's, prior to social media. But I still had a strong buzz, blazing mixtapes and rocking clubs from Jersey to New York City. In October 2001, my homie, Peedi Crakk, was signed to Roc-a-fella Records, and being the real nigga he is, he took our entire crew along for the ride. Our sole mission was to lock down the rap game and get our families out the hood. Unfortunately, in February 2003, just as my career was beginning to take off, I was arrested and charged with a murder that I absolutely did not commit. There was no physical evidence linking me to this crime: NO GUN, NO FINGERPRINTS, NO DNA, NO VIDEO SURVEILLANCE, NOTHING!!! The entire case hinged on the identification testimony of one alleged eyewitness, who initially described the shooter as *A DARK-SKINNED BLACK MAN WITH A SUNNI MUSLIM BEARD*. However, as you can see from my pictures, I have a light brown complexion, and at the time of this crime, I was eighteen years old with a baby face. I had no beard whatsoever.

At my trial, the district attorney's case relied exclusively on the testimony of this one eyewitness; the same witness who knew me prior to this incident, but described the shooter as a completely different person. This witness was a convicted felon, currently serving time for an unrelated matter. He did, however, state for the record that he was promised leniency in exchange for his testimony against me. This witness testified that at the time of this incident, he was standing on the corner selling crack cocaine and that he was under the influence of alcohol and drugs. He further testified that he only had a partial view of the shooter's face, as the shooter was wearing a hoody sweatshirt, with the hood up over his head. He also indicated that the crime scene was not well lit. During cross examination, he revealed that after this incident, he went around the neighborhood asking people "What happened?", and that another individual *TOLD* him that I was the shooter. This witness' identification testimony was so suspect and unreliable, that even the trial judge acknowledged there was the possibility of a misidentification.

In addition to shortcomings of this witness' identification testimony, the recording of his 911 call was mysteriously missing from the evidence file. Not only that, but the investigating detectives, for unknown reasons, failed to make an appearance at trial. As a result, they were never questioned about the integrity of their investigation. Even worst, according to police reports, there was at least one eyewitness to this crime who the detectives never interviewed. I made numerous attempts to have my trial counsel locate and interview this witness, but my attorney failed to do so. THIS WITNESS MAY HAVE VERY WELL BEEN THE ONLY OPPORTUNITY I HAD TO PROVE MY INNOCENCE. BUT UP UNTIL THIS DAY, HE HAS NEVER BEEN PROPERLY IDENTIFIED, LOCATED AND INTERVIEWED!!!

Sadly, despite all of the witness' shortcomings and a notable lack of physical evidence, the jury convicted me of first-degree murder. My trial lasted TWO DAYS!!! SMFH!!!!

Man, when I tell you I was crushed.... I couldn't believe it. Moreover, I couldn't understand. How could something like this happen? How the fuck could I be convicted of something that I didn't do? Excuse my language, but I'm angry as hell!! Please, try to understand.

Yet and still, in the midst of the bullshit, I knew that I had to remain humble, positive and prayerful. I knew that I had to remain diligent in my fight to prove my innocence, while at the same time conducting myself as a man, standing firm on the principles that my mother and father instilled in me as a child. I have not wavered, and I never will. I shall and must continue to fight for my freedom; that's just my nature.

I was only twenty years old when I was kidnapped by the system. I was a father of three beautiful children. I was working two jobs and busting my ass in the studio every day, primed to be the next Jay Z. I was also working with the youth in my community as an assistant coach on our little league football team. But I guess none of that mattered. I once seen a civil rights documentary where an ignorant Klansman stated: "When we get ourselves all riled up to hang us a nigger, any nigger will do." It's about to be 2018, and for nearly fifteen years, I've been in prison for a crime that I didn't commit. Maybe to them, I'm just another nigger. SMFH!!!!

You know, it's funny when I sit back and think about my life. I thought that I'd be triple platinum now, captivating audiences with my creativity and word play. I guess I still am, but instead of a microphone, I'm using a pen. Still focused on using my creativity to open the doors that confine me. Whether they be the doors that kept a young brotha locked in the hood, or the doors that currently have a brotha locked behind bars. Either way, I will be free.

To my real family and friends, fans and supporters, I love y'all from the bottom of my heart. Words could never express my gratitude. And to the big homie, CA$H, thank you bro. When I was down and out, sitting in a cell, looking for a way out, I came across *TRUST NO MAN.* In your dedications and acknowledgements, you gave me a new outlook, a new source of motivation. It was then that I picked up a pen, and I'm determined to never put it down.

Always,

Rayshon "ASKARI" Farmer

Submission Guideline

Submit the first three chapters of your completed manuscript to ldpsubmissions@gmail.com, subject line: Your book's title. The manuscript must be in a .doc file and sent as an attachment. Document should be in Times New Roman, double spaced and in size 12 font. Also, provide your synopsis and full contact information. If sending multiple submissions, they must each be in a separate email.

Have a story but no way to send it electronically? You can still submit to LDP/Ca$h Presents. Send in the first three chapters, written or typed, of your completed manuscript to:

LDP: Submissions Dept
Po Box 944
Stockbridge, Ga 30281

DO NOT send original manuscript. Must be a duplicate.

Provide your synopsis and a cover letter containing your full contact information.

Thanks for considering LDP and Ca$h Presents.

Coming Soon from Lock Down Publications/Ca$h Presents

BOW DOWN TO MY GANGSTA
By Ca$h
TORN BETWEEN TWO
By Coffee
THE STREETS STAINED MY SOUL II
By Marcellus Allen
BLOOD OF A BOSS VI
SHADOWS OF THE GAME II
TRAP BASTARD II
By Askari
LOYAL TO THE GAME IV
By T.J. & Jelissa
IF LOVING YOU IS WRONG… III
By Jelissa
TRUE SAVAGE VIII
MIDNIGHT CARTEL IV
DOPE BOY MAGIC IV
CITY OF KINGZ III
By Chris Green
BLAST FOR ME III
A SAVAGE DOPEBOY III
CUTTHROAT MAFIA III
DUFFLE BAG CARTEL VI
HEARTLESS GOON VI
By Ghost
A HUSTLER'S DECEIT III
KILL ZONE II
BAE BELONGS TO ME III

A DOPE BOY'S QUEEN III

By **Aryanna**

COKE KINGS V

KING OF THE TRAP III

By **T.J. Edwards**

GORILLAZ IN THE BAY V

3X KRAZY III

De'Kari

THE STREETS ARE CALLING II

Duquie Wilson

KINGPIN KILLAZ IV

STREET KINGS III

PAID IN BLOOD III

CARTEL KILLAZ IV

DOPE GODS III

Hood Rich

SINS OF A HUSTLA II

ASAD

KINGZ OF THE GAME VI

Playa Ray

SLAUGHTER GANG IV

RUTHLESS HEART IV

By **Willie Slaughter**

FUK SHYT II

By **Blakk Diamond**

TRAP QUEEN

RICH $AVAGE II

By **Troublesome**

YAYO V

GHOST MOB II

Stilloan Robinson
CREAM III
By Yolanda Moore
SON OF A DOPE FIEND III
HEAVEN GOT A GHETTO II
By Renta
FOREVER GANGSTA II
GLOCKS ON SATIN SHEETS III
By Adrian Dulan
LOYALTY AIN'T PROMISED III
By Keith Williams
THE PRICE YOU PAY FOR LOVE III
By Destiny Skai
I'M NOTHING WITHOUT HIS LOVE II
SINS OF A THUG II
TO THE THUG I LOVED BEFORE II
By Monet Dragun
LIFE OF A SAVAGE IV
MURDA SEASON IV
GANGLAND CARTEL IV
CHI'RAQ GANGSTAS IV
KILLERS ON ELM STREET IV
JACK BOYZ N DA BRONX II
A DOPEBOY'S DREAM II
By **Romell Tukes**
QUIET MONEY IV
EXTENDED CLIP III
THUG LIFE IV
By **Trai'Quan**

Askari

THE STREETS MADE ME III
By **Larry D. Wright**
IF YOU CROSS ME ONCE II
ANGEL III
By **Anthony Fields**
FRIEND OR FOE III
By **Mimi**
SAVAGE STORMS III
By **Meesha**
BLOOD ON THE MONEY III
By J-Blunt
THE STREETS WILL NEVER CLOSE II
By K'ajji
NIGHTMARES OF A HUSTLA III
By King Dream
IN THE ARM OF HIS BOSS
By Jamila
HARD AND RUTHLESS III
MOB TOWN 251 II
By Von Diesel
LEVELS TO THIS SHYT II
By Ah'Million
MOB TIES III
By SayNoMore
BODYMORE MURDERLAND III
By Delmont Player
THE LAST OF THE OGS III
Tranay Adams
FOR THE LOVE OF A BOSS II
By C. D. Blue

Available Now

RESTRAINING ORDER **I & II**
By **CA$H & Coffee**
LOVE KNOWS NO BOUNDARIES **I II & III**
By **Coffee**
RAISED AS A GOON I, II, III & IV
BRED BY THE SLUMS I, II, III
BLAST FOR ME I & II
ROTTEN TO THE CORE I II III
A BRONX TALE I, II, III
DUFFLE BAG CARTEL I II III IV V
HEARTLESS GOON I II III IV V
A SAVAGE DOPEBOY I II
DRUG LORDS I II III
CUTTHROAT MAFIA I II
By **Ghost**
LAY IT DOWN **I & II**
LAST OF A DYING BREED I II
BLOOD STAINS OF A SHOTTA I & II III
By **Jamaica**
LOYAL TO THE GAME I II III
LIFE OF SIN I, II III
By **TJ & Jelissa**
BLOODY COMMAS I & II
SKI MASK CARTEL I II & III

KING OF NEW YORK I II, III IV V

RISE TO POWER I II III

COKE KINGS I II III IV

BORN HEARTLESS I II III IV

KING OF THE TRAP I II

By **T.J. Edwards**

IF LOVING HIM IS WRONG...I & II

LOVE ME EVEN WHEN IT HURTS I II III

By **Jelissa**

WHEN THE STREETS CLAP BACK I & II III

THE HEART OF A SAVAGE I II III

By **Jibril Williams**

A DISTINGUISHED THUG STOLE MY HEART I II & III

LOVE SHOULDN'T HURT I II III IV

RENEGADE BOYS I II III IV

PAID IN KARMA I II III

SAVAGE STORMS I II

By **Meesha**

A GANGSTER'S CODE I &, II III

A GANGSTER'S SYN I II III

THE SAVAGE LIFE I II III

CHAINED TO THE STREETS I II III

BLOOD ON THE MONEY I II

By **J-Blunt**

PUSH IT TO THE LIMIT

By **Bre' Hayes**

BLOOD OF A BOSS **I, II, III, IV, V**

SHADOWS OF THE GAME

TRAP BASTARD

By **Askari**

THE STREETS BLEED MURDER **I, II & III**
THE HEART OF A GANGSTA I II& III
By **Jerry Jackson**
CUM FOR ME I II III IV V VI VII
An **LDP Erotica Collaboration**
BRIDE OF A HUSTLA **I II & II**
THE FETTI GIRLS **I, II& III**
CORRUPTED BY A GANGSTA I, II III, IV
BLINDED BY HIS LOVE
THE PRICE YOU PAY FOR LOVE I II
DOPE GIRL MAGIC I II III
By **Destiny Skai**
WHEN A GOOD GIRL GOES BAD
By **Adrienne**
THE COST OF LOYALTY I II III
By Kweli
A GANGSTER'S REVENGE **I II III & IV**
THE BOSS MAN'S DAUGHTERS I II III IV V
A SAVAGE LOVE **I & II**
BAE BELONGS TO ME I II
A HUSTLER'S DECEIT I, II, III
WHAT BAD BITCHES DO I, II, III
SOUL OF A MONSTER I II III
KILL ZONE
A DOPE BOY'S QUEEN I II
By **Aryanna**
A KINGPIN'S AMBITON
A KINGPIN'S AMBITION **II**
I MURDER FOR THE DOUGH
By **Ambitious**

TRUE SAVAGE I II III IV V VI VII
DOPE BOY MAGIC I, II, III
MIDNIGHT CARTEL I II III
CITY OF KINGZ I II
By **Chris Green**
A DOPEBOY'S PRAYER
By **Eddie "Wolf" Lee**
THE KING CARTEL **I, II & III**
By **Frank Gresham**
THESE NIGGAS AIN'T LOYAL **I, II & III**
By **Nikki Tee**
GANGSTA SHYT **I II &III**
By **CATO**
THE ULTIMATE BETRAYAL
By **Phoenix**
BOSS'N UP **I , II & III**
By **Royal Nicole**
I LOVE YOU TO DEATH
By Destiny J
I RIDE FOR MY HITTA
I STILL RIDE FOR MY HITTA
By **Misty Holt**
LOVE & CHASIN' PAPER
By **Qay Crockett**
TO DIE IN VAIN
SINS OF A HUSTLA
By **ASAD**
BROOKLYN HUSTLAZ
By **Boogsy Morina**
BROOKLYN ON LOCK I & II

By **Sonovia**
GANGSTA CITY
By **Teddy Duke**
A DRUG KING AND HIS DIAMOND I & II III
A DOPEMAN'S RICHES
HER MAN, MINE'S TOO I, II
CASH MONEY HO'S
THE WIFEY I USED TO BE I II
By Nicole Goosby
TRAPHOUSE KING **I II & III**
KINGPIN KILLAZ I II III
STREET KINGS I II
PAID IN BLOOD **I II**
CARTEL KILLAZ I II III
DOPE GODS I II
By **Hood Rich**
LIPSTICK KILLAH **I, II, III**
CRIME OF PASSION I II & III
FRIEND OR FOE I II
By **Mimi**
STEADY MOBBN' **I, II, III**
THE STREETS STAINED MY SOUL
By **Marcellus Allen**
WHO SHOT YA **I, II, III**
SON OF A DOPE FIEND I II
HEAVEN GOT A GHETTO
Renta
GORILLAZ IN THE BAY **I II III IV**
TEARS OF A GANGSTA I II
3X KRAZY I II

DE'KARI

TRIGGADALE I II III

Elijah R. Freeman

GOD BLESS THE TRAPPERS I, II, III

THESE SCANDALOUS STREETS I, II, III

FEAR MY GANGSTA I, II, III IV, V

THESE STREETS DON'T LOVE NOBODY I, II

BURY ME A G I, II, III, IV, V

A GANGSTA'S EMPIRE I, II, III, IV

THE DOPEMAN'S BODYGAURD I II

THE REALEST KILLAZ I II III

THE LAST OF THE OGS I II

Tranay Adams

THE STREETS ARE CALLING

Duquie Wilson

MARRIED TO A BOSS... I II III

By Destiny Skai & Chris Green

KINGZ OF THE GAME I II III IV V

Playa Ray

SLAUGHTER GANG I II III

RUTHLESS HEART I II III

By Willie Slaughter

FUK SHYT

By Blakk Diamond

DON'T F#CK WITH MY HEART I II

By Linnea

ADDICTED TO THE DRAMA I II III

IN THE ARM OF HIS BOSS II

By Jamila

YAYO I II III IV

A SHOOTER'S AMBITION I II
By S. Allen
TRAP GOD I II III
RICH $AVAGE
By Troublesome
FOREVER GANGSTA
GLOCKS ON SATIN SHEETS I II
By Adrian Dulan
TOE TAGZ I II III
LEVELS TO THIS SHYT
By Ah'Million
KINGPIN DREAMS I II III
By Paper Boi Rari
CONFESSIONS OF A GANGSTA I II III
By Nicholas Lock
I'M NOTHING WITHOUT HIS LOVE
SINS OF A THUG
TO THE THUG I LOVED BEFORE
By Monet Dragun
CAUGHT UP IN THE LIFE I II III
By Robert Baptiste
NEW TO THE GAME I II III
MONEY, MURDER & MEMORIES I II III
By **Malik D. Rice**
LIFE OF A SAVAGE I II III
A GANGSTA'S QUR'AN I II III
MURDA SEASON I II III
GANGLAND CARTEL I II III
CHI'RAQ GANGSTAS I II III

KILLERS ON ELM STREET I II III

JACK BOYZ N DA BRONX

A DOPEBOY'S DREAM

By **Romell Tukes**

LOYALTY AIN'T PROMISED I II

By **Keith Williams**

QUIET MONEY I II III

THUG LIFE I II III

EXTENDED CLIP I II

By **Trai'Quan**

THE STREETS MADE ME I II

By **Larry D. Wright**

THE ULTIMATE SACRIFICE I, II, III, IV, V, VI

KHADIFI

IF YOU CROSS ME ONCE

ANGEL I II

By **Anthony Fields**

THE LIFE OF A HOOD STAR

By Ca$h & Rashia Wilson

THE STREETS WILL NEVER CLOSE

By K'ajji

CREAM I II

By Yolanda Moore

NIGHTMARES OF A HUSTLA I II

By King Dream

CONCRETE KILLA I II

By Kingpen

HARD AND RUTHLESS I II

MOB TOWN 251

By Von Diesel

GHOST MOB II

Stilloan Robinson

MOB TIES I II

By SayNoMore

BODYMORE MURDERLAND I II

By Delmont Player

FOR THE LOVE OF A BOSS

By C. D. Blue

BOOKS BY LDP'S CEO, CA$H

TRUST IN NO MAN

TRUST IN NO MAN 2

TRUST IN NO MAN 3

BONDED BY BLOOD

SHORTY GOT A THUG

THUGS CRY

THUGS CRY 2

THUGS CRY 3

TRUST NO BITCH

TRUST NO BITCH 2

TRUST NO BITCH 3

TIL MY CASKET DROPS

RESTRAINING ORDER

RESTRAINING ORDER 2

IN LOVE WITH A CONVICT

LIFE OF A HOOD STAR